THE NINTH GENERATION

A NOVEL

John L. Owens

D1127993

JOHN L OWENS

*Dedicated to my wife, Gail
(my covenant adventurer)
and our son, Ben*

*I am gratefully appreciative
for all who gave in many ways
to make this story possible...*

It could have happened.

JOHN L OWENS

*"It was then, and later too, that the Nephilim appeared on earth -
when the divine beings cohabited with the daughters of men,
who bore them offspring. They were the heroes of old..."*
Genesis 6:4 *-THE TORAH*

1

The cry of the ram's horn pierced the stillness of the tree village, but it had come too late—

High within the branches, a hunched-over figure turned from his scroll. His eldest son was leaning against the doorway, breathing hard. "Where was she last seen?"

"Working the vines."

Methuselah quickly arose from his study seat and followed Lameck through the passageways and down. Silently they hurried through the shadows, passing beneath the other dwellings which had been built among the limbs of the huge cypresses.

A crowd had gathered around the grieving father. The wailing of women could be heard from his home above.

"Who is it?" asked Methuselah.

"My Nashta," said Olmar, his face marked with grief.

"Did anyone see her taken?"

"Come, I will show you."

Joined by some of the crowd, they proceeded east of the Grove down one of the trails into the valley. It was late in the day. The falling mist cast an eerie reflection across the fields and vegetation that supplied food for their families. Most harvesting was done by the sons but some fruits were gathered by the daughters. It was the season for sweet grapes, but to the villagers the time had suddenly turned bitter.

"There—" Olmar pointed to the partly-filled cart. "It hasn't been moved."

"Who else was with her?" asked Methuselah.

"All three of my daughters went into the valley together. They got into an argument. Krista and Kursta came home. Later they went back to help, but Nashta was gone." Olmar walked to the other side of the cart and pointed at the ground while wiping his eyes.

The sandaled impression in the dirt sent a chill up Lameck's back. He knelt and, with his hand, measured the length of it. Four spans. Six toe marks. "It's happened," said Lameck, looking up at his father. "They've returned."

Methuselah was silent.

Olmar jerked a yellow scarf from his pocket and held it out. "I found this here. It's Nashta's. She always wore it."

"We're not safe," said one of the others.

"Where will we go?" asked another.

"Back to your homes." Methuselah waved the crowd back. "The elders will meet and decide what to do."

"What if it returns tonight?" asked one.

"The wheel tracks point to the coast," said Lameck, "back to their land."

"It got what it came for," said another. "Whose daughter will be next?"

"Olmar, I am sorry…" Methuselah reached to console the father, but Olmar pulled away and along with the people turned and headed back, murmuring in dismay.

Lameck felt Olmar's grief and the helplessness of his father to stop the encroaching terror. He stood staring at the tracks. It had been almost six months since the last snatching of a Sethite daughter. They had only wanted to be left alone, but such peace had been imaginary.

Returning to the Grove, Lameck stopped beneath one of the dwellings and climbed the rope ladder to where his friend was sitting.

"What do you think they will decide?" asked Albo as he picked up one of the carved wooden balls and lobbed it from the rail. It arched downward, thudded and rolled about thirty feet from the base of the tree, just missing the marker.

"Probably post guards." Lameck took hold of a red one and gave it a toss. Too short.

Albo reached for another.

Lameck's heart just wasn't in the game and it wasn't helping him to relax. "They need to be stopped."

"Bet I could bring one down with my T-bow." Albo lobbed another, a little too far.

"Ever seen one up close?" Lameck crouched at the edge by a supporting limb.

"Not yet. Have you?"

"Close enough to keep a distance."

Albo sat, his legs dangling over the side. "How many do you think there are?"

"A lot more than we've seen," said Lameck.

"Wonder how fast they reproduce …How is Talisha?"

"Better if she were closer." Lameck welcomed the change of subject, especially the thought of seeing her. It was a day's ride.

"Close to covenant?"

"I'm not sure she's ready."

"Better not wait too long. A Ridge boy'll take notice."

Lameck was grateful for Albo's friendship, but took his counsel lightly. He meant well. It was almost dark and time to return to his family's dwelling. On the ground, he tossed the balls back up. He wanted to see Talisha again soon, but now the safety of the Grove was of greater concern.

In the weeks that followed, activities gradually resumed. The sounds of children laughing and playing could again be heard. Even the harvesting continued, but only with guards and in full daylight. A few searches had taken place, but more for the family's sake—to show concern—than from any real hope of recovering Olmar's daughter.

The elders had decided not to interrupt plans for the Sethite gathering. They would take a chance that the Nephilim would not return anytime soon. The time of celebration would help to take their minds off of their worries, and it was needed for the encouragement and strengthening of the community. For the fathers and their families that would be arriving, preparation was needed. Food had to be gathered.

Two things Lameck enjoyed doing as his part and both were at night—honey hunting and fishing. With success, a sweet supply could be jarred and fish could be smoked, enough to last for months.

Outwitting the fist-sized flyers had been learned by studying the insects' defensive behavior. In their attempt to conceal the location of their hive, the bees would overpass the nearby flowers, going to more distant fields for their nectar. Lameck and Albo had found them during the day. Catching one in their bee box, they soaked it in honey, and then released it, watching and marking the return line of flight. Capturing a second bee nearby, they repeated the process and figured from the two angles and distance between where the bee lines crossed. The triangle always pointed to the spot and told them how far.

Returning at night, when the bees were at rest, they located the tree. The comb was huge, suspended from a high limb. They slowly climbed it and struck a torch. Lameck brushed the surface, stirring the bees. Instinctively, the bees left the hive and followed the sparks to the ground. The treasure was then cut and bagged, almost more than they could carry home, an ample reward for a few stings which were quickly soothed by a honey coating. Disoriented by the fading sparks, the bees were left on the ground. With daylight, they would reorganize.

Honey hives could usually be found nearby, but for fish, travel to the cove was necessary. Lameck planned it well ahead and prepared the equipment. His brother Aril had helped him in the past and would go again. The grove and its bountiful surroundings provided well for the village families. All things considered, it was a good place to live—and peaceful most of the time.

————————

A reptilian opened its eyes on the bank. The sun was rising, but the chance of another catch tempted the night-time fishermen to delay their return. Shifting his sitting position, Lameck watched his younger brother throw the last of the bait. The surface of the bay where it scattered was like emerald— smooth and translucent with gently rolling swells. Lameck clenched a fistful of sand, and then slowly relaxed his grip, allowing the grains to drift downward, sparkling in the early light.

"Is it still safe?" Aril asked, walking back.

Lameck was silent.

"Father said they watch the beaches."

"It's barely daylight," Lameck answered. "This'll be our last cast."

Aril sat down. "I like to fish, but if we're seen—"

He was interrupted by the sudden thrashing of water. Close to shore, fins and silvery flashes signaled the final catch. Getting up they moved quickly to each end of the net where two twenty-foot poles were standing vertically, anchored in the sand at water's edge. Bending them back like bows, almost to the breaking point, they slipped the notched tips into catches and dropped the netting on top.

"Now!" said Lameck.

Yanking the release pins, Lameck and his brother stepped back. A rush of wind raised the hair on Aril's forehead as the wide net catapulted over the water. Stone weights along the leading edge splashed down first. Wood floats bobbed and held it in place. Lameck's way of fishing was unconventional but worked well.

At the cove the fish were plentiful, but it was a half day's journey from the family village down the southeast trail. They had arrived at dusk the day before and had spent all night fishing. The wide beach was bordered by palms and lush foliage, connecting around the inlet to the winding coastlands of the south.

Lameck tightened his grip, hands chafed and aching, working the lines backward against the growing weight of the catch. At 112 years of age, and muscled from hard work, he was tired. Aril, just thirty-three and lanky, was barely moving. "Final load. Let's get them in." said Lameck.

Aril frowned as he glanced across at Lameck's end of the net already on the beach. "You could've asked someone else."

"Don't give up. I need your help."

Lameck walked behind his brother picking up his loose line. Together they pulled until their catch was clear of the tide. Shimmering through the net were more fish like the others, four to five feet in length with tails pounding the beach. The brothers stood resting, deeply breathing the salt air as the fish quieted, and eyes became fixed and clouded. They then proceeded to stack the donkey cart and to dig up the equipment.

There was no noise at first, just the gentle lapping at the water's edge. It was something Lameck felt—a vibration, barely noticeable—then a sound like a rolling millstone. Both of them turned their heads toward the inlet but by the time the danger was realized, it was unavoidable. Around the bend it came.

The one approaching was big, with two dark horses in front. The brothers remained motionless, knowing they had been seen, but with no time to hide. Lameck looked at Aril. "Don't look frightened."

"What're we going to do?" Aril asked, stone-faced.

The cart with its fish was jerking back and forth as their donkey turned nervously against its harness. Lameck remembered the repeated warnings of his father to watch and stay out of sight. It was the reason they fished at night. This was what he had been trying desperately to avoid. They could be taken captive. Or killed.

When first seen, the rider had appeared of large size, but as he got closer, Lameck realized that he was a giant—one of the Nephilim. The brothers stood almost seven feet but this one was at least twice their height and he was pulled by huge horses. The vibration was from the hooves and the sound from the grinding of hard-packed sand under the wheels of the carrier.

The Nephilim were revered as god-like heroes by the families of Cain, but considered evil by the families of Seth. Unheard of until the sixth century, their origin had been a mystery. Because of their size and strength, they took what they wanted and had no challengers but among themselves.

The rider jerked the reins in front of their cartload of fish, a net's length from where they stood. With a snort the stallions halted, twisting their heads, flaring their nostrils and hoofing the sand. Lameck had never been so close to a giant. Only once, he had seen one from a river boat.

This one looked something like an ape with a wide face and angular forehead, and its size stretched beyond every normal human dimension. The head was bald and the face half-hidden behind a reddish beard. There was coldness in the eyes, which struck Lameck as serpentine.

At first it didn't move. The giant's gaze shifted from the fishermen to the cart and to the cove around them, then back to the cart. Then it stepped to the ground.

Lameck could see their donkey twisting, trying to move away. He watched as the giant reached down, grabbed the cart's underside and lifted, toppling the animal, spilling the load of fish across the sand and into the water. As the cart fell, splintering the wood, the yoke broke loose and the donkey—eyes wide with fright—regained balance and began running in the direction of the trail.

Aril was standing like a statue, looking pale, as the giant turned toward them. The eyes moved slowly, scrutinizing every detail of the fishermen. Knuckles rested on its waist while thumbs tucked its loosened tunic back into a scaly belt. The wide feet, strapped with animal hide, were placed like those of a wrestler waiting for his opponent to move.

The voice was raspy and deep. "Who gave you permission to take from our waters?"

There was silence. No reasoning was possible.

"Do you know who I am?" Arrogance and pride were in its words and countenance.

Still silence.

"I am Trog, lord of the coastlands." There was a pause as if awaiting recognition. When no response came, the beady eyes narrowed.

Lameck had never been in such a situation—Holy God —never before had he called upon the God of power and might. It was the One his fathers worshipped, but not One Lameck knew. Yet, somehow His Name came to mind.

"What are you two doing here? Show your marks."

Lameck had kept the top of his right hand turned away with hope that they might be perceived as merchants. In return for a portion of their goods, Cainite farmers and fishermen were offered protection from the Nephilim. But Lameck's family was from the line of Seth. They had not submitted to the mark of Cain and refused to pledge allegiance to their false gods.

"Sethites!" The giant glared down at the two, signaling a deep hatred, while raising both fists to his chest. "See these mighty hands. You will both die by them this day."

Lameck knew that his younger brother was trembling but he felt no fear. He had to do something. As the giant advanced, he felt one of the beachbows at his back, still upright but loosened. Turning and grabbing it, he jerked it from the ground. With no distance to throw, he thrust it outward. The giant seized it and bent it until it snapped in two. Throwing the pieces to the side, it then bolted and reached for Lameck.

Lameck struggled to get away but the giant's grip was too strong. Its fingers had found his neck and were tightening. With a grin, it was locked on like an animal watching its prey slowly die. Lameck was pinned against the ground by its weight, unable to move, and beginning to feel light-headed.

Holy God— The Name came to him again. Then he heard a sharp slap and felt the giant lurch. Another slap, like the first, and the grip loosened. A third time it happened and his attacker released its hold and stood up, twisting to locate the source of its irritation.

Facing the giant was his brother, Aril, brandishing a broken half of the beachbow and looking angrier than Lameck ever remembered. He had been smacking it from behind and now had its full attention. However, Aril was no match for the giant. It quickly seized and lifted him by the neck.

Lameck was not about to let his brother die. Pushing himself up, he felt a fishing weight in the sand. Taking hold of it, he tugged until the cord which held it to the net broke. "Holy God, give me strength," he breathed. Stone in hand, Lameck sprinted and leaped on the back of their attacker. With one arm around its neck, he swung his free hand full force into the side of its head. The stone sounded a dull crack. Immediately the giant went limp, relaxed its hold and fell forward. As it sank to the ground, its back arched upward, and then finally collapsed. The glistening point of a beachbow stuck through just above the belt.

The giant lay motionless, face down. Blood oozed from the wound and stained the sand around it.

"I think it is dead." Aril's eyes were big and his breathing heavy as he waited to be sure.

"Are you all right?" asked Lameck.

"My neck hurts."

"You almost died," said Lameck.

"It was trying to kill you too."

"What you did took courage. Thank you, brother."

Still trembling, Aril leaned over the body examining it closely. "It's a big one."

"The sons of Adam were never this size."

"Look at the fingers," said Aril. "—six on each hand."

"The toes are the same."

9

Something else drew Aril's attention—a gold ring on the right hand. Lameck had noticed it, but was now more concerned with the consequences of what had just happened. A strange heaviness was settling upon him. He was sensing fear but not for himself. It was for his family and their village. Lameck realized that this event had to be hidden, never to be discovered.

"Aril, we have to remove it."

"How?"

"We'll tie it across the horses.

"What then?"

"The abandoned well on the way home. Go find the donkey. If the cart's not destroyed, we can return it."

"The tide's taken the fish. We'll go home empty-handed."

"Be thankful we're going home. Let's hurry before we are seen again."

Soon everything was prepared for the return. The donkey hadn't run far. The cart was still usable, and the stallions had been cooperative. Using a leafy branch, Lameck swept the sand, erasing the traces of their activity and struggle. The bloody stain along with the distant carrier trail would be gone with the advancing tide.

Early evening light was streaming through the tops of the trees but darkness would overtake them before they got home. Heading northwest, Lameck walked alongside of his brother, holding the leather reins to the horses. Draped over the horses' backs hung the dead giant, twelve toes and twelve fingers swinging to and fro, the carrier behind. Aril led the donkey cart.

"Riana says they're some kind of gods," said Aril.

"Why would she believe that?"

"Some Cainite wagon merchants told her."

"Our sister needs to be more careful with whom she talks. If this was a god, it wouldn't be hanging dead from a horse."

As they neared the circular stone well, Lameck guided the stallions alongside. Lifting the strapped feet, he swung them into the opening. Aril pushed from the other side. Slowly the giant slid over the horses' backs, bumping along the lip of the well, and dropped. There was a muffled splash. Lameck and Aril stared into the dark hole. It was gone.

"Now let's break up the carrier and throw it in." said Lameck.

"Why can't we keep it?"

"Aril," The elder brother's voice was steady but forceful, "if there is anything in our possession that can be traced to this giant, our entire village and every Sethite will be in danger." It was not clear if Aril understood the seriousness. His eyes were avoiding Lameck. "Let's use what's left of the bows. We should be able to pry it apart."

The carrier was framed in iron. The sides were hardwood. Aril quietly worked with his brother until it was dismantled. An inscription in an iron plate which they had removed from the back ledge caught Lameck's attention. Etched in the surface was the mark of Cain—the crossed lines, encircled —which had become a symbol of the Nephilim-Cainite authority, and forced upon the people as a sign of subjection to their system. Lameck lifted it and dropped it into the well along with all the pieces and wheels and remnants of the blood-stained pole.

Lameck then walked over to the nearest horse and looked at it. Although some of the Cainites hunted and killed, this had never been a practice of his family.

"What will we do with them?" asked Aril.

The eyes of the stallions were large and nervous. They acted differently from when the giant had first approached them on the beach, no longer striking their hooves proudly but standing very still. They were innocent, caught in the middle of a conflict beyond their control.

Lameck was undecided. He did not want to put his family in danger by having horses that might be identified. "We can't leave them here alive."

"Then let's take them with us," said Aril.

Not wanting to destroy the animals, Lameck took hold of the reins and continued the walk home.

They were quiet most of the way, until Aril spoke, "How can we know there aren't other Gods?"

"We have the written record and testimony of Adam." Lameck remembered when the first father died at 930 years of age. He was fifty-six at the time.

"Maybe Adam didn't tell us everything."

"After all that happened in Eden, do you think our grandfather would have lied to us?" Sometimes his brother's comments irritated Lameck.

Aril was silent.

"Our fathers trust the writings," said Lameck, "It was through him that God revealed Himself to us as the Creator, the Intelligence and Power behind all that we see."

"How do we know that God was not made?" asked Aril.

Despite the annoyance of the question, there was something familiar about it. Lameck had asked a similar question when he was younger. "What do you think could have made God?" Lameck asked in return.

"Maybe another God."

"How many do you need before you get to the One who was not created?"

"Did God create the Nephilim?" asked Aril. "If God is the Creator, He must have made them."

"Not every form we see today is like it was at creation," replied Lameck. "The stallions show how a kind can change in size through selective breeding, which Cain's descendents practice. There are other variations within the plants and animals that take place on their own...but not outside their own kind"

There was a mystery behind the Nephilim. They were not a variation of any known earthly kind. Something other than their giant size was evident. There had been something in the eyes that he had seen—something other than human—chilling and repulsive.

"Aril. Don't move." Lameck saw the approaching shadow first. Sensing danger, the animals had already halted beneath the shelter of the branches.

It was a winged hunter. Lameck had never seen one going for a human, but he had heard of attacks. The behavior of some of the creation had changed over the years and it was wise not to take chances. The long dark form glided silently overhead. The creature's wings stretched the length of four men, forming a sinister silhouette against the crimson sky. Its beak, like a giant spear, pierced the night air, targeting a disturbance in the distant lagoon.

As soon as the danger was out of sight, the brothers continued, but weariness was setting in. A night without sleep, the fight, and all that followed had drained the brothers' physical endurance. It was now the flickering lights in the distance that kept them going.

"We'll sleep well tonight," said Lameck.

"Do you think that father will let us keep the stallions?"

"Not likely. I have to talk with him."

"Tonight?"

"No. I'll tell him in the morning."

"Everything?"

"Everything."

It was not the news Lameck wanted to share. He knew that they could live without fish, as they had in the past, but was not sure how a dead giant—one of the Cainite heroes—would affect their chances of survival…or how their father would react? He was too tired to find out tonight.

2

Sounds of children playing games formed familiar images to Lameck as he slept. It was a scene he enjoyed from the overlook of their home in the trees. Constructed with the help of close relatives who had also decided to settle in the Grove, the multi-roomed, two-level dwelling provided a safe haven within the massive cypress. A slatted stairway which angled to the ground could be retracted by ropes when necessary. To the east, the green valley presented a pleasant and peaceful view, dotted with reds and yellows from the ripening fruits and vegetables...

Suddenly, the peacefulness was broken as the dark image of a giant invaded the landscape. It had scaled the steps of their home seeking vengeance and had found him. The grip against Lameck's shoulder sent a wave of fear through his body, but soon subsided as the pressure became the hand of one he knew—

"Wake up, brother." It was Aril. "Are you alright?"

"Tired…" Lameck turned to face his brother.

"Father wants to see you right away."

Lameck was awake but reality seemed as dream-like as the dream itself. He wondered of he was only dreaming that he was awake. He wished it could be true, but knew that he had to confront his father with the truth of all that had happened.

He swung his legs out and his feet felt the floor. The three sons all slept in the same room. Beds had been made with smooth-split boards attached to the walls, held in place with cords from rafters to corners. Cloth mattresses were lined with ostrich feathers for comfort. The daughters' sleeping area was similar at the other end of the house. Pulling his clothing from a bin, Lameck quickly dressed and headed up the steps to his father's chamber.

"Sit down, son." Methuselah was standing as he entered. There was tension in his voice and concern in his face.

Lameck took a seat in one of the two chairs nearest the door. He was unprepared to talk.

"There are some horses in the stalls that you know about, according to your brother."

"Yes, father. I had intended to tell you but it was late when we returned and I didn't want to disturb you."

"Were you fishing in the daylight?"

"It was early and I thought that we could fill the cart with one more cast."

"What happened? Aril says there are no fish."

"Father, please sit down." Lameck motioned to the other chair.

Methuselah sat down uneasily, leaning toward his son, waiting for some answers.

"We were caught," Lameck looked into his father's eyes waiting for his reaction, "...by one of the Nephilim."

The muscles tightened in his father's neck. "How did you escape and where is it?"

"It's dead... We killed it."

"You killed one of the Nephilim?"

"It went for me first. Then it went for Aril, tried to kill him. I hit it with a stone. It speared itself when it fell on the bow Aril was holding. We used its horses to carry the body to the abandoned well where we dropped it."

Methuselah took a deep breath and let out a sigh. His brows were raised in astonishment. "Did anyone else see you?"

"The giant was alone. There were no others. Everything was put in the well... except for the horses."

"The horses? Those are the horses in our family stall?"

"Father, I know your concern. I am sorry for breaking the rule. If I had left before daylight, none of this would have happened. But I am concerned too. Something must be done to stop them. Our families can't continue to live like this."

"Those horses should be nowhere near us. You must take them to the grasslands and release them..." He paused and looked down.

Lameck took a deep breath. He was still tired and sore from the recent events, but the grasslands were in the same direction as the young woman he was planning to marry and it had been two months since he had last seen her. Their last conversation still lingered in his mind.

"…or we must bury the horses." Methuselah's words interrupted his thoughts.

Lameck reached out and took his father's right hand. "Father, it has been awhile since I have seen Talisha. Let me go visit her. I can release the stallions on the way. I will be careful, and if they are released among the wild horses, no one will know how they got there."

Methuselah's eyes were closed. He seemed to be in prayer, then looked again at Lameck. "How soon can you leave?"

"After the mid-day meal." He wanted to talk more about the Nephilim, but decided to wait until after the current crisis had passed.

The long table in the family dining area was spread with food. Smells of sauces and seasoning turned Lameck's thoughts to things more enjoyable—ripe fruits, leafy greens, cheeses, cooked vegetables and smoked fish. There was no comparison between the trail mix which had sustained them and the freshly prepared meal now in front of them.

"Can we keep them?" asked Aril, sitting alongside on the bench.

"No." The subject threatened to spoil Lameck's appetite.

"What did father say?"

"We can talk later." It was not something he wanted his other brothers and sisters to hear and would only cause fear. Father could tell them if he chose—He was now entering the room.

The youngest son was on the far side of Aril, close to the end of the table where their mother sat. Riana and her older sister seated themselves across from Lameck after setting the bread on the table. The family of seven was ready to eat.

Methuselah walked to the head of the table near Lameck and standing, lifted his hands, as was his custom before meals. He lacked his usual smile. "Holy God, all-powerful Creator and Lord, we thank you for your faithful provision. Every good thing comes from your hand of blessing. We ask you now to sanctify this food and to cover our family with your gracious presence." His "Amen" was echoed by the family.

Reaching for a platter of buttered squash, Lameck could sense the tension within his father. How apparent it was to the rest of the family was uncertain. Everyone was occupied with eating.

"Why so late getting in last night, Lameck?" asked Tamara, the older daughter.

"It wasn't late," said Riana, as she glanced at her sister and winked at Aril.

"It was after dark. I was just wondering if something happened."

"You are always worrying," said Riana.

"I do not always worry."

"Daughters. Don't argue at mealtime," their mother intervened. "Lameck is free to speak if he has something to say."

Lameck swallowed and looked at his food. He had hoped to finish his meal without discussion. Next to him, Aril was nervously picking at his plate.

"Family! Let me have your attention," Methuselah spoke. "Some events have happened recently but this is not the time to learn about them. Lameck will be leaving after our meal for the Ridge. I will speak to all of you then. So, let us finish eating and avoid any unnecessary talk."

Silence prevailed over the balance of the mealtime. Wiser eyes avoided contact while others curiously searched. Stuffing the last morsel into his mouth, Lameck arose, excusing himself to get ready for the trip.

Tossing a travel bag over his shoulder, Lameck stepped down the swaying slats leading to the ground, and headed across the Grove to the stables. The main gate was open. Entering, he looked around expecting to notice the taller stallions, but they were not visible. He walked back to the stall. Looking inside, Lameck felt his stomach tighten like a knot. It was empty... the leather reins and halters still hanging against the wall.

He swung the stall gate slowly outward. It was unlatched. He had been exhausted and could not remember, yet felt reasonably sure that he had latched it the night before. Examining the hard-packed ground offered no clue to the disappearance. Saddling his horse, Lameck mounted. He thought he might find them if they were just wandering, or that they would distance themselves far enough from the Grove so that they were no longer a problem. Either way, he would be able to spend some time with Talisha after crossing the grasslands. And while at the Ridge hopefully his grandfather would offer some answers to the questions that were bothering him concerning the Nephilim.

Lameck paused briefly at the water trough for his horse to drink. Two large dogs were curled up alongside the roots of a nearby tree. He looked upward through the branches at the homes. It was where over 300 of his Sethite relatives lived with their families, all above ground for safety. Near the west side of the Grove, within a fenced area, was where the domesticated animals were kept when not grazing.

"Where are you headed?" Albo's voice came from above.

"The Ridge," said Lameck, spotting his friend. "Have you seen any loose horses?"

"Not lately. Are they yours?"

"Just a couple strays. They're probably gone."

"When are you bringing Talisha home?"

"You'll be the first to know," Lameck replied, nudging his horse.

"Stay away from the pilgrimage," Albo called.

This was the time of year that the Cainites journeyed to Eden and back, as one of their customs. Some traveled for weeks just to circle the northern garden. Their priests required the pilgrimage of all able Cainites to insure blessings and prosperity to their cities. To the Sethites, it was all religious superstition and foreign to the instructions of Holy God.

After leaving the Grove, Lameck quickened his horse's pace in a southwesterly direction. He could see the golden grasslands in the distance, the probable way the stallions would have gone if they were on their own. The same heading would eventually take him to the Ridge dwellings and to Talisha.

The sun-warmed air felt good against his face and arms. The short journey was a time to be reminded of God's goodness toward His creation. He enjoyed riding in the wide open spaces. There was no boredom. The view was always spectacular—the flowering fields, rolling hills and crystal springs, along with the sights of fascinating animals. Some were tall and colorful, others shorter than himself with horns and armored plates. Some traveled in groups, while others, such as the bears and big-toothed cats, were more solitary. There was never a lack of things to see. Riding through the grasslands was like crossing a sea of gold. It was one of God's magnificent diversions from the details of life. Nothing equaled the relaxing pleasure of the open terrain with its unique sights and smells. Lameck was no longer bothered by the recent events and growing concerns—Here he was free. And along with this experience there was a longing deep within, a thirsting to know and communicate with the One who answered his needs so perfectly.

The sweeping vista of golden color was interrupted from the north by a stream of browns and blacks. Lameck slowed and watched the running wild horses approach and circle past. There were about fifty, including the younger ones. Studying them carefully, he saw a few large horses, but nothing close to the size of the ones that were missing. Neither did he see any during the rest of his journey.

After riding the greater distance, Lameck's attention was drawn to a spring of water at the western edge of the grasslands. It was time to give his horse a rest. As he neared the location, Lameck noticed something dark near the water's bank. Then one of the trees appeared to move… but then he saw that it was not a tree. It was a young behemoth. Its long neck was coming into focus as Lameck got nearer and noticed it eating some of the higher fruit. The body was gray and massive with a tail like a tree trunk. They were harmless to man and fascinating to observe.

His horse was not nervous sharing the oasis. Neither did the behemoth seem nervous with visitors. There was plenty of fruit and enough water to share. Bending one of the shorter trees, Lameck reached into a cluster, squeezed a large piece of fruit to measure its ripeness and pulled it free. It was yellowish-orange and had a slightly fuzzy texture. No preparation was needed. Its taste was refreshing and sweet. The juice ran down Lameck's arm.

After giving a piece of the fruit to his horse, Lameck refilled his water holder. The behemoth was resting about fifty feet away. When it was ready to move, nothing would stand in its way. There were no doubt others, much larger, nearby in heavier foliage. Their consumption of vegetation was huge. Lameck took one last look at the creature, partially submerged in the water. A slight flex of its tail sent a wave, bending reeds and washing the bank. It was time to move on.

Leaving the flatlands, Lameck had to enter the hills before reaching the Ridge. He had traveled this way before, so the path was familiar. The dense trees prevented him from seeing far ahead, but he knew that others would have equal difficulty seeing him. There were places to hide if necessary. But the thought of hiding seemed foolish. Only the Cainites and the Nephilim presented any problem and most of them were to the south. There were night-time predatory animals, but the Ridge would provide shelter before nightfall.

One stop was anticipated before seeing Talisha. A break in the trees revealed why. Cascading through the meadow, flowers of every color and design imaginable presented themselves. Lameck dismounted and walked into the field. Immediately he was surrounded by an array of God's scintillating and spectacular delights. Lameck inhaled deeply, smelling the pleasant aromas, and knelt to examine some closely. There were mysteries within the plant kingdom which encouraged detailed study. Some discoveries had already been made by the fathers with hundreds of years to explore such things, such as the numerical patterns of the petals, intriguing methods of seed dispersal, color variation, and far more. Lameck decided on a few varieties for Talisha. After gathering a bunch and tying them carefully behind the saddle, Lameck remounted and returned to the pathway.

The Ridge was now in sight and Lameck was beginning to have that buoyant feeling that was characteristic of being around Talisha. He had missed her. As he visualized her, he realized that there was no other woman who had ever made him feel this way, and thought that if this was God's way of confirming that she was to be his covenant helper, he was glad and thankful.

Daylight still lingered as Lameck approached the entrance with gift in hand. The bench swing hung motionless from a limb in front of the dwelling. It was where they had met and talked during Lameck's last visit. The planked door was shut. He knocked and heard steps. It was Talisha's father.

"Lameck! What a surprise." His face was tense.

"Lameck?" the mother's voice sounded. "What is he doing here? ...We didn't know you were coming."

"May I come in?" *Something was wrong.*

"Of course, Lameck..." Her father's words were strained as he opened the door. "...but Talisha is not in right now."

Lameck stepped inside. It was as he remembered, but everything was not the same.

"She is usually here," said the mother from her chair facing the door. Her eyes were on the colorful wildflowers. "If she had known…"

"I would have sent word," said Lameck, "but the trip was unexpected."

"Would you like to sit?" asked her father.

Lameck could see that his presence was uncomfortable to them and did not wish to delay longer. "Thank you, but I should go on to Enoch's while there is light. I can come back tomorrow." Hearing no response, he reached for the door behind him, and then remembered the flowers in his other hand. "Here…these are for Talisha." The father took them and forced a smile.

It was a short distance to his grandfather's. Most of the dwellings faced east along the mountainous Ridge. The entrances of their homes were laid with stones joining the side of the mountain and utilizing natural cave formations. A rocky trail set them apart, eight in all, with Enoch's at the southern end. It had been his grandfather's decision to build on the mountain not long after its formation in the sixth century. According to the fathers, it had been a time of frightening disturbance to the earth —eruptions of fire and risings of land masses, while rivers formed, separating parts of the mainland. Following the catastrophe, the Cainites were afraid to come near the Ridge, believing that it was cursed. For the Sethites who became Ridge dwellers, it turned out to be a blessing, as the families were safe from intruders.

After bedding his horse down in an open stall, Lameck walked to the door of his grandfather's home, seeing movement through the stone window. Enoch met him at the entrance, swinging the door wide and extending his arms. Lameck leaned down to meet the shorter man's embrace.

"Lameck, so glad to see you again. Welcome and come in."

"It's good to see you too, grandfather."

"You can put your bag in the traveler's room and join us. Your cousins and I were just finishing some discussion."

Lameck exchanged greetings with the two young men he knew from family gatherings and went to the rear cavern enclosure where he often stayed when visiting. Locating the clay lamp on the wall of the semi-dark room, he carried it to the corridor, touched the wick to a flame, and returned with it. The room was familiar—a bed, a chair and a small table. On the stone table top was the animal-skin collection of writings which Enoch had assembled from many of the fathers, including Adam. Lameck enjoyed the inspiration they imparted and appreciated the wisdom gained from spending time at his grandfather's. He replaced the lamp and left the room.

The corridor was diagonally lined with rough-sawn planking as were most of the inner walls. A large circular table in the center of the main room served as the gathering place for guests.

"Grab a cup, pull up a seat and join us." Enoch motioned to the space opposite him between Nathel and Abinar. "We have been talking about the natural evidences which communicate the glory of God. Tell us what you observed on your journey here."

Filling his cup with juice from a pitcher, Lameck thought of the sights he had encountered from the grasslands to the meadow... "I saw a young behemoth."

His cousins looked puzzled.

"How does such a beast glorify God?" said Abinar, to his left.

There was silence for a moment.

"Is it not one of God's creations?" Enoch posed the question.

"The largest," Lameck responded.

"Then what is it about the behemoth that demonstrates a quality of Holy God?" asked Enoch.

"Its unmatched size and power," said Nathel, to his right.

"The fact that no man has been able to tame one?" asked Abinar.

"Think about what you have just said." Enoch smiled. "If such is true of the created, how much more must it be true of the Creator?"

The cause is always greater than the effect. Lameck remembered the principle he had learned by observing nature and the way things worked.

"Enough for today," said Enoch. "It is late and Lameck needs to rest from his traveling. Thank you both for coming."

After escorting his two young visitors to the door and exchanging a few parting words, Enoch returned and sat down to face his grandson. Lameck's family had often commented on his grandfather's youthful appearance. He had lived for over three and a half centuries (364 years) and, even with his silvery white hair, looked younger than Lameck's own father. His penetrating blue eyes seemed able to read his thoughts.

"Was she in?" asked Enoch.

Lameck stiffened, wondering why he began with such a question…and what Enoch knew that he did not. "No," he replied.

"I am sorry. I know how you feel and it is time that you knew more about this situation." Enoch took a deep breath and continued. "It is known within the family that Talisha is having difficulty confirming her plans for marriage. I am not sure where she was this evening but do know that she has been staying with other men."

"How long have you known this?" The news took Lameck by surprise. He was aware that her upbringing had been different than his own, but did not see how this could be happening.

"I just learned of it within the last month."

Lameck was silently looking down. His grandfather gently reached out and placed his hand upon Lameck's shoulder. He was not the kind of man to speak of such a matter unless he was sure. Even so, this was not something easy to accept.

"I understand your pain."

Lameck remembered when his grandfather lost his wife during childbirth. It had been a shock to all, certainly never expected within such a righteous and exemplary household. Through the tragedy Lameck never heard Enoch ever question God's goodness. And even afterward, his grandfather was always available to any who needed counsel. Few of the elders were regarded so wise. Lameck had always looked up to him.

"It is better that you know at this point than to find out later. Talisha was hurt as a child. The enemy found access to abuse her and has affected her ability to enter into covenant with others." He paused. "This hurts me also. You both are my grandchildren and I want you to make wise choices, avoiding the suffering that has fallen upon many of the sons of Adam."

Lameck felt anger rising but it was not toward Talisha, her family, nor the men that she might be seeing. It was toward the evil that had entrapped her as a child. It was the same anger he had felt toward the evil of the Cainites and Nephilim which threatened their families and kept them isolated. "Father Enoch…" Lameck looked up at his grandfather. "There are also some things I need to tell you, matters which may affect the future safety of our families within the Grove."

The lines on Enoch's forehead showed his concern.

Lameck proceeded to tell him of their encounter at the cove with the giant, what they had done with the body, the meeting with his father and the missing horses. He then tried to express the anger and frustration he was feeling against the unknown. "I will see Talisha and do everything I can to help her, whatever our future may be, and even if there is no hope for a marriage covenant. But it is also time to do something to stop the invading menace of the Nephilim and the evil they are spreading. I want to do something … What can you tell me?"

For awhile Enoch's gaze seemed locked onto something too distant for Lameck to see. Gradually his focus returned to his grandson. "Yes," he spoke, "Tomorrow, go and speak with Talisha. The blessings of God be with you. But leave the other matter alone. It is past your present ability to even understand, much less to fight."

"But why? Did I not already slay one of them?"

"I am speaking of an evil that you have never experienced. There are powers that could easily destroy you. Leave it alone."

"But how can I leave it alone? It is threatening our families and it is destroying our plans for the future. It is the same evil. I need your help to conquer it."

"Lameck, my son, you are not prepared for this. You are not prepared to take this on."

The words echoed in his mind as he tried to sleep... ... *not prepared...not prepared...for what?*

"Hail to the gods of Eridu! Hail to our god, Azazel, and his Queen, Druana!"

"Hail to the Nephilim, the mighty Nephilim!"

Jathron lifted his hand to the crowds and the mass chanting turned into a deafening roar from the fifty thousand worshippers and spectators seated around the arena. As high priest, this was one of his favorite events. Taking his seat, he leaned back against the cushioned marble and reached for his chalice. It was an empowering moment and he felt that he had every right to share in the glory and honor of the gods, for he— *Jathron*—had been given authority over the common people and he believed that he served the gods well. *One day he too would become a god*, as Azazel had assured him.

A peaked canopy shaded the royalty on the lower level of the arena. The angelic god, Azazel, had become visible during the worship and was seated alongside Druana, a few steps to the right of Jathron. The two had been talking. On the opposite side were the lower governors of Eridu and five Cainite maidens that had been given special honor, as future wives of the gods. They would soon be taken to Phlegra, the birthplace of the Nephilim, for their nuptial ceremonies, where they might remain or relocate to rule over a city, as did Druana with her offspring from Azazel.

Reflections from golden trumpets beneath the upper arches caught his eye as they heralded the starting event. The doors swung open against the far wall of the arena floor and four carriers pulled by elephants suddenly appeared with their giant riders. Jathron knew the routine but enjoyed seeing the reactions of the people.

The giant Nephilim instilled awe and fear, which served the leadership in keeping the masses productive and obedient. Open and frequent displays of strength reminded the common people of their human weaknesses and their need for protection against warring powers. In a growing sense Jathron felt like a father to the Cainites of Eridu, offering them knowledge, guidance and protection. Stroking his trim goatee, he considered a new title… "Father Jathron." Yes, it sounded good. The more he thought about it the more he liked it.

The four Nephilim, each towering about eighteen feet, stood in four corners of the arena floor preparing for the stone-lifting. Flexing their muscles, they squatted and positioned their forearms to lift the boulders. With grunts, together they hefted the huge stones, positioning their hands beneath, and raising them over their heads. Applause was great and the four stones were dropped with thuds that shook the arena.

Again the trumpets sounded and the crowd quieted. With a deep bellowing voice, a giant in the center announced the next event. It would be a fight between two Nephilim. The city of Tarbal had challenged Eridu to a match between their strongest, the loser forfeiting a hundred bushels of grain.

Jathron thought about the grain situation as the Nephilim prepared to clash. While the fields were plentiful, the growing demand for food by the giants was creating a scarcity and a need for rationing. A hundred bushels was a heavy wager, not an easy price to pay. But the thought of defeat seemed even worse. The people would begin to question the ability of Eridu to defend itself. Such a possibility seemed intolerable, moving Jathron to glance in their god's direction. He was gone, which seemed to confirm his suspicion that Azazel would use his powers to insure victory for Eridu.

The rumbling of feet and ringing of shouts by the crowd exalted the defender of Eridu, although it was a different one than their usual hero, who had been missing. It was not unusual for Nephilim to roam; however, Trog's absence for a challenge was disturbing, especially to his mother, Druana.

Torak had brute strength but was not as quick as his challenger who gained an early wrestling lock around his neck and right arm. A backward jab from Torak's left elbow caused a painful release and the two faced each other again with defiant expressions. The giant from Tarbal jeered at the defender, taunting with his hands. The crowd's anger was beginning to rise. They shouted and stomped louder. Torak lumbered forward seeking a grip on his nimble and slippery opponent.

Jathron took another sip, looking down into the dark red wine and gave it a circular movement.

Suddenly, a crack and groan came from the arena floor. Torak was doubled over, clutching his stomach. The taunter wasted no time in delivering repeated kicks to the defender's upper body and head. Torak tried to turn but the other giant was relentless, continuing to strike, using both hands and feet with brutal force. There were no rules in such a fight. Anything might happen, including the death of their hero. But that was not a possibility that Jathron wanted to entertain.

Where was Azazel and why was he not doing anything? Jathron wondered. The crowd was no longer cheering and had begun to yell insults at their losing champion.

Then he saw it. Where it had come from was a mystery. Torak had a spiked ball and chain hanging from his hand, his bloody back to the challenger. From his crouched defensive position, he exploded upward and around, powerfully sweeping his arms in front of his opponent, the iron weapon following with deadly force. The other giant failed to see it coming and was totally unprepared for such an attack. The match was finished. A shout of victory resounded through the arena.

Jathron smiled and looked over at Druana. Her mouth was drawn tight and her gaze was intense. Within the arena, the limp body of the giant hero from Tarbal was being dragged away, leaving a trail of blood to the distant doors.

The Queen motioned for him. He got up and walked over to her. Azazel was still absent. "Sit down. There is something I just learned that you should know." Jathron seated himself promptly and gave his full attention to the Queen Mother. "As you know, Trog has been missing for two days. He was last seen heading north through the coastlands."

"Yes, my Queen. He may be exploring as he enjoys doing, or expanding our domain."

"I am not sure that my son is safe."

"Surely, Trog is able to take care of himself. Why would you have such an impression?"

"There are sources which we have among the Sethites that have informed us of a daughter who is playing with our elemental powers to charm and to influence affections."

"That is of interest, but what does it have to do with Trog?"

"She is using an object belonging to Trog as a point of contact."

"What is it?"

"That information remains hidden, so far. We are hoping, with your informants, that you might provide us with more details."

Any further discussion was cut short by the final sounding of the trumpets. Jathron excused himself and returned to his own seat. His powers were about to be exercised. Drummers on the upper level began their anticipatory roll. Sensing the right moment, Jathron stood and raised his arm three times in the air.

"Three! Three!" The crowds repeatedly chanted. There was something about the final event that intoxicated the people beyond the drinking that had already taken place. Jathron had surmised that it was the terror of seeing other humans in an inescapable situation, confronted by a ferocious beast. Above all the events, it generated the most fear. And it was the fear of a gruesome death that kept the people subject to authority. Such a spectacle served to remind everyone of the consequences of rebellion.

Three of their own who refused to bow to Azazel and Druana could now be seen standing alone at the arena's edge. The escapes were closed and the heavy rope that angled up from the hinged cage door in the floor of the arena was slowly tightening.

As the iron bars lifted, the scaly green spines of Gorgon came into view, a vicious beast with wide jaws, teeth the length of a man's forearm and four muscular legs that looked strangely human. It had been presented to Azazel as a gift from the god of Phlegra, Semjazza, for use in the arena.

A collective gasp was heard as the crowd tensed. With a sudden leap from its hole, it landed level with the three desperate captives. Jathron lifted his goblet, savoring the dark red remnant. The pursuit and brief struggle had become a familiar scene. Still, his hand tightened twice, reactively, around the neck of his goblet. Shifting his eyes toward Druana, he saw that their god, Azazel, had returned. They were both gazing as the last fleeing rebel was overtaken by Gorgon. Then they smiled.

Jathron pursed his lips as he delighted in Druana's news… *a Sethite daughter who is playing with the forbidden powers. At last—a doorway past the Sethite God's Watchers.*

3

"Let's run to the peak." Talisha tossed her long dark hair to the side and took a few steps, smiling back at Lameck. She was the same as he remembered, beautiful and impulsive.

He quickly caught up and took her hand. It felt good as she held tight. Together they started up the familiar Ridge trail. "I've missed you," said Lameck.

"Thank you for the flowers. They were…"

"A little crushed?"

"Maybe a little, but you found my favorite colors."

He helped her step carefully around a rock as they continued.

"I'm sorry that I was out," Talisha continued. "You've been gone a long time and …your visit was a surprise."

"It has been too long."

Talisha was silent. She brushed a low branch to the side as she walked. With winding paths, rocky steps and some narrow passages, the trail took some energy and attention. Because of the distance it took some time, but being with Talisha, Lameck was enjoying the journey as much as the destination.

The more they walked and climbed, the more panoramic the view. The trees no longer blocked their vision and they could see to the west of the Ridge, beyond the river, to the great forest.

"Do you remember our last river trip?" asked Lameck.

"The one when I fell in the water. How could I forget?"

"Thankfully, we pulled you out safely. But I was thinking of another part of the trip."

"Our kiss?"

"That…and our conversation. It was the first time we shared our hopes and plans."

Talisha was silent again as they continued up the final slope to the peak. Reaching the upper ledge, they walked over to the log bench and sat down next to each other. From their vantage point, they could see from the Ridge in any direction.

"The pilgrimage has begun," said Lameck. A long line of people, carts and horses snaked from the south along the merchant highway. It continued west of the Ridge and along the river, winding north.

"They have been doing it every year as long as I can remember," said Talisha.

"The Cainites follow the ways and teachings of their false gods. They have been deceived."

"Have you ever wondered," asked Talisha, "if they could be right?"

Lameck was stunned by Talisha's question. "Did your father not tell you of the record of the creation of the kinds by God?"

"I heard something about it, but father said that the original inscription no longer exists, so how can we know?"

"It is true the original tablets have been missing for many years. They were stolen from Adam's third son, Seth, but there are writings taken from the tablets which are trustworthy. They are often read at our family gatherings."

"Sometimes I wonder what to trust. Don't you?" Talisha looked questioningly at Lameck.

He was searching for the best way to respond when Talisha suddenly stood up. "We have talked about that enough. Wait here. I have a surprise for my future husband."

Lameck watched as she spun around and walked behind the peak of the Ridge, out of sight. He was concerned that Talisha had no certainty of the creation record or, possibly, even of Holy God.

After a short time, Lameck heard her steps and looked around.

"Lameck, it's your Talisha."

He suddenly realized that neither his father nor his closest friends had ever prepared him for a moment like this.

"Lameck, do you find me attractive?"

"I have always thought you were beautiful," Lameck responded, "but what are those shiny things on your ears and what keeps them from falling?"

"They are ornaments which go through my ears."

"Through holes in your ears?"

"I had it done for you. Do I look like a classy temple girl from the city?"

"What happened to your eyes? Did you hurt yourself?"

"Lameck, don't you ever get out of the Grove?" Talisha was looking at him sideways and tilting her head strangely. It looked like someone had punched her. There were dark smudges around her eyes and her lips appeared to be bleeding. Her clothing was pulled to one side and she walked with a jerking motion toward him. All he could do was stare as she reached out, placing her hand on the side of his neck.

She spoke with a different kind of voice…a low whisper. "Wouldn't you like to taste the pleasures of marriage before we actually commit?" The fragrance of myrrh was about her and stimulating to the senses.

"Why not…?" The thought was tempting. But a vision came to Lameck of a deep swirling well, like the one in which the giant lay. Holy God was giving him both a warning and a choice. He could obey the will of God or give in to his own immediate desires and live with the consequences. *Which will it be?*

Taking her hand firmly but gently, Lameck lifted and cupped it within his own hands, looking into her eyes. "Talisha, I love you; but covenant pleasures are designed by God for the enjoyment of those who are already in covenant. To do this would be like stealing fruit from the One who desires to give before He has the opportunity. It will only turn bitter."

Talisha pulled her hand free and glared at him. "You can't love me, Lameck. You already have a lover—that God of yours!"

Before he could say any more, Talisha turned and started running down the trail. "Talisha!" Lameck called after her, "be careful. I want to see you again."

Lameck returned to Enoch's. He was gone. It was just as well. He did not feel like talking to anyone. After packing his bag, Lameck went to the stall, readied his horse and started home.

The words, ...*ever get out of the Grove,* played in his mind. *Maybe he should have stayed in the Grove. Things might have turned out better if he had.*

The palm-thatched hut was not visible to outsiders. That had been part of Enoch's intent when building it. No one but Enoch knew it was there on the upper east side of the Ridge, nestled within the foliage. It was his secret place, a small simple structure. Needing no furnishings for distraction or fleshly comforts, Enoch was there solely to meet with his God. At first, following the loss of his wife, he began going there once a week. But soon he realized that was not enough and started to take every opportunity.

Stretching his hands upon the earth floor, he groaned deeply. There were times when no words could express his thoughts and emotions. But he knew that his Maker, the One with absolute knowledge of him, was able to understand and interpret. Enoch's cries were never ignored and an indescribable sense of love and peace would often flood his being. He had the inner assurance that Holy God, the Almighty Creator of the universe and Father of his soul was not only listening but present and waiting to respond.

While in such holy contact, Enoch had hardly any sense of passing time. Even his awareness of material things which could be seen or touched receded with the appearance of the Eternal One, the Beginning and the End of it all. The revelation of His Being had not occurred all at once, but little by little, as occasions were sought within the secret place. Such periods alone with God had become immensely valuable to Enoch, for in such times he received awareness, renewal and purpose from the very Source of life, in ways that no man, angel or other created being could ever supply.

Today had been different, although every encounter was somewhat different. Enoch was agonizing over something he felt was grieving God and it involved his family—*Methuselah and his sons and daughters, Lameck and his future wife*. He was also concerned over the killing of the giant. A struggle was taking place which involved the safety and future of them all. From the beginning, territories had been established by God and angelic Watchers assigned to the families of Adam. Those who had remained faithful in honoring Holy God were kept safe and allowed to live in peace. However, when families stopped looking to God and began looking elsewhere, their defenses were weakened and ultimately lost, replaced by Lucifer's Watchers, those rebellious angels who had followed him. Now, something was giving Lucifer's forces an opportunity for encroachment within the Grove.

Wrestling within the heavenly realms between powerful angelic beings - He was aware of it, though not through human eyes. Enoch strained within his spirit, interceding for Methuselah's family. At times he felt helpless, and then God reminded him that physical strength was of no use in such a battle. It was his faith in the One he knew.

The struggle continued. Then quietly and calmly the words came and he recognized their origin from Holy God:

"Enoch. Thank you for striving for my glory and grieving over the things that grieve me. Continue to be strong and watchful in prayer. Testing will come and the faithful will

rejoice. The battle belongs to me. You will soon see these things as I see them."

"But, God, my Father—is there nothing more that I can do?" Enoch asked. "Whatever this evil is, can I remove it from my family?"

"I have put within every man a sense of good and evil. Even if they have turned from me to follow other gods, they still have a voice inside which is calling them to return. But they must, each one, make their own decision. That is the way I have chosen to create man, according to My likeness. One day, that which was lost will be restored."

Enoch was saddened by the choices that so many of Adam's children had made. He only desired to show them the wisdom and rewards of walking with God rather than after one's own selfish desires and the temporal attractions of the world. The glory of His presence had been so satisfying it was worth the sacrifice of anything and everything. And yet, the sons of man were turning to beggarly things attempting to fill their needs, ignoring the only One with the power and desire to restore true happiness and fulfillment—that which their first parents enjoyed in the beginning.

Words of praise flowed effortlessly as Enoch lifted his arms in worship. Although his eyes were open, he did not see his physical surroundings but was spiritually beholding the face of Absolute Love. Tears streamed down into his beard and his body began to tremble. A pure, almost blinding light, and fragrance sweeter than any imaginable flower filled the room. So transfixed and consumed with awe had he become that he was no longer able to speak but only to bask in the unsurpassable magnitude of God's glory.

He wanted it to last forever but knew that he had to return to his earlier state. How long he had been there was uncertain. He remembered that Lameck had gone to see Talisha shortly before he had left the house. Brushing the dirt from the front of his clothing, he gathered his writings, returning them to a cloth folder, and headed down the hill to his dwelling.

The door was partly open.

"Lameck, are you here?" he called as he entered.

There was no response and after briefly checking the rooms Enoch realized that his grandson had departed for home. He would have liked to have talked more but he would see him again in a few days at the gathering for Methuselah's 300th birthday.

Settling into a chair, Enoch tried to relax, taking a deep breath and letting it out slowly. The sky, a grayish-pink, was visible through the small window. His mind was attempting to process the revelations he had experienced. Suddenly his peacefulness was broken by voices, mischievous in spirit, coming from outside—then two sharp raps against the door. Going to the front, he could hear the crunching of gravel and rapid beating of feet. He lifted the latch and pushed open the door. Several children were running away on the trail that connected the Ridge homes. Something else caught his eye, on the ground next to him—two crushed egg shells. The glistening contents were streaking down the outside and dripping on the ground.

Cleaning the small mess was not a big problem, but it bothered Enoch as he thought about it. The Ridge children were his descendants and this was not the first time such disrespect had manifested. Among the children of Cain, such behavior, and far worse, had come to be expected; but to see it among the children of Seth, especially his own, was disheartening. Enoch had tried to gather his full family for godly instruction with limited success, but over the years some had married outsiders without the same values and had become less communicative. How his heart ached for his family to be once again united in obedience to Holy God.

"You are experiencing heartache for your family. My heart aches for all mankind."

The words dropped suddenly into Enoch's spirit and he knew in part what God was feeling. How limited his own awareness had been. Of course, he knew that the Father Creator was intimately concerned for all of His children. Having been created in His image, Enoch was sharing the feelings of his Father, but on a smaller scale. The spreading waves of violence had to be grieving to Him—so unlike Him. Man was becoming like the beasts—yet worse, for at least the beasts usually acted in the way for which they had been created. But man had removed himself from the ways of God and only a few that he knew still called upon His Name. Like some of the fallen angels, and possibly through their influence, man was in rebellion.

As to a restoration, Enoch wondered if it could be and reasoned that certainly the all-powerful, all-wise God had a plan that would restore His very good creation - and the glory of the Lord that Enoch had so wonderfully experienced would cover the earth, that all of His children might know Him and be united in His love. Was it just a dream, Enoch wondered, or was it a vision of the future? But what if man still chose to reject Him even after such glory became visible? It was incomprehensible that anyone would react in such a way.

———————

The radiant warmth of the sun felt good against Lameck's back, as he approached the Grove. He looked forward to some rest, not only from his ride, but from the frustrations he had experienced. He hoped that in a couple more days Talisha would be back to normal and he could spend some time with her at the gathering. He was still puzzled by her behavior on the Ridge.

"Go away, Nephilim killer." The voice came from high in the trees. It sounded like a child. A dreadful realization swept over Lameck—*the secret had been discovered by others outside of his family...*

As Lameck entered the Grove, the absence of people and activity on the ground added to his growing discomfort. His attention was drawn to the movement of a rope ladder being swung and jerked upward to one of the dwellings. Two figures above, handling the ropes, were quietly occupied. There were no welcoming calls, only an unusual silence in all directions.

Ladders were already up at other homes. Tree-top eyes followed him as he rode through the Grove to the family stable. It was not very far...only one more turn in the trail.

Suddenly a rustling of leaves caused the horse to react, tossing Lameck backwards. Then a stone flew past his head, barely missing him. At the corner of a dwelling, someone ducked from sight. He knew the family and was surprised at their actions. Lameck placed his hand against the neck of his horse, calming...then continued on and quickened the pace until the stable came into view.

Alongside the stable, Aril and two of his friends raised their T-bows, aiming at a circular target painted on a distant tree. One after another, the metal darts whistled through the air finding their mark.

"Good shooting," Lameck called out, while dismounting.

Some mumbling could be heard, as the two turned and walked away. Aril looked down, adjusting the tension of his weapon.

"Isn't anybody talking?" Lameck asked, releasing the reins and walking toward his brother. "Aril, what's happening? Why are the weapons out?"

Aril's face was flushed. "What makes you think we're safe?"

"Safe from...?"

"Of course. Why else would we need to get ready to defend ourselves?"

"Did you tell the families what happened?"

"They came to me asking questions. I could not avoid it."

"So, someone else told them first? Who else did you tell? Was it Riana?"

Aril glanced away, then pulled again on the tension line. "What if I did? Someone would have found out anyway, sooner or later."

Lameck realized that the damage had been done. The news of the slain giant had sounded an alarm throughout the Grove and now everyone was in a frightened, defensive position, expecting the worse. And Lameck was being blamed as the cause of it all. "What about Father. Has he talked to the family heads?"

Aril rested his T-bow across his shoulder. "They talked, and then decided to prepare family defenses."

"Have any giants been seen?"

"Not yet, but they must be coming."

"How do you know?"

"They will. They have ways of finding out... Riana..." Aril stopped himself.

"Riana? What has our sister been saying?"

"Not much. But she knows about things that are happening."

"What else is happening?"

"Nothing, yet."

Lameck knew that Aril and Riana enjoyed talking, but he had his suspicions that the content of their conversations was not always beneficial to themselves or others. "Where is father?"

"At the altar."

The billowing smoke at the edge of the Grove had become a familiar sight to Lameck over the years. Sometimes he or another family father would assist, but on this occasion Methuselah was alone. Lameck watched at a distance as his father knelt at the side of the stone altar. Flames licked the sacrificial animal which had been spread open across the surface.

The smell of the cooking flesh to Lameck was a bitter-sweet event. It meant that an innocent and often favorite animal had been slaughtered, which was a sorrowful process. But it was the way Holy God had established to obtain His forgiveness and blessings. For that reason it was needed, though he did not understand it fully. Since Lameck knew his God to be good, he also knew that there was a mystery yet to be revealed, *the reason for this repeated, seemingly pointless bloodshed.*

Lameck sat under the cover of a long cypress bough, watching thoughtfully, until the offering was completed and the smoke faded away. He stood to meet his father.

"Welcome home, son." Methuselah held out his arms. His embrace was comforting, causing Lameck's eyes to moisten. How he needed that from his father. Together they walked back up the path. Nothing more seemed necessary to say.

Riana sat out of place during the evening meal, avoiding any conversation or contact with Lameck. Few words were exchanged. Aril excused himself early from the meal picking up his T-bow which had been leaning against the wall and joining some other young men for guard duty through the night. Without the same sense of imminent danger, Lameck took his time and decided to enjoy the food. It was his first good meal since the start of his trip. Father was friendly but reserved in his comments, with tension still evident.

Following the meal, after returning to the sleeping area, Lameck stretched out on his bed. It was quiet. Spots of moonlight played patterns on the leaves outside his window. Finally, to go to sleep, he rolled to the darker side, facing the wall. How long he slept was uncertain.

The wail of the ram's horn caused Lameck to suddenly sit up—then came Aril's voice of alarm— "Get up! Quickly! The Nephilim are attacking!"

Lameck dropped to the floor, threw on his robe and hurried outside following the running footsteps of his brother around the deck. Aril was positioned against the east rail with his T-bow pointing into the darkness. "What did you see?"

"They're out there, at the edge of the Grove. I heard them and saw one. They're twenty feet tall."

A dog began barking and another horn sounded from a dwelling to the north. Soon their father came to see what was causing the alarm. "Where is it, Aril?"

A crunching sound…then *another* was heard like bushes being crushed under heavy weight. Lameck strained his eyes peering through the trees. He saw the shadow of something large moving. Aril's hand went to the release trigger of his weapon.

"Wait," Methuselah spoke, putting his hand on Aril's shoulder. "It's not what you think."

With more crashings, the shadow slowly moved into the clearing, next to the stone altar. They could see it in the moonlight, standing high on its two rear legs.

"A carnivore," said Aril.

"Probably attracted by the lingering smell of the burnt calf," said Lameck. "It won't bother us."

"We can safely go back to sleep," said Methuselah. "Thank you, Aril, for your alertness."

"Go back to bed, children," their mother spoke, motioning the younger brother and sisters back through the doorway. "It's only a dragon."

"Don't feel bad, Aril," said Lameck. "You were right about it being twenty feet tall."

4

"Our daughter 's a disgrace to us. Her nightly involvements bring shame to our family."

"You don't understand her. Talisha is young and unsettled. She just needs a husband like Lameck and children of her own."

"Talk to her then. Maybe she 'll listen to her mother and you can put some sense of proper behavior into her head before it's too late."

"She's only forty-nine. What's the hurry? I was eighty and you were over ninety before we married and we did the same things. You knew more than a few women as I recall."

"That's all in the past. We have a daughter to consider now. Just talk to her. Is it too much to ask?"

Talisha rubbed the side of her face while listening to her parents in the next room. It was morning and it hurt where Derrin had hit her the night before. Her plan was to get up and act good, like nothing happened. Then they would soon calm down and forget about it.

After throwing on a loose red-dyed garment, Talisha picked up a small cloth bag and proceeded into the main room where her mother was busy preparing food for the gathering. She seated herself on the opposite side of the table. "Where's father?"

"On the hillside, gathering pods." Her mother looked up sharply at her. "What kind of trouble have you been getting into?"

"None. What makes you think I am in trouble?"

"Where did you get that bruise on your face? Don't lie to me."

Feeling her left cheek, Talisha glared back at her mother. "Why do you and father always try to control my life? You did the same things when you were my age."

"I never dressed or behaved like a temple prostitute."

"I don't have to stay here and listen to this."

"Where do you think you can go? Who will take care of you?"

"I know plenty of men who would like to marry me," Talisha paused, "including Lameck." Looking down, she reached into the bag on her lap and pulled out a string of colored beads. At the same time, her mother took hold of another pod, the size of her forearm, snapped it in two with both hands and shook the peas into the big wooden bowl in front of her. "But I'm in no hurry." Talisha's words sounded like her mother's she had just overheard. "I am young and attractive. I may just look around until my first hundred and find a more mature man."

"Lameck may not want to wait that long."

"Why are you always talking about Lameck? I may not be interested in him any longer."

"Lameck is quite handsome at his age, and he did ask you to marry him. He also comes from a very influential and prosperous family."

"Is that why you and father want me to marry Lameck, so that you can get some of his belongings?"

"Talisha, there is more to think about than that. We want you to be happy."

Pushing a shiny green bead onto the end of the twisted threads, Talisha thought about the word...and if she ever really knew what it meant to be happy... *Would having a husband make her truly happy?*. "Like you and father?"

Her mother was silent, continuing to snap pods.

"Well, I may talk to him again, tomorrow at the gathering. But I am not ready to commit to covenant."

"You better cover up that mark on your face. No decent man wants a wife that's been slapped around by other men."

"It was just an accident, mother. Accidents do happen."

A bump at the door interrupted her thoughts as the father stepped in with a bulging sack upon his shoulder. "I see that our nocturnal daughter finally decided to arise with the day." His words pierced like a needle.

Stuffing her almost-finished necklace back into the bag, Talisha tossed it onto the table and briskly walked out the door, with no acknowledgment of him.

Her head felt like it could split as she walked up the rocky slope. She only wanted to get away while trying not to think. Thoughts were painful.

It was a trail to nowhere in particular. Talisha walked it when she wanted to be alone. This time she was barely conscious of her surroundings or how far she had gone.

"Where are you going?"

With all the confusion she was experiencing, Talisha was not sure if the voice came from inside or outside of her head.

"Can you help a lost Cainite?"

This time she stopped and looked around. An elderly man was sitting at the base of a tree near the edge of the trail. She wondered what a Cainite was doing on the Ridge, and if he had wandered this far from their pilgrimage.

"Do you know the way?" the man asked.

"I'm not going your way," Talisha answered.

"Which way are you going? Up or down?"

"It doesn't matter. I'm just walking."

"Would you like to know the way up?"

The question irritated her as much as this outsider who, she thought, pretended to know all about the Ridge. "How is it that you, a stranger, can tell me how to find the top of the Ridge?"

"Finding the top of the Ridge cannot make you happy. I am speaking of a different mountain."

Now she was even more confused and felt annoyance at this personal interruption. "Old man, I've lived here all my life. If there was another mountain, I would certainly know about it."

"You are talking of things which can be seen and, one day, will perish. I am speaking of things which are not visible to human eyes, but spiritual and eternal."

She felt anger rising at this Cainite who was telling her, a Sethite, of spiritual things. "You must be a fool," Talisha replied. "There is no other mountain. See that path. It will take you back down the Ridge to your own people. I have no time for your nonsense."

Talisha turned away and continued walking. She glanced back after a little distance and was satisfied to see that the intruder was gone. As she thought about the encounter, she was struck with the strangeness of it…how such an old man, especially a Cainite, had wandered so far away from the merchant highway…and why he had spoken in such a way with her. It appeared to be nonsense; yet, the thought of another mountain, *the possibility of a place that provided happiness*, caused her heart to warm. But then the thought was gone. *Other things* rushed in to occupy and bring back her former state of confusion.

The throbbing soreness within her cheek caused her to remember the night before. Returning to Derrin she knew was unwise, but something within kept drawing her back. She knew better, but the brief pleasures seemed to outweigh the pain.

She had given Lameck an opportunity to share in the same pleasures, but he had refused. She wondered how she might persuade him, and gain more control over the situation. Actually, she thought that she could be quite comfortable married to Lameck, if only she felt the same way about him as she did about Derrin.

A strange sensation swept over Talisha as she thought about the approaching gathering and how she could use it to her advantage.

"How many will it take to provide a defense for our families?" asked Kenan.

"To cover the perimeter of the Grove, at least a hundred. The problem is we don't know how they might attack," said Jared.

"The danger has been exaggerated by the families that live here," said Methuselah. "Only one giant was slain and the location of its body is not known outside of my family. There is no reason to believe that anyone outside of the Grove has any information that could identify us as the ones responsible for the giant's disappearance, much less his death."

Lameck stood with his father along with the two elder Sethite fathers on the front overlook of their home. With silvery-white hair and beard, Kenan was a fourth generation father, just over 660 years of age. Jared, rugged in appearance, was of the sixth generation at 527. Methuselah was quite youthful by comparison, though none lacked energy or wisdom.

"Let the five youngest generations be responsible for supplying twenty sons each," Kenan spoke. "We will all feel safer."

"I agree," said Jared. "Even if there is no attack, having the archers in position will help to remove the fears of our families."

Lameck interrupted, "Grandfathers, forgive me for any danger I have brought upon the families…and my own father, for spoiling what should have been a joyous celebration for you."

"Son, you did what you had to do. There is no reason for guilt," Jared spoke, looking straight at him.

"It was only a matter of time," said Kenan. "We have all been trying to adjust to the encroachment of Cain's system along with the Nephilim. Let us pray that God's blessings and protection will remain upon us."

"My son, go on down and assist the arriving families," Methuselah said, patting him warmly on his back. "The gathering and celebration will go as planned."

Lameck felt better as he stepped to the ground and walked among the people. They were already setting up their temporary bedding and privacy shelters. A few spare stalls were offered for the animals, but most were left loose or tied to stakes. Tables were being erected, fire pits were being dug and the smell of food was in the air. Activity was everywhere and still more families were arriving…carts being pulled by horses and other kinds of tamed beasts, children showing off their pets of all descriptions, colorful birds, small fuzzy rodents, even an upright lizard which one boy was chasing.

"Hey, Lameck. Got any room upstairs?" It was a cousin from Mahalaleel's family.

"Sure. Bring the whole clan on up," Lameck replied, facetiously.

"We may have to do that, from what we have heard."

The meaning of his words cut like a knife. The joy that had started to return was departing. *Would the whole gathering be affected?*

Enoch's families from the Ridge were beginning to settle along the eastern edge of the Grove, facing the valley. In the distance, Lameck spotted the wagon that belonged to Talisha's family. A cooking fire was going. He thought of what the best way might be to approach her and had an idea -

"Hop in."

Talisha smiled and looked surprised as Lameck pulled up alongside her in the slidecart.

"Is it safe?" she asked, sweeping her eyes past the two horses in the front to the sleek wooden cart in which Lameck sat, motioning her to join him.

"Most certainly, and an experience I promise you will enjoy."

"I won't get thrown out, I hope." Talisha stepped cautiously onto the flat outside rail and let herself down slowly on the bench next to him.

Making sure she was ready, with the bench cord secured around her waist, Lameck popped the reins and they started to move. He waited until they had passed through the Grove before increasing their speed. After entering the open field, he began to shift the steering arm from one side to the other and felt the cart respond. "Would you like to try it?"

"No, thank you. You can do it."

"Okay—hold on." With the horses running at a fast pace, Lameck pushed all the way to the right, shifting the gliding tracks in the same direction. The cart swept to the right, building speed. Then he thrust it to the far left and the cart slid to the opposite side with even greater speed, swinging on the connection at the rear of the galloping horses. Talisha's hair was streaming behind her and her eyes were open wide. Adding to the excitement were rises in the field which projected the cart upward and sent them soaring through the air.

After awhile, Lameck could tell that Talisha was ready to slow down. Pulling back on the reins, he brought the horses to a medium trot. "Had enough fun?" He turned to see her response.

She was nodding, so they returned.

Lameck disconnected the slidecart at the rear of the stables, leaving the horses tied to a drinking post. Together, he and Talisha walked up the steps to his home and around to the rear deck, overlooking the valley.

"Would you like to sit?"

"I'm a little sore. I think I'll stand." Talisha brushed back her hair, and then rested her hands on the rail, looking off.

They both were silent.

Talisha reached over and placed her hand in his. "Lameck, I do not know why I behaved the way that I did on the Ridge the other day. Did you think I was crazy?"

"Of course not. I have never thought that. I must confess, though, that you were tempting."

"Do you really mean that?"

"Talisha, you have always attracted me, ever since the first time I saw you."

She turned to face Lameck closely, eye to eye. "And you have attracted me." She paused for a moment, looking down. "I have found it difficult to be apart and to wait so long for us to become one."

"Are you talking about …?"

"You did ask me. Is the offer still open?"

Lameck was caught by surprise, never expecting so sudden a change in Talisha. She was like the Talisha he first knew, and this seemed to be the response for which he had been waiting. There was hardly time to think…"There has never been anyone other than you, Talisha. I have always wanted you to be my wife and helpmeet."

"Yes Lameck, I accept."

Their lips met. It brought back memories of the river trip and all the adventures they shared together. A feeling returned to Lameck which had earlier been quenched by circumstances.

Jathron slid the blade slowly along the edge of the scroll breaking the wax seal. "That will be all for now," he said, casting a glance at the one standing. He waited until the messenger's footsteps could no longer be heard and the chamber doors had fully closed, then turned to face the large figure seated at the end of the table. Savoring the attention of the council, he briefly scanned the writing, then began reading from the top:

"Father Jathron—"

"Is this a new title?" Azazel interrupted.

"Nothing is meant by it, my lord, just a term of respect."

"Continue reading."

"Payment has been received. The rulers can be confident; I am in position to know what is happening among the Sethites. A gathering is planned within the Grove on the day of the new moon. I will make contact with the daughter you mentioned. If property of one of the heroes is in her possession, I will soon discover it.

Your indebted servant, Derrin"

"It should not be long. We are in position."

Azazel's hand reached out, snatched the paper from Jathron and crumpled it in his fist. "Position? You call this position? You have much to learn, father Jathron."

The other dark figures around the table chuckled and mumbled in agreement with their leader. All eyes were on Jathron.

"You were chosen to be part of the council as the high priest of Eridu and our human representative," Azazel continued. "Perhaps we have expected too much by asking you to obtain information."

"Azazel, my lord and our god, please have patience," said Jathron. "We should have what you need within two days. Derrin is a loyal contact."

"Jathron, my servant, patience is not one of my attributes. I have tolerated such sluggish communications in the past only out of necessity. Now that a doorway has opened through occult involvement, our own Watchers are gaining position." Azazel opened his hand, letting the ball of paper roll down his fingers and drop to the table. "We have just removed two days from our delivery time."

"Does this mean that Derrin is no longer of use to us?" one of the council asked.

"From what we are learning about Derrin," said Azazel, "he may be of great use to us, but not in the way that he thinks."

"I say that we remove him," said another one. "He knows of us and has no power or influence among the people."

A ruffling noise came from the rear of the room and suddenly another dark figure appeared like the others. Taking a seat opposite Jathron, he did not wait to speak. "Azazel, we have located Trog. It is as Queen Druana feared. He was killed."

Jathron could feel the tension of the council.

"Where is he now?" asked Azazel.

"His body…in an abandoned well—but Trog's spirit is wandering in the guarded zone southeast of the Grove, within the Sethite valley."

"Get Druana," Azazel spoke to the figure on the far end.

Soon, she entered. "I want to know who did it." The words skewed from a contorted face, barely recognizable as the Queen Mother.

"The name we have heard is Lameck," said the late arrival. "He is a Sethite, the eldest son of Methuselah."

Jathron had never seen such hatred as that seething from the face of Druana.

"Azazel, I want vengeance. This one is mine. I will repay this Sethite." The words hissed through her teeth. "Find out all you can about this Lameck as quickly as possible. I will tell you what I want done."

"My Queen, you will have your way. We will soon be avenged and Trog will have another body."

Druana turned and stomped out.

"Just a suggestion, my lord," said Jathron. "Surely, with our Nephilim, we could easily conquer such a small clan of Sethites. Why not use our superior force and remove this irritation once and for all?"

Azazel's brow was trenched with shadows. "Mortal fool," he said, glaring at Jathron. "You cannot see their spiritual defenses. You have never felt the spiritual sword. Wait until you are disembodied. Then you will know the forces of our world."

"Azazel is right," said another. "Leave the battle tactics to us."

Growling and guttural beast-like noises caused Jathron to shudder. The rebukes hurt his pride and the thought of being disembodied was making him nauseated. "Master, if it is acceptable, I am not feeling well and would like to step outside for some fresh air."

"You may leave us for now."

Pushing open the heavy door, Jathron passed from the council chamber to the hall and inner stair passages. Heading for the opening to the ziggurat's outer levels, he almost collided with a temple girl carrying an armload of candles.

"Priest Jathron, I am sorry. I did not see you coming."

Jathron remembered her face and, unlike the others, her simple way of dressing. She was a good worker. "It is not the time to replace the candles. The council is in session."

"I will come back tomorrow."

"That will be better," he replied, turning to continue.

"Excuse me, but may I ask of you a question?"

Bothered, he turned back. "Can you be quick?"

"I am seeking the truth. Are the Sethites the enemies of our gods?

"It is as you have been taught, unless they have renounced their false god."

"Do you know what they are like? Are their ways different from Cainites?"

"What is your name, candle girl?"

"Bathenosh."

"Bathenosh, if you desire to keep your job, you will inquire of me no more about this matter."

"I am sorry for any offense. I was only interested in—"

"Learn from your teachers. That is enough." Jathron walked hastily out onto the open upper level, breathing deeply. He leaned against the outer brick ledge.

All of Eridu could be surveyed from the lofty position. Located at the mouth of the river, Pison, the ziggurat temple towered three-hundred feet into the heavens, a construction of cut stones, bricks and mortar, erected with help from the Nephilim. At the base were buildings and storerooms and accommodations for priests and others connected with the temple. There was little activity in the market places. The reason could be seen beyond the rooftops—streams of people flowing through the city gates to the north, and slowly returning—the pilgrimage.

Jathron recalled how his life had been changed by the same event that had taken place when he was much younger. Two boys, a little older, while on pilgrimage had stopped to talk. They told him of the freedom and excitement of living in the city. He was angry with the Sethite family that had raised him, upset at their accusations and restrictions upon his life. When invited to go away with the boys, he accepted and never returned.

His birthparents had never been known by him, nor did it matter. In his mind, he was fully Cainite. *Thirty years' service as high priest was enough evidence to all of his loyalty and commitment.*

The beliefs of the Sethites he considered foolish…and now that he was enlightened by the revelation of the gods, he found satisfaction in using his knowledge against those he disliked.

5

A marvelous use, Lameck thought as he studied the huge tortoise shell with strings stretched tightly across the opening. It resonated harmoniously in the skillful hands of the musician.

> *"Hallelujah, Hallelujah,*
> *Almighty Holy God,*
> *Wondrous Creator of all"*

The voices of praise, accompanied with instruments, instilled an unnatural peace. No longer noticing the faces of the singers or rows of relatives seated about him, Lameck was swept up with the worship. It lifted the heaviness that he had been shouldering and filled a void which had long been empty.

> *"By Your Word the world was formed and the countless starry hosts,*
>
> *By Your Breath our life was given and all the earth was good,*
>
> *Hallelujah, Hallelujah"*

The singing had stopped. Those in the front returned to their family groups as attention was now being given to the eldest of the fathers, Grandfather Seth. Positioning himself behind the wood stand, the old man looked up. His eyes communicated authority before the gathering as he spoke—

"Let us never neglect to give praise to our good and all-powerful Creator God." Seth waited for quiet, then continued—

"My children...after 857 years, I still stand before you, a testimony to the goodness and faithfulness of our God. I have lived to see nine generations along with my father, Adam, and...

even with the difficulties from the curse, I am thankful every day for the blessings of a caring Creator.

"As I look about, my heart is encouraged to see my family, so many now, gathered together and giving honor to our Maker. If only my brother, the father of the Cainites, had turned to Holy God, our gathering today would be far greater, and the struggles we face would be far fewer. However, the crops reveal the seed and the times reflect the choices we all have made."

Lameck remembered the word spoken by Adam years earlier. Having lived nine hundred and thirty years, he was dying and in despair over the evil that was spreading throughout the earth. Gripping Lameck's hand and with quivering lips, he spoke the word, *conqueror*. It was the meaning of his name, but for what reason was unknown to Lameck. Nothing he had done seemed worthy of such a name. Even the recent killing of a giant was not the act of a conqueror, but one of defense to save a brother.

The skin of writings, which had been inscribed by Seth from the original tablets of Adam, was laid across the stand by Enosh, Seth's firstborn son. Lameck wondered what difference it would make if Seth were reading from the tablets that had long ago disappeared. Assurance had been given by the fathers that utmost care was taken in preparing copies, even to the numerical placement and checking of symbols, and that confidence could be given to the meaning of the words *as breathed by God*. One of the copies was in their own family's possession which Methuselah kept in his study. Others were held and shared by the Sethian patriarchs.

"In the beginning God created the heaven and the earth..."

Grandfather Seth had started the traditional reading of the creation account. The words were familiar yet always instilled a sense of awe. Lameck wondered at how great God must be to have spoken everything into existence—the heavenly lights, the great trees and animals, and all the wondrous details of creation by the power of His word.

"...And the evening and the morning were the fifth day..."

It took years for their family to construct their home, but God in a single day of darkness and light did all this. Lameck mentally struggled but was unable to comprehend it, concluding that such a miracle had to be simply accepted by faith.

"...And God said, Let the earth bring forth the living creature after their kind..."

Lameck considered the distinctive kinds. Some of the animal kinds were varied but all that were within the kind shared common characteristics.

"And God said, Let us make man in our image, after our likeness; and let them have dominion...and the LORD God formed man of the dust of the ground, and breathed into his nostrils the breath of life; and man became a living soul."

A frown was noticeable as Seth looked up from the stand. "My beloved family, beware of the lies being taught as truth among the Cainites. As we have just heard, man was created from dust, separate from the beasts. Father and Mother were made in the Creator's own likeness, a little lower than the angels. But all are created beings. There is none equal to God and none who will ever gain omnipotence with God, despite what they claim.

"As we look about the earth today, the fathers' hearts are heavy to see how far we have fallen in the nine hundred and eighty-seven years since the beginning. Some of you remember how it was before the great corruption by the fallen angels. At one time man's thoughts were upon the glory of Holy God. Now, to our shame, man's thoughts are upon evil and our families live in danger because of those trained in violence and the Nephilim, the giants of those fallen ones.

"The first human death of my brother Abel was a dark lesson that carried lasting consequences. Even to Cain it was a shock to see the results of yielding to pride and anger. There was no death in the beginning and one day—it is our hope—that death will be no more. Until then we must endure this human struggle, knowing we are not alone. God will not forsake those who seek to live righteously, in accordance with the writings and a clear consciounce."

Lameck recalled how Adam had described his walk with God in Eden—the glorious companionship, and the light that had enshrouded their nakedness. How perfect it sounded, without evil, without suffering, without death.

Seth looked down again continuing the reading—

"...And the serpent said unto the woman, you shall not surely die; for God knows that in the day you eat thereof, then your eyes shall be opened, and you shall be as gods, knowing good and evil."

A sharp sting caused Lameck to slap the back of his neck, interrupting his thoughts. *Biting insects.* They were like thorns, part of the curse brought upon the earth by man's disobedience.

Lameck leaned forward to hear every word as Seth concluded with his favorite section—the judgment upon the serpent pronounced by God in the garden—

"Upon your belly shall you go, and dust shall you eat all the days of your life. And I will put enmity between you and the woman, and between your seed and her Seed; He shall bruise your head, and you shall bruise His heel."

"In my lifetime," Seth spoke, "I have seen the curse upon the serpent come to pass. That colorful and cunning upright creature has lost its ability both to walk and to talk. That once eloquent mouth will no longer charm but is doomed to the dust of the ground, despised for its venomous bite. Many a human heel has been struck and many a serpent's head has been crushed in retaliation.

"The Seed promised to woman remains a mystery. According to father Adam, it is the promise of One who will come to restore the righteousness, peace and joy that were lost. Let us hold fast to this word. It remains our great hope."

Lameck had read the prophecy of the coming Seed but had not found much comfort in it. He watched as Seth's eldest sons carefully rolled up and removed the skins. The old man continued—

"Many of you are fearful for your family's safety and with reason. Two of our own daughters have been taken. The Nephilim have come close to this village…but we have cried out to our God and believe that with God's protection that they will now leave us in peace. So, let us get on with what we have come to do, the bestowal of honor upon one of your fathers, and one of my sons, who has reached his three-hundredth year… Methuselah, please step forward."

Lameck observed the elders as they gathered around his father, who knelt before them for the ceremonial laying on of hands, and spoke their blessings. Tears welled up in his eyes. Lameck was the ninth generation—all but Adam were present, the centuries portrayed by the progressive whiteness of their beards. He wondered if he also would live six hundred, eight hundred, or close to a thousand.

The thought of his future brought Talisha to mind. He had not seen her all day. Sights and smells of food being readied for serving were making the children squirm. As soon as they dismissed, Lameck decided that he would go find her.

The sun's diffusion through the atmospheric heaven produced a twilight panorama perfect for Enoch's star talk. Seated before him on the darkening ground in an opening among the trees were close to a hundred children. They had already eaten and their attention was being held by the one who was telling stories displayed in the sky. For some it was their first time to hear the names and meanings of the stars and star-groups as first revealed to Adam and later to Seth.

Enoch, as a child, had sat enthralled at the feet of Seth, listening to the same descriptions and stories. When he became older, he was invited by Grandfather Seth to come and study the stars with him. Together, over the years, they sketched and compiled charts with detailed calculations relating to the movements of the celestial bodies. Blessed with the gift of teaching, Enoch was soon given the responsibility and honor of passing on this knowledge to the younger generations.

"Look up there to the north. Can you spot that old serpent, Draco?"

In the dimming light, Enoch's hand could still be seen directing the children's gaze. Their heads moved together.

"Good. Now this evil one must pay for all the suffering he has caused. Just to the east, what do you see? Connect the stars to see the great warrior, and his foot—where it is placed— on the serpent's head!"

A spontaneous cheer erupted from the children. It always happened at the end of the story, every time it was told.

Grandfather Enoch gave them all a warm hug as his little family swarmed around him before returning to their shelters. It was also time for him to go to Methuselah's house for the evening.

On the way, Enoch was troubled in his spirit. Earlier in the day he had felt that he needed to pray, but with all the activities, had ignored that inner signal. He was almost to the top of the steps…when another invitation came.

"Father, come join me in the study before going to bed," Methuselah said, rising from his seat on the front overlook.

"Son, I am tired, but always glad to make time for you." Following Methuselah through the house to the upper level, Enoch entered the room and sat down.

The flickering lamplight illuminated the writing on the wall—*Faithful is God who has promised the Seed of deliverance.* It had been copied from one of the scrolls that rested on the shelves, words once spoken by Adam.

"It was a joy to have a part in your celebration today," said Enoch.

"Thank you, father. If only I could undo Lameck's encounter and that we had the peace again that we have enjoyed in the past."

"It could have happened to any one of us. Although he took a chance by not returning before daylight, Lameck cannot be blamed for what happened. Son, we have never enjoyed peace with Cain's family and the Nephilim are worse than beasts, driven by hatred and greed. If you are speaking of earthly peace, there has been none since the beginning."

Methuselah was silent.

"I share your concern for the safety of our families," Enoch continued, "and desire deeply to offer some words of assurance for us about the future, but I sense that the angelic and human rebellion that is escalating on earth can only be met in a tragic confrontation with Holy God which will impact us all."

"Can we do nothing?" asked Methuselah.

"Not in our own strength. The powers of evil are beyond our comprehension."

"Then, how?"

"We must cry out to God and seek His face. He is our only hope of deliverance."

"Can we do that now?" The two knelt side by side and began to pray…

"Father! Father!" The voice shrieked from outside the room, startling Enoch.

Methuselah scrambled to his feet and swung open the door. "Riana, what is the reason for such a disturbance? Why are you not in bed?"

"It is Lameck. He will not stop asking me questions and is calling me a liar."

"Where is he now?"

"The family room."

"Go find him son," said Enoch, "I will stay with Riana."

A strangeness in her eyes bothered Enoch. Fear was present and she could not sit still. Attempting to calm her, he met with resistance and a different granddaughter than he remembered.

After awhile, Methuselah returned to speak with his daughter. "Riana, tell me exactly what questions Lameck was asking."

"Didn't he tell you?" asked Riana.

"No. He has gone somewhere."

Riana looked away from her father, moving her hands nervously.

"What was it that he asked?" Methuselah repeated.

"It was about Talisha. He wanted to know where she was."

"Were you able to tell him?"

"No." Riana's lips were tightly pressed together.

"Have you been with Talisha?"

"We talked a little."

"When did you see her last?"

"Father, you are sounding like Lameck."

"Riana, it is important that you tell me."

"It was near sunset."

"Was anyone else with you?"

"Just a cousin from the Ridge."

Enoch interrupted—"What was his name?"

"Derrin, I think."

The name caused Enoch's stomach to tighten. Derrin was a family outcast who lived alone. His presence at the gathering was unusual. "If you will excuse me," said Enoch, "I need to go check on some of the family and see what I can learn of this situation. It may be late when I return."

"Please let me know. I will be awake," said Methuselah.

Holding an oil lamp, Enoch stepped carefully down the rope ladder and onto the path leading to the northern edge of the Grove. All was quiet except for the distant hoots of the owls. Most of the shelters were darkened along the way to the Ridge families' tents. As he got closer, Enoch heard some voices. Then he recognized Talisha's parents. "Is there a problem?" he asked.

"No problem here, Enoch," the father answered, motioning his wife into the tent. "We were just getting ready to lie down."

"How is Talisha?"

"She is the same."

"May I see her?"

"Can you wait until tomorrow?"

"Is she in the tent?"

After a nervous pause, the father answered. "She has not come in yet, but that is no cause for alarm. Talisha often takes walks."

"Here, at this time of night?"

"She is not a child. We let her do as she wants. What business is it of others?"

"Have you seen Lameck?"

"He was here. We assured him that their plans would work out."

"What plans?"

"For marriage. Talisha is ready for covenant."

"Do you know that Derrin is here at the gathering?"

"Derrin? What difference does it make?"

"We are not ignorant of his involvement with Talisha on the Ridge. You need to be talking solemnly with your daughter about the sacredness of covenant, which God does not take lightly.

"Have a good night, old man," said the father, entering his tent and letting the flap close between them.

Enoch turned and walked slowly back to Methuselah's, the light in his hand growing dim.

———————

Lameck moved slowly up the last steps to the passage that led to his father's study. It was morning and he had not slept. His search for Talisha had not gone well, hindered by the hostility he had encountered among the families. The resonance of Enoch's snoring could be heard through the passageway.

"Any success?" asked Methuselah, standing to greet his son.

"Not yet, father."

"Did you get some help looking?"

"No. The families were not cooperative."

"I am sorry."

"It is not your fault."

"Neither should you be blamed. The threat of the Nephilim has been growing. It could have happened with any one of us. But I must talk to you about Talisha."

"Do you know where she is?"

"I do not. But Enoch has told me some things that I must share with you."

"If it involves her past, I already know. That has all changed. Talisha and I are ready for covenant."

"Are you aware that one of those men was seen with her at the gathering?"

Lameck was silent.

"His name is Derrin." Methuseleh looked steadfastly into the eyes of his son. "I hope that you are right and that she has changed. We want you to be blessed."

"Thank you, father. If there is nothing else, I need to keep looking."

"Just be prepared. Your brother, Aril, may be of help with your search."

Lameck decided to check back again with Talisha's parents, thinking that she must have returned. Quickening his pace, he tried not to think about the man his father had mentioned. He thought, instead, of their recent time together on the overlook deck…and how pretty she was, just as he had always remembered. They had shared their feelings for one another, and Talisha had communicated her readiness for covenant. How right everything seemed for their future.

Approaching their former campsite, Lameck noticed that many of the structures were already gone, including the tent belonging to Talisha's family. Then some movement—a family wagon, heading his way—caught his attention. The man seated in front of the enclosure pulled back on the reins. It was Talisha's father. Lameck raised his hands as they slowed to a stop.

"Lameck, we were hoping to see you."

"Is Talisha with you?"

"No. Her mother and I have decided to go home. It is where she must be. She just returned early with some friends."

"How can you be sure?"

"Talisha is a wanderer, but always comes back."

"But would she not have told you that she was leaving, or at least sent word?"

"Not our Talisha. She is impulsive like her mother. But don't worry. You two will make a good partership. Come and see us soon."

Lameck stepped back as the wagon rolled past, then continued walking.

"Are you two any closer?" It was his friend, Albo, approaching from the opposite direction. When Lameck failed to reply, he continued, "Remember? You said I would be the first to find out."

"A good covenant takes time, Albo."

"That Talisha is a pretty one. You better latch on to her."

"Have you seen her lately?"

"I have barely seen anybody, except from the trees. The gathering was too short and I have had watch duty. Maybe next time this Nephilim scare will have passed and we can all relax and enjoy a week or two together, like we used to do."

"Albo, tell me when was the earliest you saw people leaving for the Ridge?"

"It was after sunrise when most of the families pulled out with their wagons. Only one left much earlier."

"A wagon?"

"No. Just a rider on a horse."

"Could there have been two on the horse?"

"Just one, I think. But it was still dark."

"Did you see anything else unusual?"

"Like a giant?" Albo forced a grin. "No."

Something within wouldn't let him rest from his search for Talisha. Even if she had gone home without telling her parents, after Lameck's last conversation with Talisha, impulsive or not, it seemed inconceivable that she would have left without a word to him. Returning home, Lameck found his brother.

"Not another fishing trip."

"Aril, I need you to help me look for Talisha."

"Give me your word that we will not go fishing."

"You have my word. Get your horse."

The search proceeded slowly. Riding about fifty feet apart, they moved from one end of the Grove to the other, then back again, until the full area had been covered. The few families remaining from the gathering were friendlier than those Lameck had encountered earlier, but had no news of Talisha.

After a final sweep of the perimeter, the two paused at the northeastern corner where a trail led into the valley.

"Could she have been riding?" Aril asked.

"Why?"

"Those look like horse tracks?"

Lameck had not seen them before, but now noticed the depressions. Dismounting, he leaned down to examine them. The pressed grass was a sign they were less than a day old. Clearly, they were hoof prints going east through the valley, not the direction home for any Sethite.

"We're not going to follow them, are we?"

"We are," Lameck replied.

Aril said no more, probably preferring to stay, but followed anyway.

The north valley trail was lengthy and ran like a tunnel through thirty-foot high corn plants. Eventually, the corn ended and the trail widened, then parted into a section of golden grain. A pair of dragonflies darted in front of them, their fibrous wings the length of Lameck's arm.

Aril's horse moved up alongside. "How much longer do we follow these?" he asked.

"To the end of the valley, if we must. But don't worry. We won't go near the cove."

The trail turned to the south, intersecting the end of the mid-valley trail and continuing on. In the distance could be seen the tree line that marked the southern edge of the valley. As they neared the end and the last intersecting trail, a second set of hoof prints appeared, identical in size and markings, but returning to the Grove on the south valley trail.

"Our rider has made a loop," said Aril. "Can we turn back now?"

"Not yet. Let's see where else these prints go."

The area was familiar to Lameck. It was the way they returned from fishing. It was also close to the abandoned well where they had dumped the giant. Lameck nudged his horse out of the valley and up the slope. A musty odor was in the air and late afternoon shadows from overhead branches cast a giant web over the ground. Aril was no longer riding alongside but was slipping behind, with worry on his face.

Lameck pulled back suddenly on the reins. It was where the prints circled before heading back.

"Lameck, look up," Aril spoke with a loud whisper.

Sitting above them on the branches were six huge black carrion eaters, furling their wings and shifting their gaze between the intruders and something beyond them in the grass.

Lameck slowly got down from his horse and began to walk through the high grass. They had come this far. Now he wanted to see what had brought the mysterious rider to this point. At first nothing was visible. He was prepared for the ugly sight of a dead animal, half picked apart.

Then he saw it, partially hidden at first. Walking closer, his muscles tensed. Doubling over, he dropped to his knees.

"My God!" he cried— "Why? Why?"

In front of him in the grass, in the same red clothing he remembered, lay Talisha, pale and lifeless. Tightly knotted around her neck was something that sent a chill through Lameck's body—a scaly belt, like the one worn by the giant they had killed. And the smell of myrrh.

6

The two brothers lifted Talisha's body to Lameck's horse. Nothing was said. Nothing was known. Stuffing the belt into his pocket, Lameck walked slowly toward the well—*it had to be checked.*

As he got closer, the chill he had felt earlier returned, accompanied by an oppression. The sides were covered with vines. Tendrils pointed with thorns had crept over the top. Lameck carefully pulled them apart and peered down through the opening into the swirling darkness. A stench caused him to hold his breath. *It must still be there*, he thought, but he had to be sure. A tree branch lay nearby. Using his flints, Lameck ignited the wood and carried it flaming back to the well opening, dropping it. He watched it descend, dim, then sizzle at the bottom, faintly illuminating the crumpled mass of the giant's body. He turned away. There was no need to remain.

"What are we going to do?" Aril asked.

"Take Talisha home."

"Tonight?"

The reddening sky reflected the lateness of the day. There were animals that prowled in the dark.

"To the Grove," Lameck replied. "I will take her to the Ridge, tomorrow."

"What about the giant?" Aril's nervousness was apparent in his voice.

"The giant is dead."

"But, the belt. Where did it come from? Could there be another one who came looking for this one?"

Lameck had no answer.

As they started back, Lameck tried to discern what had happened to Talisha...*Had she just wandered or had she been brought to this spot? Why did this happen to the one he was to marry?* ...His next thoughts were chilling. It was as if something knew. *Out of vengeance something had drawn her here—taking blood for blood.* But how such a thing was possible, he could not fathom.

The riders returned to the Grove together, bearing the body, along the twisted and darkening valley trail.

"Go and get father and bring him to the stable," said Lameck.

As Aril rode on to the house, he entered the wooden enclosure, and in the dim light, slid Talisha's body from his horse and gently laid her upon a ledge. Lameck took a blanket down from a hook and spread it over her body, leaving her face visible.

Death among the animals had become a common sight, but human death was something rarely experienced among the Sethites, especially killings. The natural life of man extended hundreds of years, with some close to a thousand. A married couple might expect to be blessed with twenty or thirty children. Eve had fifty-six in all. But Lameck's hopes of having a family with Talisha had been destroyed.

Her face was different than he remembered, so pale with the life and spirit departed. It was the first time he had experienced such loss and emptiness. How helpless he felt. There was nothing he could do—no way to bring her back—to once again enjoy the wonder of her uniqueness, her smile and laughter. How tragically final death appeared. What a terrible enemy to have entered a world that had once been described as being *very good*.

"Where was God now?" Lameck wondered. "What was He thinking about this? Did His heart ache too? Why didn't He stop it from happening?" So many questions and so few answers added to his helplessness.

"Son…Aril told us," said Methuselah. He felt the hand upon his shoulder. His father's presence brought comfort. His mother's arm on his waist caused him to turn and embrace them together. Tears trickled down his face and into his beard.

Together they stood for some time looking at Talisha's still form. Then his father walked over and pulled the gray blanket all the way up. "It will be all right to leave her here for the night," Methuselah said. "I will secure the stable."

"Where did Aril go?" asked Lameck.

"I told him that I wanted two loyal men to accompany you tomorrow on your trip to the Ridge. He was going to make arrangements with Albo for the three of you to go."

"You can walk back with me," said his mother. "Some dinner is waiting for you and your brother. You need to eat."

Lameck had no hunger but for his mother, sat down at the table. His sisters were still busy clearing the other places following the evening meal. He pushed a piece of bread into his mouth, remembering his encounter with Riana the night before. Lameck was surprised when she came up to him and spoke.

"There was something I did not tell you."

"Why are you telling me now?" Lameck tried to sound kind.

"I'm sorry, Lameck. I thought it would make you angry. But now, with Talisha's death, maybe it will help for you to know."

"You knew where she went?"

"No, I had no idea where they were going."

"Sit down, Riana. I am not angry. I just want to know everything you can tell me, beginning with the one who was with her."

Riana remained standing, fidgeting with her waist apron. "I only know that it was more than a casual friendship. It was obvious."

"Who are you talking about?"

"Derrin. I thought you knew."

Lameck felt a gnawing pain. It was the same one his father had told him about the night before.

Aril entered the family room taking a seat next to his brother.

"We were just talking," said Riana.

"I'm glad to see that. Thanks for keeping the food on the table," said Aril.

"Mother did that."

"You were telling me about Derrin," said Lameck. "What were you doing together?"

"It was a family gathering. We were just visiting and sharing news like everyone else. I really don't know much about him, but I could tell there was closeness between the two of them, almost like covenant."

Aril was face down, gulping his food, not showing any attention to the continuing conversation.

"How did you happen to meet with him?" Lameck asked.

"I don't remember ever seeing him before, but he called me by name and said that he knew me. Talisha was like a different person with him, and I felt it too…like some kind of control that he had over those around him."

"What else can you tell me? Did he have a horse?"

"We all walked. I didn't stay with them long and was surprised that Talisha was with him, since you two were making plans for marriage. He was not the sort of man most girls would choose to be with."

"Why was that?"

"There was something about him I can't explain…and his clothing was different."

"In what way?"

"One thing was his repulsive belt. It looked like it was made from a serpent's skin."

Lameck reached into his side pocket. Feeling with his fingers, he untangled it, then stretched the scaly belt across the table between the platters of food— "Is this Derrin's belt?" Lameck asked, staring at Riana.

Her eyes grew big and Aril, with a gagging sound, looked up from his food.

"H-How did you get that?" asked Riana, backing away.

Later, in the darkness of the stable, a lone figure slipped a T-bow and several arrows into a saddlebag and returned up the steps to the tree.

"Are you sure they are Trog's horses?" The high priest scrutinized the face of the keeper.

"There is no doubt, father Jathron. The size and markings are identical."

"No one brought them here?"

"They just showed up in the night, by themselves, without the carrier. I hope to get it back. It was one of our best."

"Interesting. Something caused them to return all the way to Eridu," Jathron thought, as he walked over to the stall. An unnatural restlessness within the horses, which increased with his proximity, raised the priest's suspicion.

"Who are you?" Jathron spoke, catching one of the horses' glances.

The one shook its mane while the other started to tremble.

"You can either tell me, or I will summon Azazel to deal with you."

Pupils widened as the horse's jaw muscles moved. A whining noise turned into distinguishable words— "No-o-o. Don't disturb Azazel."

The keeper stood at a distance, his mouth agape.

"What are your names and how did you enter?" asked Jathron.

The horse's mouth moved again— "Pride and Rampage, two of the greatest Nephilim to ever fight in your arena. Trog allowed us entrance."

"Trog is dead," said Jathron.

"I know. We saw it happen at the hands of Sethite fishermen. Let us stay in the horses, and I will tell you more."

"Very well." Jathron agreed, then turned to face the keeper. "You will not speak of this to anyone, if you value your position."

"I understand, father. This secret will remain concealed."

After hearing the story of the two Sethites who killed and disposed of Trog, along with his carrier, and listening to Pride brag of their escape from Methuselah's stable, Jathron returned to the temple for the scheduled assembly.

This was not the first time he had encountered Nephilim spirits embodied within animals. Although Azazel did not like familiar spirits affecting his livestock, Jathron saw no harm in allowing them to remain. Sometimes they could be a source of knowledge, that is, if their information was true. And getting them to leave was often a struggle, requiring angelic intervention.

Reaching the top of the temple steps, Jathron proceeded through the hallway to the inner chamber. Lifting the hinged knocker, he struck the brass plate three times and waited a moment for the door to swing open. The wail of pipe music greeted him and a tall guardian, standing inside the doorway, directed him to a seat. It was not the seat he would have preferred but he had learned not to dispute Azazel's arrangements of the assembly.

All ten apprentice priests in their hooded robes were gathered around the circular stone table in the center. Among them was where Jathron sat. Surrounding them all, on an upper level, were the gods and their winged assistants. The piping continued from a dark corner with its discordant and mesmerizing magic. Combined with rhythmic beating, it was a powerful tool used in channeling the emotions and energies of man, one of the mysteries revealed by Lucifer to the select priesthood, of which Jathron was a part.

When Azazel stood, the music receded, and full attention was given to the god of Eridu. The elegant Queen Mother was poised in her chair, alongside of him. First taking time to gain eye contact, Azazel then addressed the assembly.

"I welcome the visiting gods to our inner chamber and trust that they will be pleased with what they see. I also welcome our apprentice priests on this occasion, as well as our high priest, to reestablish their commitment to the work, and their worthiness to obtain the status of the gods.

"The City of Eridu continues as a leading power under the principalities of Lucifer. As additional rights are gained to more worldly ground and souls of men, we will expand dominion until all are brought into unity and submission. Only then will the promised peace and utopia be obtained. The gods are pledged to cooperate and network together with the Nephilim for the success of the plan. The priests are essential. The rewards for all will be great.

"Before continuing, do any of the apprentices have any anxieties or concerns that you would like to express? If so, it will be perfectly in order for you to speak."

Japheth was surprised that Azazel would invite such a response during a meeting like this. The apprentices had all been thoroughly interviewed before and after their selection by him and others. Their commitment to the plan had to be resolute.

Azazel's eyes moved around the lower group, then seemed to remain fixed on one at Japheth's right who was staring downward. "Do tell me if you have a concern," Azazel spoke, waiting.

"I just don't understand, my god, why we are not allowed to hear the teachings of the Sethites. If we can learn more about them, then could we not live together in peace?"

With the apprentice's words still hanging in the air, there was a cough, then silence. The piping had stopped. Japheth had never felt such tension in the assembly. The first movement was by Queen Druana who rose and whispered into the ear of Azazel. The god of Eridu then lifted his wings—A rustling sound was heard to Japheth's right— and an empty seat was all that remained of the questioning apprentice.

The piping resumed and the assembly continued with its purpose. At one point, Japheth tried to recall the words of the young apprentice, but could not. His lack of memory concerning the event seemed strange, but he was soon called upon to lead the apprentices in reaffirming their vows of dedication, after which Azazel again spoke.

"I trust we all have heard of the disappearance of Trog, but not everyone is aware of the details. Our sources tell us that Trog was murdered by Sethites. In great number they attacked him while he was sleeping, killed him and threw his body into a well, stealing his horses and carrier. It is obvious that these people do not want peace and that their teachings are false and corrupting. Rejecting the true gods, they make enemies with the world. Does light have fellowship with darkness? Can we make friends with such evil?"

"No! Never! Death to the Sethites!" the assembly yelled.

Azazel smiled. "I am glad that we are all in agreement. The Queen Mother now has something she would personally like to share with you." Turning to Druana, Azazel took her hand and escorted her to a position in front of the head table and the wooden cask which contained the covenant drink. On the table next to the cask was a vial with crimson content.

Facing the chamber guests, Druana was elated. "I have waited too long for this moment. I am delighted to report within the assembly that the blood of my son, Trog, has been partly avenged and his spirit has found another body, a human on our side." Taking the crimson vial, she held it out for all to see. "This is the blood of a Sethite who was involved with the death of Trog. It was extracted from the very spot where our precious hero was dropped. This life was taken for the life of my son and represents the one closest to the heart of the chief murderer. I want us all to savor the taste of vengeance this day."

As Azazel lifted the lid to the cask, Druana poured in the blood.

Soon, everyone was served and, as chalices were lifted, words flowed in unison over the discordant noise of the piping— *"To the success of Lucifer's plan."*

"...the treasure of human life." With his concluding words, Enoch nodded to the four men who lifted the grave box and slowly lowered it with ropes into the dark opening.

A small circle of Talisha's relatives had gathered for the morning burial service, along with the parents. As the dirt was being shoveled back into the earth, Enoch recalled the events from the day before.

The father and mother had been brought to Enoch's house shortly after the arrival of Lameck and others with the body. At first, they refused to believe that their daughter had been murdered. Then, when Lameck showed them the belt that he and Aril had found around her neck, they got angry, shouting accusations at Lameck for failing to protect his future bride. Both Aril and Albo had tried to defend Lameck, but had only created more friction. Enoch had persevered much of the evening trying to calm and restore peace to his injured family.

How the murder had happened was as great a mystery to Enoch as to the others. He knew of that one angel, Lucifer—also called Satan (the adversary)—who, beginning with Cain, had revealed himself as the father of murder, and was the same one who had deceived Eve in the garden. The Cainites had, over time, turned the truth into a lie, making Lucifer their god, Cain a hero, and Abel into the enemy who had threatened their freedom. This corrupt angel was also the father of lies, a master of deception.

But knowing that God had assigned Watchers to protect them, Enoch was not sure how this murdering spirit had done his work in their midst. He suspected that Talisha, or someone close, had given legal ground. He had seen others afflicted with calamity and disease after living in opposition to the teachings of Holy God. Some had died young.

Lameck had told Enoch that his sister had seen the scaly belt being worn earlier by Derrin; but, since his last encounter with her at Methuselah's, Enoch was not sure that Riana's words were true. He had decided not to mention this report to the parents. They were thinking it was one of the Nephilim and, to Enoch, it seemed far more likely.

The grave work was finished and a stone marker was set at the end. A prayer of closure was said by Enoch, after which the people began to exchange condolences. He started to approach the parents but waited, seeing Lameck walking up to them with his arms extended. There was no sign of emotion on the father's face. The mother's eyes were fixed on the grave. Suddenly, as if repelled, the father grabbed her by the shoulders, and both turned and walked away abruptly. No one attempted to slow their departure.

Following the incident, the relatives soon parted to their homes. Albo and Aril walked over to give support to their friend and brother who had lost his bride. Enoch also went and embraced him. Lameck stood stiff, barely responsive, his eyes distant.

"We could all use some rest," said Enoch. "There is enough room and food in the house for everyone to stay longer."

"You are kind to offer, but the day is early and I must return to help my father," said Albo.

"We should also go back," said Aril, looking at his brother.

"Whatever you decide, you have my blessings," said Enoch, waiting for Lameck's response.

"I will stay with Enoch," said Lameck. "Aril, Albo, thank you for coming with me and you can tell father that I should be back in a few days."

Enoch was glad to hear Lameck's response and sent him back to the house to give the others some food for the journey, while he remained a little longer at the gravesite.

Scattered stone markers cast their short shadows on the familiar ground. Stepping past the fresh dirt, Enoch walked to the marker that brought back the deepest emotions—his wife's. His heart was still full of the memories of their years together. Methuselah's wife had the same name, Edna. God had blessed them with three sons and two daughters. It was with the birth of their third son that he had lost her, the one who had shared his love and interests in life, leaving a void in his heart which resulted in a struggle with his God—a desperate search for answers. The result was an encounter with the Holy One, and an ensuing relationship that had continued to grow and fill his inner man with immeasurable peace. After awhile, he knelt and thanked God again for allowing him the years of fulfillment with Edna, for their love, and the simple but profound blessings of life.

While rising to his feet, a movement among the far trees shifted Enoch's attention to the edge of the clearing. It was someone on a horse, receding through the thicket, and then disappearing. The image, though broken and brief, brought to mind just one individual—Derrin. The name was a grief to his spirit, causing earlier questions to resurface. "How long had he been watching and was it him?" Though possible, the Ridge-dweller's involvement was not an admission Enoch was ready to accept.

Later at home, following their mid-day meal, Enoch sat opposite Lameck at the table, studying his countenance.

"Son, you are not to blame for any of this. You tried to share comfort with Talisha's parents, but they were not ready. They took out their hurt on you, for which I am sorry."

"If I had stayed with her…"

"For how long, Lameck? You could not have protected her indefinitely. Talisha's past made her vulnerable."

"What about my past? Do you not think that a dead hero made me vulnerable?"

Enoch was silent.

"Tell me about the One who watches over us," Lameck continued. "Why did God let this happen?"

Enoch did not have the answers to satisfy his injured grandson. He knew that there were mysteries not yet revealed to man and that faith in God was not always easy.

As night turned to morning, Enoch stirred from his sleep. Obeying an inner urge, he got up to check on his grandson. The light from his candle probed through the doorway into the dark traveler's room. All that was visible was a wrinkled depression in the bed. This time, he knew that he would not wait to pray.

7

Having been informed where Derrin lived, Lameck arrived at the western edge of the Ridge by moonlight. Descending to the end of a rocky trail, he spotted the cave entrance, a door and small dark window framed with logs, built into the front, similar to the others. Scraps of wood were scattered in the tangle of overgrowth in front of the doorway. A snorting noise called attention to a horse in a stable at the side.

Easing down from his saddle, Lameck tied his horse to a tree, and then stepped quietly through shadows to the stable. He lifted the catch, swung the gate open and led the horse away, far enough to be sure that it would be out of sight. He then walked back to his own horse, reached into the saddlebag and pulled out the T-bow. After stretching and setting the tension, he inserted an arrow, then sat down on a rock and waited.

Lameck had no doubt that this man was involved in Talisha's murder. His earlier attachment with her, his unusual appearance and departure from the gathering, and the belt that he had been seen wearing were enough. The more he thought about Talisha lying lifeless on the ground, the more hatred rose up against this one who was responsible. Vengeance was in Lameck's nature. It was easy to obey and imparted its own energy and direction.

Jagged streaks of light projected like pointed fingers over the Ridge peak, illuminating the distant forest and the dividing river. The merchant highway between the river and the Ridge was empty, still too early for travelers. Lameck turned his attention back to the house. It was time to do what he had come to do.

Standing to the side of the window, he called with a loud voice.

"Derrin!"

There was no response.

"Derrin!"

Still silence.

Armed with the T-bow, Lameck moved to the door and, taking hold of the handle, slowly pulled. Unlatched, it squeaked open, releasing an odor like decaying meat. Cautiously, he stepped inside the semi-dark room, straining to see any sign of human presence. As he looked around, Lameck noted the absence of furniture, as well as the circled markings of a star on the wall. A broken bench seat, remnants of clothing and other debris cluttered the floor. Seeing no movement, he crossed the room to an opening at the back. Something sent a shiver through him.

There was a passageway faintly illuminated from within. Feeling the T-bow's trigger, Lameck took a deep breath of the putrid air and proceeded through the inner doorway. If he had stopped long enough to consider what he was doing, he might have turned back, but the memory of Talisha was sufficient to keep him going. Her blood cried out for justice and Lameck was the one to bring it. His plan was simple. Confront Derrin with the evidence and avenge Talisha's murder. Though he had never killed a man before, he felt capable.

A tickle against his forehead caused him to jerk backward. Then he spotted the shimmering strands of web stretching from the overhead darkness to the cave wall. Dangling from the strands were the unfortunate insects enshrouded in their silk prison while venom worked internally. The spider was partially hidden in a crevice. Using the T-bow, Lameck brushed the way before him and continued.

The entrance to the first room was dark. The faint light was coming from a room at the end. He kept going, listening. The stillness itself was disconcerting. *Had he entered an empty house? If Derrin was here, was he asleep, or waiting to surprise his unwelcome visitor?* Whichever was the case, he would soon find out. With his shoulder against the outside of the last doorway, Lameck pivoted slowly around, his finger tensing against the trigger of the ready T-bow.

He was unprepared for what he saw. It was a man fitting the description of Derrin, sitting rigid on the floor, facing a flaming lamp on the opposite wall. Half-naked, he appeared to be in a state of meditation with arms folded and legs tucked beneath. The only movement was the swaying flame. Surrounding the lamp were markings similar to the ones in the front room. Lameck was unsure if the man was even aware of his presence behind him.

"Derrin!" Lameck spoke.

The name produced no response.

"You murdered Talisha!"

Digging into his pocket, Lameck grabbed the scaly belt and threw it on the floor next to the man.

Suddenly the man's head turned unnaturally around, his eyes locking onto Lameck. They were serpentine like the giant's he remembered, and the furrows in his face conveyed a depth of hatred that surpassed anything Lameck had ever witnessed. Then a voice sounded—more beastly than human—

"You come to accuse me. Do you know who I am?"

Lameck was paralyzed, his mind filled with fear. He could neither think nor move. The flame instantly went out and the room turned to darkness. As quickly as it happened, a hand clutched him powerfully by the neck and lifted him from the floor. Another hand pinned him to the wall.

"I have waited for you, fisherman. My name is Trog. Yes, I killed your bride, and now I will kill you for what you did to me."

In the dark, the words and grip of the giant were unmistakable. It was the one he and Aril had killed in self-defense. Somehow it still existed in the body of Derrin, and had the strength of ten men. The pressure against his throat was too great. Lameck knew that he was about to die, but he was helpless.

Suddenly his arm felt the recoil and he heard a groan as the T-bow he held discharged. The hands released him.

Dropping to the floor, Lameck desperately crawled and groped his way through the doorway. Seeing some light, he scrambled through the passageway with only one purpose—to escape. Bumping the walls, he ran, finally making it to the front door and slamming it behind.

Outside, he grabbed up a piece of wood. He thrust one end into the rocky soil as an anchor, and angled the other end against the door, pounding it tight. Lameck then ran to the trees, where his horse was waiting, quickly untied the reins and mounted.

Before he could get away, a frightening noise of smashing wood caused him to turn. The door was broken in two on the ground. Crouched in the open hole, peering into the trees at him, was the Nephilim-possessed wild man, the shaft of an arrow protruding from his thigh. Lameck kept looking as Derrin bounded up the slope, barely limping, to the trail—blocking his escape and moving toward him.

There was no other choice and no other way to go. Slapping his horse on the flank, Lameck started down the western side of the Ridge. He held tightly while driving his horse down the rocky incline to the road below, but not so fast as to lose footing. Several times he glanced back and, each time he did, fear rose within him. His pursuer was still after him on foot, leaping and moving like a mountain goat, with speed almost keeping up with the horse. The thought of revenge had now given place to the hope of escape. If only he could make it to the road, then he should be able to outrun this thing which would not slow, despite its wound.

Near the foot of the Ridge, as the incline lessened, Lameck broke his horse into a run. The road was ahead, with the decision whether to flee north or south. It was not a safe place for a Sethite, but better than crossing the river. Approaching it, he could see that the north way was blocked by wagons— Cainites accompanied by Nephilim, heading toward Eden. Lameck could not risk going in their direction and being seen by them. Halting, he looked to the south. What he saw caused his heart to pound. Loping toward the road and cutting off his escape, was Derrin—the crazed superhuman had trapped him.

Running his horse across the road, Lameck paused at the river's edge. The Gihon was not like the Pison, further to the south, but was still a dangerous river to cross. If there was any other choice, he would have taken it. Kicking off his sandals, Lameck led his horse quickly down the bank. His only hope now was to lose Derrin in the forest, to find a place to hide until he could return safely. As the river rose to his chest, he began swimming alongside his horse, keeping one hand on the bridle. His father had told him of river fish that ate living flesh, and had once watched them strip an animal to its bare bones. There were other predators that lurked within the river, reasons to get to the other side quickly.

The current of the Gihon was pushing them northward as they swam. Trying to ignore the pain in his neck from the earlier struggle, Lameck pulled and kicked across the flow. They were almost to the middle of the river when he felt the bridle jerk from his hand. The horse threw its head back, eyes filled with fright at something in front of them. Lameck saw it as the tail trailed down the bank and disappeared below the waterline. Protruding nostrils followed by two bulbous eyes were all that showed, and Lameck knew that it was a crocodile moving toward them.

There was no stopping the horse from turning back, churning the water in its retreat. With his hands free, Lameck took a deep breath and ducked beneath the surface. If he tried to return, he felt he would die for certain. Continuing to the forest bank, at least he thought he would have a chance. Pulling with all his might, he stayed underwater, guided by the current against his body. The crocodile was watching the surface and, he hoped, would not see him. Lameck held his breath until he felt that his head would burst, then his fingers touched some roots. He had made it safely. Pulling himself out of the water, he looked back through a low branch. The crocodile had not changed direction, and Lameck estimated its length at forty feet. It had followed the horse and was almost to the opposite side when the horse came out of the water and quickly climbed up the bank. The crocodile then submerged.

It was the former danger that concerned Lameck the most. Scanning the opposite bank, he could not see Derrin, and dared not to underestimate his abilities. This being had pursued him this far. "Would he stop now? Could he already be in the forest?" Lameck wondered, but had no weapon and decided not to stay where he was—too easily to be found. Though wet, exhausted, and in pain, he hurriedly strapped his feet with leaves and made his way into the forest.

The enveloping silence of the forest depths was broken only by the muffled crunching of his footsteps and the overhead shrieks of furry and feathered creatures among the limbs, either swinging or nesting. As a child, he had ventured a few times into the forest to explore with his father. They had crossed the river by boat to get a closer look at some of the greater creatures. It had been fascinating, but was also a place where the curse upon the earth had proven deadly to man. Slithering and crawling kinds, some with wings, possessed poison defenses that one had to be careful to avoid.

Lameck stepped carefully as he went, looking for a spot that would provide good hiding. The vegetation of the forest offered some concealment; but it was the root systems of the massive cypress trunks that contained crevices deep enough for any security. Finding a hole the right size, Lameck used a branch to brush out the foot-long beetles, then crawled into the depression between the gnarled roots, pulling the branch over the opening.

Hidden in the shadows of his dirt retreat, Lameck rubbed his neck. It throbbed with pain, as did his ribs, where he had been pressed against the wall. He wondered how such strength was possible from a man smaller than himself. Then he thought about the voice of Trog. For a moment he felt fear—then doubt, concerning the things he had been taught. What kind of powers were at work upon the earth? Why did he feel like an animal, cowering from another creature more powerful? These and other thoughts were stilled in an instant by a light so bright that it penetrated his covering.

"Is this the conqueror, Lameck, who hides himself in the dirt?"

It was not the voice of the one he feared. Whoever it was, in such light, knew the identity of Lameck's name as well as where to find him. Slowly, he moved the branch.

"Come out of your hole."

Lameck lifted himself, gazing upon the most glorious being he had ever beheld. He had heard the fathers tell of angels, though he had never seen one, or imagined such radiance. He felt compelled to bow before him, and did so, lowering his face to the earth, hesitant to speak.

"Do you know who I am?"

"Are you an angel of Holy God?"

"Lameck, you have been deceived, but are wise to bow before me. I am the god of this world, with the power to deliver you from the danger you fear."

"Forgive me, but I have been taught of only one God."

"And you do well to bow before him. I know of your loss which the God of the Sethites lacked the power to prevent; neither does he intend to avenge the one who murdered your bride. Why should you continue to see injustice?"

"If I have been deceived, have my fathers also?"

"They are only men, with limited understanding. They did not intend to mislead you, but I have appeared to give you the illumination they failed to receive. You have been chosen to receive special knowledge and power."

Lameck remained silent with wonder.

"It is time, and the decision is yours. Do you want to continue in suffering and humiliation, or are you ready to see justice and vengeance upon your enemies?"

"*Vengeance*." The word slipped from Lameck's tongue with hardly a thought.

"It is done. Blood will be your sign. And, in return, all that is required is your loyalty. Do you covenant with me as the true god, and renounce all others not aligned with me?"

"I do."

"Excellent. It is sealed. To help you, I have assigned a spirit. Become familiar with it."

Lameck inhaled and felt his body strengthen. The pain and tiredness were amazingly gone. "Can you help me safely return?"

"Go back the way you came. When you reach the river bank, continue south and you will find a vessel with which to cross. Your horse will be waiting."

"But, what if Derrin..?"

"Do not worry about him, my Lameck. He is no longer a danger."

"How may I call upon you for help?"

"If you should need me, just call upon the name of your god, Lucifer."

After the luminous being departed, Lameck returned to the river bank and followed it, as instructed, a short distance. There he found the vessel, a dug-out log and paddle. Pushing it into the river, he noticed that the water was crimson at his feet. Curious, his eyes followed the red trail along the river bank to its source—the closed jaws of the crocodile, its head resting halfway in the water. The rest of its body stretched up the bank and into the forest. Its size was greater than Lameck had imagined and the belly bulged out of proportion a distance of about six feet. There was no movement from the full predator as Lameck slid the vessel into the water, and none as he continued back across the river to his waiting horse.

The words came back to him as he paddled—*Blood will be your sign*. It was then that he realized that his feet had stepped in Derrin's blood. Lucifer had obtained his covenant loyalty through vengeance on Talisha's murderer.

A slight smile came to his mouth.

———————

Bathenosh held the reins on the riding board. It was near the end of a three-day journey from Eridu, and the misty contour of Eden's mountain loomed in the distance. Her father was seated alongside while her mother and younger brother rested in the wagon's rear enclosure. To their right, a Nephilim-driven carrier passed the north-bound pilgrimage raising a trail of dust. Bathenosh's family was traveling with the final group of Cainites that had duties in the temple, and the Nephilim had been instructed to guard them safely to and from their destination.

"You're a good driver, Bathy." Her father used the shorter, affectionate name.

"Father, have you heard of anyone, other than the gods, ever seeing inside the garden?"

"Not since our first parents."

"Can the Nephilim go inside?"

"I do not know," he replied, reaching over and taking the reins. "Maybe you can help your mother get ready."

Bathenosh turned, lifted the corners of the cloth enclosure and stepped back into the wagon. A low moan was heard as her sleeping brother rolled away from the light.

"We must be getting close," said her mother, looking up. She was just finishing her work on a basket.

"The shrine is not far. Let me help prepare the offering," said Bathenosh, sitting down next to her. With the basket between them, they placed and arranged the gifts within it—the sticks of spice, two jars of oil, and three small bread-cakes. Bathenosh gently squeezed one, feeling its freshness and enjoying its sweet nutty aroma. "Do you think the gods will be unhappy that we have no gold or onyx stones to offer?"

"It is the best that we can do. They should understand," her mother replied, spreading a white cloth over the top and tucking it into the sides.

The wagon jerked a few times as it slowed behind the large pachyderm. Through the front opening the towering cedars of Eden could be seen, enveloping the procession in a sky of green. The lush beauty and majesty of the region was wondrous to behold. Stretching her arms, Bathenosh felt like she was in a different world. "It's so peaceful, mother. Why can't it be like this in Eridu?"

"We would be too busy to notice it."

"Maybe we should make our home here." Her mother did not reply and Bathenosh knew that it was an impossible dream. After presenting their offering at the garden shrine, they would circle the mountain and return to Eridu, as they had done in the past. She would return to her duties in the temple and everything would be the same. At least she could carry the memory of Eden back with her.

After leaving the main roadway, the pilgrimage wound through the trees and into the eastern campsite, where they would stay until the next morning. Bathenosh's family wagon pulled into a space among the others, near the stone wall that bordered the shrine. An open gate in the center allowed people to enter the shrine area.

"Garden mushrooms!" came the familiar yell of the hallucin hawker.

"Can we get one?" asked her younger brother, Rushton, who had finally awakened. "My friends eat them."

"No," came the quick response of their father.

Many people did eat the speckled mushrooms, which were known to produce unusual visions, but Bathenosh's family was different. For some reason her father did not allow them to participate, and she thought well of him for this.

"Get your mushrooms and see the glory," the hawker's voice faded as he walked on through the site, a full leather pouch on his waist.

"Are we ready?" asked her father. "The shrine is open."

"I will be happy when this is finished," said Rushton.

"Just be respectful," said his mother. "We don't want an incident report from the priest."

"Is that understood?" asked his father, waiting for an acknowledgment from Rushton.

"Yes." The word finally came.

Being the eldest child and a temple worker, Bathenosh had accepted the responsibility of presenting the gift at the shrine. Lifting the basket this time seemed easy compared to the weight of the oil and candles she sometimes had to take up the temple steps. After walking with her family through the gateway, Bathenosh proceeded by herself to the table where the priest was stationed, taking her place in line. The rest of the family seated themselves to the side on one of the viewing benches. In front, a lower spiked wall prevented anyone from getting any closer to the ancient garden boundary which was several hundred feet further. Bathenosh strained to see the place she had been taught that man and woman had first developed, with the help of the gods, from another form of life. It was dense with foliage.

The dark marble shrine stretched upward from a broad triangular base to a narrow apex, with sixteen steps leading up to the feet of the gold-winged god—a statue, and the place where the gifts were laid. In the grass to the left of the shrine, three Nephilim sat talking loudly among themselves.

"Name?" The voice of the priest startled her. It was her turn.

"Bathenosh, daughter of Milcah," she replied.

Scrolling through the names, the priest placed a mark, and then looked up. "Your offering?" She set the basket in front of him, waiting, while he lifted the cover and scrutinized the contents. The corners of his mouth tightened to a thin line. "Is this all that you are giving?" he asked, still gazing into the basket.

"Our family is not wealthy. The gods should understand that it is the best we can do."

"How would you, a common Cainite, know what the gods understand?"

Bathenosh remained silent, not wanting to irritate the priest.

"Take it and present it, but I cannot promise a blessing."

Taking up her family's offering, Bathenosh secured the cloth cover and began the walk up the marble steps. On the way she wondered about the reaction of the priest—the first time disapproval had been expressed—to the same modest offering that they had given in the past. The thought troubled her that the gods might this time act differently and withhold their blessings toward her family, but concluded that perhaps it was the priest who did not understand the gods.

Thirteen...fourteen...fifteen... Bathenosh took the last step into the shadow of the gold image. Bending, as instructed, with her face down, she set the basket by the others, then slowly turned away and began her descent. When she was almost down, she heard a deep voice from below but ignored it and continued on. After stepping onto the lower walkway, her return was blocked by one of the giants.

"Look at me. I am Ugar, speaking to you."

Bathenosh had no choice but to stop for the giant. She preferred to stay away from them, considering them vile creatures. This one was no different and, in his eyes, appeared to be devoid of sense.

"Ugar gets what he wants," the giant continued with a gruff voice, his hands on his waist, "and what I want now is a pretty Cainite bride."

"Don't listen to him," came the voice of another giant, seated on the ground. "Ugar eats too many mushrooms."

Whirling around and almost losing balance, Ugar drew his sword, pointing it in the direction of the other giant. "No one gets in Ugar's way," he growled, then looked back at Bathenosh, extending his hand. "Come. Ugar will give you all that you want."

Urgently and silently, Bathenosh appealed to any God with power to help, and instantly an idea and words came to mind— "How do I know that Ugar can get me anything I want?" she asked.

"Name it and it is yours," the giant replied.

"A piece of fruit from the garden," she paused, "unless that it is too difficult for the mighty Ugar."

"Nothing is too difficult for Ugar, my bride will see."

Bathenosh watched the creature turn in the direction of the garden, sword still in hand. The people watched from the benches. The other Nephilim watched. Ugar took a big breath, then began running, gaining speed as he went, stomping past the great trees and into the thickness surrounding the garden. Just as he disappeared from sight—a *SWISH*, like a quick wind sounded, and a fiery arc of light flashed in the distance. Everyone waited, but nothing more was seen or heard.

Shaken, but grateful to the God who saved her, Bathenosh returned to her family.

8

Enoch sat still, listening to Lameck, as he told of his encounter with Derrin, the sudden change and manifestation of superhuman strength, his retreat into the forest, and finally, the evidence that the Ridge-dweller had been devoured. Nothing was said of Lucifer's appearance or the covenant into which he had entered. Lameck lifted the cup to his mouth, savoring the juice, as he waited for a response from his grandfather.

"What did you hope to gain by going to Derrin's?" Enoch asked.

"He was responsible for Talisha's death," Lameck replied, bringing the cup down with a thud.

"Was it your intent to kill him?"

"I would have."

"Did you consider the council?"

"Reconciliation would not have worked."

"The council will take action when it is needed."

"Could they have punished a giant?"

Enoch paused, "That is unusual…the possession that you described…at least among Sethites."

"So, is there no justice? Do the Nephilim simply go to other bodies when they lose their own, to work their evil? Surely, you have all the answers, great teacher." The words were sarcastic and, for a moment, Lameck wished that he had not spoken them. But he was angry, and frustrated over his lack of understanding as to how these things happened—things he could not see or control.

"I do not wish to have all the answers. There are hidden things that belong to God alone. Do you recall how you reasoned with your cousins at this table?"

Lameck was silent.

"You used the logic of cause and effect to show the greatness of God from the things that He created. Using the same logic, who do you think placed a sense of justice within you— knowledge of right and wrong—even from childhood? If the created image has such an attribute, then how much greater is the attribute of justice within the Creator?"

"Why don't we see it?"

"We do not see the wind. Neither can we see the ways of Holy God. They are not our ways and His purposes are accomplished in His own time, not ours."

"Are you saying that vengeance is wrong?"

"I am saying that God has ways of dealing with injustice and that we should trust His ability to act, no matter how painful the wait may be. Our part is to release the evil-doer into His hands."

"What if we are His instruments?"

"We are all His instruments—some for honor, others to bring dishonor. There is a price for putting ourselves in God's place to bring judgment. I am not talking of defending our families, but of acting out of hatred. Our natural urges do not speak with wisdom, often leading us to do things destructive to ourselves and to the ones we love."

"It is the ones I love that I desire to protect."

"Then learn first to walk in the ways of Holy God."

Shoving his chair back, Lameck stood and turned away, moving toward the door. "I am no longer sure that this God of the Sethites is the true God, or even exists."

"Lameck, please come back and sit. Let us talk more about this."

"It is all you seem able to do—talk," Lameck said, as he walked out through the doorway. "I need some fresh air."

He had to get away from Enoch for awhile. He felt his heart racing and the trickle of sweat on his forehead. For some unknown reason, he was afraid to face his grandfather. It was as if Enoch knew everything about him, even his secrets. The thought of being judged by someone able to discern the intent of his heart was more than uncomfortable, it was terrifying. But, rationally, there was no reason to fear Enoch. His grandfather had never done anything to cause Lameck to be afraid of him. He had only offered to help.

As he walked along the trail in the gathering darkness, night birds swooped about him, like the thoughts darting through his mind, bringing only confusion. At one point, on a rocky overlook, Lameck stopped. *What was happening? Where was the confidence he used to have?* An impulse came to call upon his newly revealed god, the one with whom he had covenanted, for assistance—

"Lucifer."

He waited, remembering the promise he had been given.

"Lucifer!" He tried again, louder, still waiting.

"Lucifer?"

Searching the darkness but with no response, Lameck decided to return once again to the dwelling. Perhaps Lucifer had other more important business as god of the whole world. It was incredible that Lameck had been able to see him even once, he thought, with so many places to rule.

The door was already slightly ajar when Lameck opened it further and stepped inside. He felt relief to see that Enoch was not waiting up for him, though the lamp had been left burning on the table. Extinguishing it, he went to his room. After lying down, Lameck still could not rest. *Something in the room was disturbing him.* Finally, he realized that it was the collection of the fathers' writings on the table next to him. Without knowing why, he moved it to the far corner of the room. He felt better and returned to his bed. Thoughts continued to trouble him, but eventually he shut his eyes.

The eyes of the high priest popped open. His bed was wet with perspiration and his breathing rapid. It was not the first time the dream had awakened him, and he dared not mention it to Azazel. Both times it was a great white throne, before which all humanity was bowing. The terrifying part was that the One enthroned was not aligned with the god he knew, and the judgment of everyone was in that One's hands.

Deciding again to ignore it, Jathron forced himself up and across the stone floor to his wash basin. He could not afford to be occupied with thoughts that contradicted everything he had been trained to believe. After drying, he slipped into the white full-length robe, for the dawn sacrifice. A reddish-brown stain near the waist annoyed him which had been the result of a careless apprentice. A replacement robe had not yet been delivered and the appearance bothered him as he hastened to the site.

It was a short walk from the priests' quarters to the south side of the temple and the River Pison, where the human sacrifices took place. Young women were the usual offering; but on this occasion, Azazel had informed him that Lucifer wanted an infant. Preparations had been made the day before with little difficulty. An unmarried woman had been shamed into giving up her baby. Some did it for freedom from a constrained life-style, or as a noble deed. Most likely, she would not be present to watch, heeding the priest's advice, nor would her guilt be removed. Guilt was found useful in obtaining sexual favors.

Two assistants were standing in their dark robes on the sacrificial platform ninety feet above the river channel. The supporting timber structure leaned outward from its base in the river bank. Nearby, giants were still arriving from Phlegra through the underwater tunnel, a project constructed prior to Jathron's arrival, following the breakaway of the southern land mass. It had taken decades and required the diverting of the Pison until a trench could be dug and stone tube completed, reconnecting the two mainlands. Thronged behind the Nephilim and sloping up from the water's edge, were the people of Eridu, sufficient in number to fill the area.

"Is everything in place?" Jathron asked, approaching the stepway that led up to the platform.

"Everything is ready, Father Jathron," said one of the priests.

Gripping the rail, he began the climb. On the horizon, an orange orb bridged the eastern inlet, Pison's portal to the sea, casting illumination on the high priest's ascent. To his left, on the upper ledge of the temple, Azazel and Druana sat with other dignitaries in their favored positions. Some nervousness was suppressed as Jathron reminded himself of his own position and set his mind to mechanically follow the routine.

Upon reaching the platform, he proceeded to the stand for the incantation. He withdrew the scroll from the leather sleeve and unrolled it to the familiar words. Pausing a moment to look over the ground-level assembly, he then spoke with a voice loud enough to be heard. The two others stood waiting, the sacrifice and instruments in front of them.

"...to the glory of our god, Lucifer." The reading was completed.

Jathron turned and faced the sacrificial table. At his nod, they executed their solemn duty, and the collective chanting of Lucifer's name began. There was a time when the helpless cries bothered him, before he had been fully indoctrinated. But now he had proudly received illumination and was no longer subject to petty human emotions. His higher rationale was able to disconnect from that which was only flesh. One day, he would be an immortal god, sharing Lucifer's command and respect.

The chanting continued as they waited.

The push of air was felt against Jathron's face and a hush fell upon the assembly. The luminous winged creature appeared, hovering above the sacrifice. It was Lucifer. To Jathron, his presence and voice conveyed his godly authority over the world—

"My Nephilim, and people of Eridu, you have done well in carrying out my instructions. Continue to worship me, and obey those I have empowered over you. Under my rule, receive the protection you need and the pleasures you enjoy from the secret things I reveal. Be loyal and you will discover great rewards when my plan is consummated and the resistance is removed. Now, let your eyes behold the power that you serve."

Jathron watched with awe as Lucifer, wings outstretched, gradually descended and disappeared into the depths of the Pison. The priests then tied the end of a rope to the handle of the basket containing the sacrifice, and swung it from the end of a wooden arm, out and over the river. Taking up a cup of blood, the high priest poured it over the side into the river, and then stepped back.

The rolling movement on the surface of the Pison could be seen in the distance. A serpentine path was being traced from the inlet by the turbulent force beneath, sending swells splashing against the bank as it approached. As it neared, the long twisting shadow parted the water with a snort of smoke. The assembly, along with the Nephilim, cried out and shifted away from the river bank. Jathron moved to the back rail, along with one of the priests, while the other priest, an apprentice, remained at the front edge looking down. "He will learn to step back," Jathron thought, "after his first experience."

Its dark glistening back was lined with scales like armored plates, sliding and whipping one way then another, following a horned head of great size. Of all the creatures on the earth and in the sea, there were none that inspired such dread as Leviathan, extending over 300 feet in length, and thwarting any deep-water expeditions by man.

The low rumble of voices from those watching had been heard since it was first sighted, but now everyone was quiet. It had gone under about a hundred feet away.

"What's the matter? Come on," said the apprentice, pushing on the arm and causing the dangling sacrifice to swing.

Jathron had decided not to say anything, preferring to let this one learn a lesson. The high priest's hand was on the rail and holding tightly.

"Maybe the old fellow isn't hungry," the apprentice spoke again, turning to the other priests with a smirk—

As the words left his mouth, a chilling roar erupted from below. The platform shook, causing Jathron almost to fall. A scream and collective gasp broke the silence of the crowd. Jathron saw the terrified expression of the apprentice as he turned back to face the creature he had treated so casually. Leviathan's head and long neck had risen to the height of the platform. Eyes like the morning sun were fixed on the basket, still swinging, and upon the apprentice, whose hand had dropped from the wooden cross member. Leviathan continued raising himself up, looking down at the trembling apprentice huddled on his knees at the platform's edge. The jaws had been shut, but suddenly they opened like iron gates. Rows of swords sent shivers through the high priest's body. Then sparks of light within ignited a burst of flame. Jathron turned, clutching the rail with both arms. The blast of heat could be felt against his back and legs. Behind him there was a shriek, then a splintering jolt to the platform, followed by the crashing rush of water from below

Jathron slowly turned his head and looked. A jagged blackened edge was all that remained of the river side of the platform. Trembling, he returned to the temple.

"Is insubordination an issue within the priesthood?" Azazel asked, tapping his fingertips on the chamber table between them.

"It was foolish behavior," Jathron replied. "He was a useful apprentice, but was taking awhile to develop."

"The incident was an embarrassment to the council and must not ever happen again. Am I understood?"

"Of course, my lord."

"There is another one who has outlived his usefulness to us, your contact among the Sethites—Derrin, I recall, was his name."

It bothered Jathron that he was late in learning of such news. "That is unfortunate, but I have other sources of information that should be of help to the council, details of the family that was involved with…"

"It will not be needed," Azazel cut his reply short. "Lucifer has become personally involved in the matter. We now have our own contact within.

"Excellent." Jathron tried not to appear self-serving.

"Yes," Azazel said, his wings expanding into view, "Now you can devote yourself more fully to your primary duties, the preparation of the priests and the subjugation of the people. You are still the high priest."

Unnerved by the word (*still*), Jathron thought it better not to reply.

"Let the people enjoy their simple pleasures and provide them with plenty of pharmako. That way they stay more controllable. Remember what you have been taught by those of us with far longer experience in manipulating human nature. Continue to keep them occupied with images and events of our choosing. Too much musing and they may see through your persuasive techniques and become less useful to the plan."

Gimlet's loft was on the Grove's west side, a short walk from the stable. Overhanging the lower limbs, it had been built as a night-time get-away by old Gimlet himself with the help of companions.

It had been late when Lameck arrived. Enoch's prodding had stirred up voices within, and such tension that he could not stay at the Ridge any longer. He had departed mid-morning without breaking bread, though his grandfather had insisted that he take some with him. The loft was not the place Lameck often visited, but he was not yet ready to return home.

"What will you boys have?" They were all boys to Gimlet at around 300 years of age. His wrinkled face, furrowed with anxiety, gave the appearance of a far older man.

"Bring us a pitcher of your best", Albo replied. He had joined Lameck upon seeing him, leaving another table nearby.

"So, did you have a chance to see Talisha's parents again?" asked Albo.

"Not yet." The question irritated Lameck. He looked around the room. Everything was pretty much as he remembered, even after a year. The animal carvings were still gathering dust and the sketches on the walls still bragged of Gimlet's adventures. A fishing spear and hunting bow hung from a beam in front of the mounted head—Gimlet's central trophy.

The beast's mouth was spread and its rows of teeth illuminated by the lamps on the overhead wagon wheel. Lameck recalled the story Gimlet told of how he had tracked and killed it, almost losing his life in the final confrontation. Another report was that he had found the animal already dead, then severed and brought back the head, inventing a heroic lie. The head had been coated with clear resin and the eyes had been replaced with painted rocks.

"How was your trip back?" Albo asked, still trying to make conversation.

Lameck tried to recall any significant details, but could not. He had been pre-occupied with past events throughout the trip.

"Here you are, boys." The owner had returned with the drinks. "Enjoy Gimlet's best, a better batch than the last time you were here."

Before Lameck could dig into his pocket, Albo slid a small piece of gold across the table. "Let me take care of this. I don't get to see you here that often," said Albo, smiling and reaching for the pitcher.

Except for the bubbles, it looked like just a citrus drink. But Lameck had noticed how it changed people's perceptions, making some happy, while having an opposite effect on others. Methuselah did not speak well of the loft and cautioned his family against going, claiming that it weakened integrity and produced laziness. While respecting his father, Lameck had not always heeded his words. "What if it did change his perceptions," he wondered. "Reality had not been very enjoyable lately. Maybe it would improve his feelings."

"Let me tell you about my trip back with your brother," said Albo, taking a swallow. "We had just left Enoch's and were almost down the Ridge when we spotted movement in the grasses. You know Aril. He's like you, wanting to investigate…"

Curiosity could be deadly, Lameck thought. How close he had come recently to finding that out. Grotesque images of

Derrin pursuing him down the slope jumped through his mind. Sensing moisture on his hand, he recaptured his thoughts and the realization that he had sloshed some drink from the cup. "Sorry…you were telling of Aril. I got distracted."

"There was a group of them we chased through the grasses. They were quick and running at angles, but we were gaining and having fun." Albo paused to refill both of their cups, and then continued with the account.

Lameck was thinking of Talisha, the fun times they had spent together, their walks together, the ride in the slidecart—then the tragic sight of her lying strangled in the grass. Suddenly he felt sick.

"Are you feeling alright," asked Albo. "You look pale."

"I think so…still going through all that has happened recently. Go on."

"As I was saying, we found ourselves facing a three-horn, and it was ready to charge…"

The juice was making Lameck light-headed. He realized that he had not been listening. Occasionally he looked at Albo, with his mouth still moving, then glanced around the room. The talk from other tables was like a waterfall of voices, surging and receding, then surging again, building in volume with the passing time. Smoke pots on tables slowly blanketed the air as people inhaled and blew from long reed extensions.

The atmosphere of the loft had changed since Lameck had first entered. A collective consciousness was pulling like a whirlpool, sedating and sweeping everyone along into a mindless flow of participation. Something within was wanting to relax and to be a part, but something else told him that it was foolish and destructive.

"Isn't that Methuselah's boy, the one who killed the hero?" The words came like a dart from another table. Heads turned.

Lameck sensed the hostility. Groggy from the juice and smoke, he tried to focus, but the figures were like a mirage with indistinct movement.

"That's the one that put our families in danger."

"What is he doing here?"

They were becoming more challenging and, like a shadow, closing around him. In Lameck's mind there was no way to reason, no single person with whom to talk. They were each part of a whole, with a stalking, animal-like nature, moving in unison.

Albo stood and tried to intercede.

"Get out of the way, Albo," one of them spoke. "You're not part of this."

Lameck could no longer sit still. He had only wanted to be left alone, but now he felt trapped like a creature surrounded by hunters. At first he was confused, then he rose with anger. Mentally he did not know how to respond. It was the rage within him that took control, summoning a strength and sudden response that surprised himself.

He spun and reached, his hands tightening around the necks of two men, one on each side of him. Jerking them upward and swinging them together, he cracked their heads and dropped them to the floor. Grabbing another by the beard and belt, Lameck tossed him through the air and onto a table, splitting it with the fall. Sensing something behind, he started to turn when something struck him, causing everything to disappear.

9

"OOOOOYAAAA"

Enoch's groanings arose from the depths of his spirit. Human language could not convey the anguish he felt for his family, especially for his grandson, Lameck. He knew that something had happened. On his face in intercession, Enoch was detached from the time that had passed.

The knock was barely discernable until he heard it again, louder. With some reluctance, he pushed himself up from the mat and made his way through the hall—the sunlight in the front room, his first awareness that it was day. Anticipating a call to mediate a family squabble, Enoch parted the door.

It was not what he thought. The warmth that he felt from his father's eyes, and his grandfather with him, was a rush of joy unexpected. They lived near Seth, Adam's third son, two days north, and saw each other about twice a year. With smiles, the three embraced.

"What brings my fathers to the Ridge and where did you spend the night?"

"Son, we have come to see you. There is no need for lodging," said his father, Jared.

"Will you come inside? There is bread to be shared."

"Come with us. We can talk on our way back to our campsite."

Closing the door behind, Enoch joined his two fathers, walking between them, as they proceeded up the trail through shades of green. He felt at peace, yet curious as to the reason for their trip.

For awhile they walked quietly, then Mahalel spoke, "Word has come that the Nephilim are constructing new weapons."

"More swords and carriers?" asked Enoch.

"These are reported to be different, able to bring great destruction."

"Do we know how or when they will use them?" asked Enoch.

"Not exactly," replied Jared, "but we have known for some time that the Nephilim are not likely to remain in Phlegra. Their consumption of land and food increases every year as they grow and multiply."

"The Cainites are unable to meet the growing demands from their own storehouses, though they are being pressed to do so," said Mahalel.

"What does the council say of this?"

Jared answered, "They believe that we may have only a short time until the Nephilim move to take our lands."

"As you know, the Cainites will not help us. They all serve the same false gods," said Mahalel. "In another hundred years, these Nephilim could subdue the earth and the human population."

"With this weaponry, it could be much sooner," said Jared.

"Do we know any more about them?" asked Enoch.

"They have been a mystery since their first appearance, about the time you were born," said Mahalel. "I have heard that an angel named Semjazza, one of the Watchers over Phlegra, was responsible, though he is not alone. As everyone knows, their evil continues with the daughters of men. The giant offspring seem partly human, but are not our kind."

Enoch felt a familiar grieving within his spirit. He was convinced that an unspeakable evil and violation of God's boundaries had transpired by His creation, both angelic and human, and now all were suffering as the evil progressed.

The pace of the three had slowed as they continued uphill, approaching the Ridge summit and place where the fathers had camped. At the edge of the clearing, overlooking the eastern slope and the distant plains, the fathers seated themselves across from Enoch on log benches.

"Does the council have a plan?" asked Enoch, his eyes briefly sweeping the panorama of the golden plains.

"There is no human plan or weapon that is able to succeed against the Nephilim. They have supernatural help," said Mahalel, steadying his attention on Enoch.

"That is why we are here, son," said Jared, also looking intently at Enoch. "Ever since you were a child, it has been evident that God was drawing you into a favored place with Himself, a special relationship which few of us have ever experienced since the earliest days in the garden."

"We need Holy God's help," said Mahalel.

"Of course, my fathers. I will do whatever I can."

"There is something else," spoke Jared, "a dream that came to my father. He wants to share it with you. Perhaps God will reveal the meaning, as He has done through you in the past."

"Tell me the dream."

Mahalel pulled at his beard and looked away thoughtfully. "It was a firstborn son… I am uncertain as to identity. He was bound head to foot with grave wrappings and faced a turbulent and rising sea. Everywhere was darkness. A second man appeared who loosed the son's bindings and sent him into the waters. After an uncertain time, the darkness receded and the man returned with a woman. They were riding the back of a bird with luminous wings." Mahalel gazed at Enoch. "When they returned, the second man was gone, and I awoke."

Enoch had been prayerfully listening and immediately discerned some of the meaning, however there were parts not yet so clear about which he still wondered.

"Can you tell us who the men are?" asked Jared.

Without hesitation Enoch replied, "The first man is Lameck."

"Methuselah's firstborn?" asked Mahalel.

"Yes…and I am the second man who looses him and sends him," said Enoch. "Somehow, Lameck will be used to set back the threat we are facing."

"And the woman?" asked Jared. "Who is she?"

"I do not know, but the two of them will be delivered out of great danger by the hand of Holy God. That is all that has been revealed to me at this time."

"Son, before we leave, we must do one most important thing," said Jared, rising with Mahalel from their bench. "Let us give you our blessings."

Enoch slipped to his knees, bowing before his fathers and felt their hands rest upon his head and shoulders.

By faith he received the words of empowerment that he would need for the task ahead. He was confident that the fathers' authority to speak was ordained and would be honored by God.

"Your father has compensated Gimlet for the damages." It was the familiar voice of Lameck's mother as she drew the damp towel out from under his head. The throbbing pain would not let him rest.

"mmm… damages?" Lameck murmured.

"Albo said you threw a man through a table and seriously injured two others."

"I do not remember." Lameck smelled the balm and olive oil that had been rubbed in. It was their family remedy for injuries, though it was not working as well as usual.

"You are fortunate to be alive. You know how we feel about Gimlet's place."

"Gimlet's… How did I get here?"

"With the help of Albo and another. Promise us you won't go back."

"Did he say what happened?"

"Someone clubbed you. They said you lost control and just started fighting."

Lameck tried to move but the pain from the back of his head pierced like a knife through his body. The dark wooden beams overhead formed double images to the right, then to the left…back and forth….

"This is not like you, Lameck," she continued,

"You're not fifty anymore.

"What were you thinking?

"Why couldn't you have—"

"Mother," Lameck interrupted, but he couldn't think of a satisfying explanation.

"Here," she said, lifting his head and positioning a fresh towel. "Just think about what you have done, not just to yourself but to your family." After looking at him a moment longer, his mother turned and walked out of the room.

Disgrace. The word was as clear as if it had been heard, stinging deeply as an arrow that had been dipped in poison. Lameck felt it sink within. Like a fool, he had shamed his family. His actions had brought disgrace. It wasn't like him, she had said. How did she know? How could anyone know what he was like—what he had gone through since Talisha's murder? Emotionally detached images of his family members—mother, father, brothers, sisters…one-by-one, passed by like painted figures. He knew of them but no longer was part of them. Why, he did not know.

Something was wrong, but he was still Lameck, the eldest son. This was his home. Whatever had happened, he would make himself go on, swallowing the pain and the guilt.

Footsteps in the hall.

Lameck knew *it was the father coming to reprimand the son for the disgrace he had caused.* A flash of fear brought back an image of the giant as it stepped from its carrier and approached them on the beach. The approach of the father connected the same fear of confrontation to his indwelling shame. Like a wave it enveloped him, causing his heart to quicken, his breath to shorten.

The familiar and dreaded steps slowed, and then stopped. A door opened, and then closed. Methuselah had entered his study.

At first Lameck sensed relief—then the jolt of rejection. *The shame he had caused had been so hurtful that his father refused to see him.* Though the words had not been spoken, his isolation was painfully evident to his mind that it was true. He lay still, just staring.

Gradually, he moved his foot to the floor. With resolve, he raised himself. The room swayed as he stood. He then proceeded slowly to the doorway and into the hall. Passing the closed door of the study, Lameck continued down the steps and through the family room to the outside front deck. He went to the bench and just sat.

As he stared, vacantly looking out, something caught his attention—a low, soaring bird, but too rigid. Abruptly it landed and without motion lay in the clearing in front of their tree. Moments later, Aril appeared, walking toward it. Lameck watched curiously as his brother bent over and picked something up. From the overlook, he couldn't tell what it was. The object was hidden from view.

He called to Aril but got no response.

Again he called, louder.

This time Aril paused, and with a surprised expression looked up.

"What do you have?" Lameck asked.

The reply was too low to be heard.

"Wait, I'm coming down."

Aril stood still while Lameck carefully descended the stair-ladder and stepped through the grass to his brother.

"What is it?"

"Something I made."

"Let me see it."

Reluctantly, Aril held it out. It reminded Lameck of a T-bow, but in place of the bow there was a long thin piece of wood. A similar but smaller structure with a vertical section was attached to the opposite end. The main body of wood looked familiar. Lameck took it in his hands.

"It is called a wooden bird," said Aril. "They sell them in Eridu."

"You have been to Eridu?"

"No, I heard about them."

"How far will it go?"

"Farther than a leaf whistler."

Lameck started to toss it, but the pain was too sharp in his shoulder. "Where did you get the wood?"

Aril was silent, his eyes shifting.

"The slidecart?" Lameck knew.

"I…uhh…didn't think you would care. You haven't used it since—" Aril stopped his words but not soon enough.

The recall of his last ride with Talisha caused Lameck to stiffen. He felt his grip tightening around the body of the wooden bird. With a grunt of anger, he snapped it in two, then threw it to the ground and stomped on it.

Aril stared at the ground, then at Lameck, before turning and walking away.

They didn't know her secret. Bathenosh had told no one, not even her family. "You have a good job," her father had often said. "Don't risk losing it." That was not her plan, but her curiosity could not wait another day since their return from Eden. "I still have some time," she said, scrubbing.

"Go on. I can finish these," said her mother, taking the platter.

Bathenosh wiped her hands, went to the mirror to check her appearance, then picked up her candle bag, straightening the strap over her shoulder and left the house.

Puppet-like, trailing brief shadows, the people passed her on the pathway leading to the temple. Food and ware vendors spoke in their superficial language in their artificial world. Her mind was preoccupied with an image of a curtain and the horrified expression on the face of a priest who had drawn it closed.

A month earlier, she had entered the lower chamber-room by mistake. It was outside of her assigned area and she was quickly escorted out after interrupting an assembly of priests, but not before she had seen it—a black, full-length curtain against the far wall. The harsh reprimand she received had made her even more curious as to why the room was kept secret from temple workers. If she was going to investigate, it would have to be when the area was vacant, a time she already had in mind. But now there were official things she was required to learn.

"Implements"

The class responded by taking up their writing sticks. Impression sheets lay before them on the tables for writing their notes. Attendance was compulsory for temple workers.

"We will continue the lesson on earth's origin," said the instructor, one of the temple priests, "remembering the digression of the heavenly spheres, and earth being the lowest."

Those around Bathenosh acted as though they were paying attention, but the weekly lectures were boring to her and made no sense. She had heard it all before.

"…and over countless ages it slowly formed, and with the help of the gods life emerged…simple forms at first. Then gradually, with more infusion, complex forms arose…the animals, and with more time…."

It seemed strange how he spoke with such confidence, as if he had been there to see it happen, thought Bathenosh while scratching a few words.

"…our hairy ancestors—" He paused, making eye contact, waiting for a reaction from the class. "Does anyone fail to see our ape-like image?"

There was some fidgeting, but no response.

"You are all animals—nothing more—made to serve the winged gods. This is their earth. The heavens and stars are also their possessions."

"Excuse me." It was a young man at the table behind Bathenosh. "What about the stories the fathers tell?"

"Myths!" The priest retorted with an irritated look, "All lies—fabricated by the Sethite fathers, who did not understand the eternal cycle of death, to cover their own insecurities." The priest waited, but it was obvious that no further exchange was welcome. Satisfied that he had made his point, he continued —"The destiny of man is in the hands of Lucifer. Serve his priesthood well and you may move on to a higher sphere. Serve poorly and your next existence may be here again…perhaps as a frog. Let me add that if any of you, as temple workers, are ever heard discussing the ancient legends, you will be severed with disgrace from your privileged position."

Bathenosh breathed a sigh when the word of dismissal finally came. Class impressions were collected which would later be reviewed and entered on their records. Taking up her bag, she merged with the stream of workers funneling through the doorway.

The temple corridor emptied quickly as everyone went to their duties. Bathenosh went to her supply room where the oil, candles and equipment were kept. She reached into her bag, removed the candles from home, and added them to the inventory. The art of candle-making had been learned from her mother and was the part of her job she did at home and enjoyed most.

After gathering her supplies, she began her routine of servicing the lamps, beginning on the upper level. She did not want to appear nervous or in a rush, and had to catch herself once—even twice, to be careful to fill them all to the top and to wipe all the smudges from the bases. As she worked she wondered if the god of Eridu might know her plan. She kept her eyes averted as the priests walked by on their way to the festival of grains. They would all soon be taking part in the city-wide procession and celebration. Then no one would notice.

Eventually, Bathenosh worked her way down to the lower level. The corridor was empty. Pausing a moment, she reconsidered her decision. She was finished and could go home, and avoid the risk. *Was it worth it?* she really wondered, but her legs kept moving, drawn by her deep curiosity.

The end of the corridor had been darkened, the lamps extinguished. A dampness caused her to shiver. Rotating and sliding the metal latch, she felt the heavy door release and creak inward. She stepped inside.

A dusty shaft of light from a narrow opening in the wall shone over the table and high-backed chairs that occupied the center of the room. Careful not to trip, Bathenosh moved further, following the beam that oddly landed on the very spot in the corner that she remembered. She would not have to use a lamp.

The pull-cord was within reach. Grasping it, she drew it down, folding the concealing curtain to one side. Behind the curtain was a recessed area, and embedded in the wall, an arrangement of flat clay pieces. Each piece contained etched inscriptions—words enough to fill the space. Above them all, in large letters, was painted, "The Sethite Lie of Creation".

Bathenosh had heard of the lie, but had never known there was anything in writing, nor had any idea where it could have come from. Rising up on her toes, she stood as close as possible, straining to examine this claim for herself.

IN THE BEGINNING GOD CREATED THE HEAVEN AND THE EARTH. —the Sethite answer to how it all began... with their God.

...THEN GOD SAID... —a God who spoke all things into being. How terribly powerful He would be, Bathenosh thought, *if it were true.*

...EVENING AND MORNING... —actual days of creation, instead of unknown eons of time.

...SEA CREATURES AFTER THEIR KIND...BIRDS... CATTLE...AND THE BEAST OF THE EARTH ACCORDING TO ITS KIND... —all the kinds, created during the first days of earth's existence, with no record of one kind arising out of another. What a lie, contradicting everything she had been taught.

...THEN GOD CREATED MAN IN HIS OWN IMAGE, TO HAVE DOMINION OVER THE EARTH... —What was this? Man, not an animal, or from the animals? A special creation in God's own likeness, with authority to rule the earth? Bathenosh could not believe what she was reading. It was obvious to her why the gods didn't like the Sethites.

Glancing over the other tablets, her gaze fell on the words,

...YOU SHALL SURELY DIE. —A point in time when death entered the world? Just another lie. She had been taught that death had always been part of the eternal circle of life. What a strange teaching it seemed, that man might have never died. The truth was that something inside Bathenosh longed to believe everything she had read.

Suddenly, a rustling sound from somewhere near made her jump. Bathenosh drew the other cord, walked to the door and pulled it shut behind her, latching it.

10

Lameck sat staring into the dark, his left arm propped against the slidecart frame, his right hand feeling the gap in the seat where Aril had taken a slat. It had not moved from alongside the stable since the last day Talisha had ridden with him. Like a carving, he was fixed in time, with no desire to go forward and no way to go back, to recapture the happiness. The door had been closed. Recent events within the Grove, and now within his own family, caused him to question whether he even belonged… or if anyone understood him.

The family meal had long been over, avoided for fear of confrontation. Lameck did not want to hurt anybody else. Why he had done it, he didn't know. Thoughts would come, causing him to react with rage. Just a word made his muscles tense, start to do things he would not normally do.

Voices in the distance, low but familiar, caught Lameck's attention. They were outside, not far away. Slowly he got out of the cart and followed the faint sounds until he saw some strips of light coming from between the boards of a crop storage bin. Approaching quietly, Lameck pressed his eyes against one of the wider cracks. Seated on the ground around a star-shaped marking with flaming candles in the center were his sister, Riana, his brother, Aril, and another man from the Grove. Riana was chanting, while the other two repeated the words after her.

For awhile he listened and watched, with growing uneasiness. Then a sparkle—something metallic near the candles caught his eye—a reflection from a large ring. He was attracted to it. Something stirred within, something that wanted to take control. Lameck's hand stretched upward involuntarily to a corner of the bin. With a surge of rage he splintered the wood, shattered the latch and flung the gate open.

"Lameck!?" Riana shrieked, her face filled with fright.

Aril grabbed the ring attempting to conceal it, but Lameck flew on him like a cast-net, seizing his wrist and prying open his fingers. The other man, with an opportunity to escape, scrambled away in the dark.

With a cry of pain, Aril released his hold and backed away, trembling in the corner with his sister.

"Where did you get it?" Lameck asked, holding the ring out and glaring at the two.

"I-I was going to tell you," said Aril, "He was dead. I didn't think it would matter."

Lameck looked closely at the Nephilim ring. He had seen it only once at a distance, yet he felt a strange attachment— *the impulse to put it on*. He studied it, waiting—he sensed an inward resistance. He turned it in his hand, wondering, but could delay no longer. Too large for a finger, the ring slipped snugly onto his thumb. Suddenly a sensation like liquid fire surged through his body. *It was reconnected.*

"Lameck?" Aril spoke weakly. Terror was on their faces.

"Disgraceful dogs. First you steal from me, then you use what you have stolen to charm and cast spells. SSSSSethites," the words were not Lameck's. "How dare you to meddle with the dark powers. When Methuselah hears of your abominations, it will shame his household. There will be no end to the grief you two have caused." He stood above them gazing down.

"But, if you don't tell," said Riana.

"You are cursed. I will bear your secret to everyone in the Grove."

"Why?" Riana pleaded. "What do you want from us? What can we do?"

"Go."

"Go?" asked Aril.

"GO!" The force of his word made them jump. *"Get out of the Grove!* If I were not restrained, I would avenge myself now." Kicking the candles into the dirt, he whipped around and departed, giving the broken gate another shove.

Lameck trodded back toward the house, but something jerked him in a different direction. Surprised by the power of the inner impulse, he gave in, not feeling much like sleeping. He felt the ring and remembered putting it on, but that was all. As he walked he tried to think. *The problem was in his family, and how he might change them.*

Moonlight illuminated the site of Methuselah's altar. Knowing what needed to be done, Lameck approached it. The thought of the blood that had been shed and having to touch the rocks that had been splattered made him cringe. But with ample strength he knocked them loose, and continued to tear the altar apart—throwing it down, stone-by-stone, until it was done.

Standing on the vacant mound, the lone figure raised a defiant fist in the night.

The creaking sounds from below the temple drew Jathron's attention to the grain carts rolling in tandem toward the tunnel. It was done by night to avoid angering the citizens. They labored hard planting and harvesting and would not understand the need for so much of their food going to Phlegra. Neither did Jathron fully understand.

He was irritated. It was well after midnight and the assembly had not yet called him in to join them. Standing on the upper level of the temple, he stared over the rooftops at the distant outline of the arena. The image of the cheering crowd and himself as high priest made his wait even more painful. Why, given his position, was he not invited to hear everything? Was Azazel displeased with his performance? Certainly no one else could fill his place. None of the other priests had the connections or the access to information that Jathron had. Though plagued with questions, he was confident that he would continue unchallenged despite the recent embarrassment during the morning sacrifice.

"They are ready for you," came the voice behind him.

Relieved to have his thoughts interrupted, Jathron turned and followed the tall sentry inside and through the corridor to the chamber room where he was directed to his usual seat. Azazel and Druana were at the head of the table, next to each another. The other winged assembly members occupied the sides. Glancing about, he attempted to discern the mood of the meeting but saw no clues except the tapping of Azazel's fingers.

"Jathron," Azazel spoke. "You are in the position of high priest because of your obedience to the assembly." There was an awkward silence. It was as if his earlier thoughts had been perceived. "We would like your comments on the festival, and the mind-set of the people."

Leaning back, Jathron took a moment to organize his recollections, but not too long. "The festival of grains was carried out as planned, maintaining the traditions of previous years—"

"Traditions of men," interrupted one of the members.

"Let him continue," said Azazel.

"The count was down but the procession was well attended," continued Jathron.

"By how many?" another asked.

"At least half," he responded.

"Why were half of the people missing?" the same one asked.

"The lingering effects of the pharmako, as well as what they drink. It induces complacency."

"Let them stay that way," said Druana, "as long as they continue to work."

"Increase the distribution," said another.

"You are forgetting the purpose," said Azazel. "It is to keep them in submission while molding them to the plan. If they are absent from the functions this will be more difficult."

Jathron knew Azazel's concern over the rebellious and often independent human nature. It was the reason for feeding the people's sensory appetites—to quench organized unrest and to provide a reward in return for service—but it was not without its problems. "It is a difficult balance," he replied.

"One you will figure out," said Azazel, pausing. "How did they react to the Nephilim show of force?"

"It was an unusual part of the procession and achieved its purpose by instilling fear."

"Do the priests feel at ease with the Nephilim's growing powers?" asked Azazel.

"We all have our places…it is understood."

"Good. The priests will all be visiting some sites in Phlegra as part of their indoctrination, and for a demonstration of weaponry."

Jathron had seen one of the new weapons in the procession and understood that they were part of Lucifer's plan for earthly dominion. "It appears that the Sethites are about to face bigger problems," said Jathron. "That should please the Queen."

"I am already pleased," said Druana, with a slight grin.

"Already?" Jathron prodded cautiously for information.

"My Trog got back his ring," Druana spoke boastfully, "and what better revenge than to have control of the one who took his life, and to have the Methuselan house divided."

"You were able to cross their spiritual defenses?" asked Jathron.

"My Queen, let me answer our high priest," said Azazel. "The daughter's activities have given us legal ground, lifting their defenses and allowing a gateway to the family. Lucifer's masterful timing and covenant with the eldest son provided the sweetening to the cake. Derrin was of use for awhile. But now, firmly entrenched within Lameck, Trog will be our gatekeeper."

"And Semjazza will soon have a Sethite daughter for breeding—" The other member's comments were cut off.

"Enough!" Azazel spoke. "The assembly meeting is ended. Bring father Jathron a celebratory libation."

He was flattered to hear Azazel call him father, a sign of deeper recognition within the assembly. Indeed, he deserved a drink, something to take his mind off of the things that had concerned him.

"Before you leave, there is one small matter to discuss," said Azazel, as the cup was set before him.

"Regarding?"

"A temple worker."

Aril and Riana were gone. Unseen by them, Trog had watched them pack their horses before morning light, then climbed down and followed them far enough to be sure, before returning to his hideaway in the rafters. His hand jerked compulsively, tearing at his blood-smeared clothing. A rodent's half-eaten body lay in the straw.

Lameck was frightened, unable to control his actions, or to understand what was happening. While conscious of some events, he could no longer put them together. There were missing segments. Earlier, he thought he had heard his father's voice distantly calling. For what purpose was unclear. In his mind, he was unwanted and had to be separated. That much was his choice.

As the shadows shifted, so did Trog, restlessly crawling back and forth over boards, peering out through openings in the vaulted side of the stable, studying the Sethite activity like a stalking cat, waiting and curious. The numbers had been growing steadily since dawn. Some were running, others walking. Most were gathered in front of Methuselah's place.

Any thought of Lameck returning home was overcome by the scene before him of family and neighbors angrily yelling, motioning with weapons, and the wrenching guilt within that he was the one responsible for it all. "It was too late to return. Whatever he had become was being hunted."

Trog gnashed his teeth while watching the lines of Sethites organizing, stretching, and sweeping outward in all directions. Reed fire was brought in and passed between torches, flaming their way. Commands came, some distant, some closer. His ears lifted slightly as they approached. No movement was made other than the methodical rubbing of his ring.

A moving gate and the entrance of light signaled their presence in the stable below. "Lameck?" came a voice, "Are you in here?"

Silently watching, Trog breathed faster.

"Think he killed them?" asked another.

"He could have."

"See anything?"

"Bring the torch over here."

"Just the animals."

"Hold it there."

"Where are you aiming that thing?"

"Up there—Lameck?"

Trog remained crouched, and Lameck unaware.

"Want us to go and get the old man?"

"No time."

The recoil of the T-bow made a muffled *twang* and a grunt came from the rafters.

Reactively, Trog reached for the shaft of the arrow that had struck his left shoulder, pulling it out. He let it drop, then took hold of a heavy piece of wood, yanking it loose with no difficulty. He held it high for a moment, eyeing the ones below, then flung it through the air down upon them. With a cry, the man released the torch and darkness swallowed the stable.

"Get another torch," one yelled. "Go tell the others."

Trog groped his way back along the upper wall. *Twang —Thunk*—another arrow sank into a beam near him. Feeling the inside corner, Trog backed into it as far as he could retreat, waiting. He could see the blood now, streaming down his arm. The stable entrance was soon ablaze with light. A line of Sethites readied and raised their weapons.

Unconcealed, with no other place to go, Trog hammered his right arm backward with fury, dislodging a board in the wall, then jumped and kicked like a goat, cracking and sending wood flying outward. The opening was enough. Seizing the edges, he thrust himself through and leaped. Forty feet he fell, maneuvering in the air like a tree creature, positioning for impact with arms and legs. He hit the ground and spun around.

"Look. It's Lameck," came a voice.

"Stop him," said another.

Trog's escape was blocked by a multitude of people surrounding and closing in on the stable. Surprised by his jump, they were not ready with their arrows, but were swarming toward him swinging poles, fists raised with rocks. With no other escape, Trog flew directly into their ranks, snapping poles and tossing men with the ferociousness and ease of an angry bear. Before they could regroup he had broken through and was running with such speed that no man could overtake him.

Trog could still hear the distant yells and bristling of arrows through the leaves as he headed to the edge of the Grove, but his pursuers were far behind. Only a glow through the trees from the stable fire was all that could be seen.

The hammock of trees ended and an open field stretched before him beneath a hunter's moon. Into the grasses he ran, toward a large waiting shadow. Climbing upon it, he gripped the leather harness and held on as it spread its wings, leaped forward and left the ground.

11

Trog yawned, tasting the upper night air. The creature's beak homed south toward Phlegra while its rider lay forward to rest, his eyes rolling upward.

Lameck felt the movement and saw the sweeping wings. He did not budge and kept his grip where he found it. His shoulder throbbed with pain. To be flying on a reptilian was beyond his understanding...as was his destination.

While considering his circumstances, the vision came of a dark winged figure drawing Lameck toward him. As he got closer, bars of iron rose up preventing him from turning away. It reminded him of a trap he had once made. But this time he was the unfortunate animal. Then the bars changed shape and became Nephilim lining the way as he was being dragged in shackles. They shouted and waved for one of their own who returned as a victor. The vision ended.

Lamack was aware of his danger, that something powerful was controlling his actions, causing him to do things and to go places he would not have chosen. He had heard of evil beings using the bodies of others. What made it worse was that he had no ability to stop it.

The smell of the bird was putrid and with every lift of the wings Lameck grew more and more nauseated. Repeatedly he convulsed, desperately clinging for his life, wondering if it would be better to let go. Like a flight of death, his passage provoked thoughts of his past, images of those he knew and had mistreated, words he had spoken—all violations of his conscience—but the most painful was the covenant he had made with Lucifer. Suddenly he knew that this was the one in his vision, no longer a manifestation of light, but darkness.

He had been deceived—*Why had he done it? Why had he been so quick to accept such a lie?* There was no other God. He had been taught the truth as a child, but had trampled it. He despised himself. Lameck coughed and convulsed, again and again, with every rise and fall.

"Holy God," he breathed. "Forgive and save me."

As quickly as the words were expressed, a whistling sound and something brilliantly white came from above at such speed Lamack had never seen. He marveled at it for a moment, and then realized that it was coming toward him. Lameck felt the muscles in the creature's back strain as it shifted its wings, sensing its danger. Tightly he held on, as they swooped to the side.

"WHOMP!" –Feathers flew and the massive bird carcass tumbled downward.

The impact tore away Lameck's grip. His arms and legs reached for anything but there was nothing. He had fallen from a tree once, and felt the same fear…but far worse was this. Moments were measured by the rush of air and the flapping of clothing. *How would it feel to die? Where would he go?* Whatever the answers, it was out of his hands.

Suddenly the light that had struck returned, surrounding him like the sun, slowing his descent and filling him with such peace that he no longer cared whether he lived or died.

The angel carried the unconscious figure to a place not far from the Ridge, gently setting him down in the grass alongside a merchant roadway. The winged warrior then touched Lameck's injured shoulder and departed.

It was just before morning light that an early traveler slowed and stopped his cart. Walking over to the still figure, he paused as though waiting for some response, then crouched down and slipped something shiny from Lameck's thumb, dropping it into a pouch on his side. The traveler then returned to his cart and, with a strange twitch of his head, continued on.

"Lameck!" Enoch quickly arose from his table. Leaning against the doorway in torn, blood-streaked clothing was his grandson, looking like he had crawled through thorns.

"Can I stay a few nights?" His voice was weak.

"Excuse us," said one of his guests as they also got up. "We'll come back another time." The two men passed around Lameck on their way out, nodding without speaking.

"Sorry to interrupt," said Lameck.

Enoch walked over and ushered his grandson inside. "You are always welcome to stay here."

"A lot has happened."

"It looks that way. We can talk after you get cleaned. Do you want to eat first?" Lameck sat down. Enoch cut bread and cheese and watched him as he slowly ate. Then, in a basin, he poured water and helped with a towel. Afterward, he brought him a clean white garment to replace the rags he had worn.

With the evening lamps lit, Enoch sat down and listened as Lameck unfolded the events that had occurred since his last visit—the incident at Gimlet's, the growing hostility at home, Aril and Riana's dark practices, and the large crowd with weapons.

"Where was your father?"

"At the house."

"And you?"

"The stable."

"Why?"

Lameck seemed to be searching for an answer.

"The scar on your shoulder," Enoch motioned. "Where did it come from?"

"They were hunting me."

"For what reason?"

"Something inside of me…"

Enoch squinted as he listened to Lameck describe his loss of control and his sense of some entity using his body. He knew there were spiritual barriers established by God against such things, but also knew that human choices could allow openings. He had suspected a problem earlier, but needed to know more.

Lameck then told of his unusual flight, and how he had awakened later near the Ridge and walked most of the day to get to his grandfather's.

"You described a figure in a vision—one who was drawing you. Who was it?"

"I believed him."

"Who?"

"Lucifer."

"Tell me what happened."

Lameck related his encounter in the forest with the being of light, after running from Derrin. Then he told of Lucifer's covenant into which he had entered—

Enoch believed that he had what he needed. His grandson had given legal ground for the deceiving one to work. "Do you know the seriousness of what has happened?"

Lameck was silent.

"Have you asked for forgiveness from the true God?"

"Yes."

"We need to do more." Enoch got up and stood before Lameck, watching his face. "Pray with me—"

"Holy God, I come to you through the covenant blood —" Suddenly, Lameck's body lurched forward, his pupils narrowing. "…covenant blo—" He tried to speak, but the word would not come out.

"Foul spirits of the Nephilim," said Enoch. "Release this son of Adam."

"By whose authority?" The hate-filled eyes locked onto Enoch as the spirit manifested its defiance. "Thisss is our home now."

Enoch showed no fear. It was not the first time he had found unclean spirits trying to hide within humans, posing as personality traits, while carrying out their deadly directives from Lucifer. He looked straight into Lameck's eyes. "I speak to you from the highest authority—the Lord God Almighty. And by His covenant blood, I command you to leave! **Go!**" Enoch knew that they had no choice but to go. The spirit creation was under different rulers, but all had to answer to Holy God. Having confidence in the power of the Promise, Enoch was joyful for the freedom that was coming to his grandson.

Lameck's body stiffened. The muscles of his face contorted. His mouth stretched open. "eeeeaaAAANOOOooo…" the trailing wail of voices sent a chill to Enoch but he continued to praise and thank his Deliverer.

With a final sigh, Lameck loosened and relaxed—his face and features as Enoch once remembered. A smile appeared across his face and his eyes were clear.

"Thank you, grandfather. I never realized—,"

"Thank our Lord God."

They both sat quietly enjoying the peace, with a sense of awe over what had transpired. Then Enoch led Lameck in the declaration that had been interrupted, confessing and renouncing the covenant he had made with Lucifer. This time it was completed.

"Am I prepared?" Lameck leaned back.

"What is in your heart to do?"

"Stop the Nephilim."

Enoch reflected on the visit of his fathers and the revelation of Lameck's destiny. "You will be ready," he replied.

It was the first sound sleep that Lameck had gotten in weeks. Refreshed, he was ready to begin preparation under the guidance of his grandfather.

Enoch reached up and removed a panel of wood revealing the ends of three scrolls. Pulling them down one-by-one he handed them to Lameck who placed them on the table, then stepped down from the stool. "Have you studied the writings?"

"Father read from them."

"But, have you?"

"No."

"You must do this."

"Read them all?"

"Not just read, memorize."

Lameck looked up from the scrolls into the face of his grandfather. Enoch was serious.

"It will help you to discern God's voice from the others."

"That could take a long time," said Lameck.

"Three days," said Enoch.

"Between visitors?"

"There is a secret place I go to pray. No one will disturb you there."

With the first scroll under his arm, Enoch led the way to the nearby thatched hut surrounded by fruit trees and foliage. There he left Lameck, seated on a bench, unrolling the scroll.

It contained the writings of Adam and the record of creation, as revealed by God. The words had been copied by Seth from the original tablets. With interest, Lameck began, and with each consecutive reading and repetition, the message burned its way deeper into his heart.

His emotions were affected as he read and recalled the events that occurred in Eden with the first parents—God's goodness and close companionship, the serpent's deception, then the sin and separation—and the entrance of death. Tears rolled down his cheeks as he pondered the bloody skins given by God as a covering.

At the end of the day, after Lameck had completed the scroll, Enoch returned and together they walked back to the house. After a meal came the review of all he had studied— *Describe the sixth day of creation. What were the freedoms and restrictions given to Adam? State the promise of the coming Seed.*

The second day was like the first, but the next scroll, instead of coming from Adam, came from Seth. It told of how his family began to call upon the Lord, as Adam did in the beginning, and the relationship they enjoyed. The acceptable sacrifice was described along with the need for faith. Words from God were recorded, providing direction, comfort and hope. Wisdom writings were included from Seth and the other fathers.

The more that Lameck read and committed to memory, the more life and energy he felt…and the more he sensed the holiness of the Godhead. He trembled, yet felt safe. That evening Enoch smiled as though he knew what Lameck had experienced.

The third day he opened the final scroll, and was surprised to see that it came from Enoch's hand. He did not remember seeing such a scroll in his father's study or hearing of the things that were in it. The appearance of the Nephilim was described as the dark mystery, taking place during the six-hundredth year. They were said to be the result of an ungodly union between some of the angels that had transgressed their lawful boundaries, and the daughters of men. Judgments and things to come were also written. But the relationship that Enoch had with God was of most interest. Lameck pulled on his beard, incredulous at the revelation imparted by his grandfather. The knowledge Enoch had of God and His attributes was as if he had been visiting with Him in person.

Lameck waited until evening to ask, "The third scroll, the attributes and ways of Holy God—"

"You are wondering how I know," replied Enoch. "The same way you can, by going to Him."

"How do you mean?"

"God is not a respecter of persons. Anyone can draw near if that is their desire."

"But how?"

Enoch paused, "In Spirit, through the blood."

Lameck mused over Enoch's words and all the writings being held within his heart.

"We will continue tomorrow," said Enoch.

"But I am finished."

"You are just ready to begin—the journey of faith."

The next morning they left the house following the narrow Ridge trail that wound through the densely-wooded area on the eastern slope. Before departing, Enoch had prayed.

It started as a pleasant hike. The early light sparkled on the dew drops imparting brilliance to the colors around them. Fragrances were sweet. The cries of the birds signaling their territories caused Lameck to think. As they continued, they talked. Lameck wondered at his grandfather's powers of observation. Questions that had never before come to mind arose and were answered in such a satisfying way by his grandfather that it was better than food. He was amazed. And the things Enoch asked in turn, inspired him to search for even more answers. Lameck felt a new freedom and zeal to seek truth and a new-found depth of joy.

Then he stopped. A huge tree to his left caught his attention. Its massive trunk and broad limbs stood unique among the others and the ridged pattern of its bark reminded him of the skin of a creature. Leaving the path, he walked over to look at it more closely and its texture. As Lameck placed his hand against the tree, something didn't feel right. He glanced around and did not see Enoch.

"Why did you turn back?" The familiar voice startled him.

Above, seated on a limb, was the one who had appeared to him in the forest. It was Lucifer—that evil angel surrounded with light. Lameck became fearful.

"Do you really believe that Enoch's God has any power over this world?" The words resonated with authority, intimidating him for his foolishness. Suddenly he could not think, much less speak. "Foolish Sethite, you know nothing," said Lucifer, spreading his wings. "You are in covenant with me."

"It…was broken." said Lameck, weakly.

"You cannot get away that easily. I have the power to destroy you."

"The only power you have… is what Holy God gives you." Something else was now rising up within Lameck, supplying his words and opposing the fear.

"Why be deceived?" said Lucifer. "Renounce this Sethite God now, and return, or be destroyed."

"You are the deceiving one. I will never again renounce the one true God."

As the light from Lucifer faded, his form took on a different shape— Stretching from the limb around the trunk and across the ground to Lameck's feet was a serpent of such size that it appeared able to crush a behemoth.

Before he could move away, its tail coiled around his ankles, holding him fast. Lameck pushed on it and tried to loosen it but was unable. His heart raced as he watched the multi-colored bands slide down the tree and across the ground toward him.

Lameck struggled as the coils moved slowly up his legs. Not only was he powerless to stop it, but he could no longer keep his balance. He swayed then fell to the ground. Suddenly his arms were fixed to his sides and he felt the clammy pressure advancing above his waist to his chest.

In vain he strained with all the strength he had, using every bit of remaining energy. With each small breath he took, it tightened, until he had no more air. Lameck was not afraid to die, but he did not want this to be the time or the way that his spirit would leave. Still, he could do no more.

It was then that he realized that if Holy God wanted his life, He could have it. God had given Lameck his life and this life was rightfully His. It was now in His hands, *fully surrendered*.

"ZZIIING," came a metallic sound.

Lameck took a deep breath where he lay. The pressure was gone. Standing in front of him was a mighty angel with a gleaming sword in his hand. He watched him sheath it and then vanish.

At the foot of the tree was the severed head of the serpent. The coils around him were loose and writhing, slapping the ground. Lameck felt hands pulling under his arms and saw the face of his grandfather bending over him. He slid free from the dead mass.

12

Bathenosh felt safe sharing her secret with her father and mother, and they were intrigued by the tablets. However, they had concerns. If it was discovered that their daughter had gone into a restricted temple area, things could happen—to her and to her family.

As she went about her temple duties, Bathenosh had little worry. She had been careful to choose a time when the area was vacant, and had left everything in the room undisturbed. Her thoughts were more on the inscriptions she had uncovered, the incredible creation. It was an account she had never heard before and it went against everything she had been taught. Yet, there was a fascination—something about it that attracted her. If such a God did exist, who brought all things into being by the power of His Word, she had to know.

"Stand to the side," came a voice through the corridor.

Bathenosh backed to the wall, which was customary when subjects were being moved under guard. She watched as the five were taken past her. Three of them looked like the usual misfits, probably being brought in for disciplinary action. But two were different. Their faces, and the way that they walked were not like Cainites.

Interested, she took up her bag and followed them at a distance, pretending to be about her lamp work. Turning a corner, they came to the section containing the holding chambers where the guards opened two doors. Some angry remarks were exchanged by the misfits as they were pushed into the first room. The young man and woman were put into the second one.

Pulling out a cleaning tool, Bathenosh worked on a wall lantern nearby, waiting as the two guards secured the doors and returned in her direction.

"Going home after work?" she asked, smiling at the one who looked less stern.

"Usually do," he replied, slowing.

"Who were the two?"

"Sethites"

"Where are they going?"

"Him, the arena. The girl, Phlegra. They have been wanting one like her."

"We have to report back," said the other guard, with a tap on his arm.

Bathenosh turned her attention back to the lamp as the two continued on their way.

It was later, toward the end of her work, that Bathenosh was approached by one of the apprentices.

"The high priest has summoned you."

"I am almost finished with my tasks."

"Immediately," said the apprentice. "I will escort you."

Tucking the bag under her arm, Bathenosh followed. She wondered what it could be about. Temple workers were rarely called into the high priest's chamber. Obtaining a job required an interview with a work supervisor. Job reviews and corrections were also handled at lower levels.

She was motioned into the outer room, where a seated guard stood up.

"It's the lamp worker," said the apprentice, "to see Father Jathron."

"You may go in."

It was the first time she had seen the chamber with its gold lamps, and ornate stonework on the walls, ceiling and floor. An angular table, that looked well organized, occupied the center. She heard the heavy door shut behind her.

"Bathenosh," said the high priest, entering through a rear archway.

She bowed, as instructed, and carefully lifted her eyes. He had a slight smile that looked out of place, as he slid into his chair.

"How long have you been a temple worker?" No seat was offered, or expected.

"Four years."

"According to our records, it has been three years and ten months. Have you been well compensated, in your opinion?"

"Very adequately."

"And for the candles?"

"Most fairly, father Jathron."

"Bathenosh," he paused. "We pride ourselves in being generous with all of our workers. There is no other place in Eridu that offers as many benefits and as much security as the temple."

She nodded.

"In return, we expect more from our workers, and, above all—trust."

Bathenosh was silent.

"The temple," he continued, "is a sacred place. There are areas, as you know, closed to all but our priests. The reasons for this are too involved to explain." Jathron had been shifting his gaze, but now looked with close attention at Bathenosh. "During the festival—the day of the procession—was there a reason you might have had for visiting a restricted area?"

"None." She tried not to show any surprise, or fear.

"You are aware that the gods monitor all of our activities, are you not?"

"Of course." She was not, but recalled the sound she had heard before leaving the room, wondering if she had been seen, or had accidentally left something.

"Of course," repeated Jathron, as if to mock her. "We felt sure that none of our own would be so foolish.

"My purpose in summoning you at this time is to inform you, that after a careful evaluation of your performance, we have regretfully found your work below our acceptable standards. Furthermore, your class instructor informs me that, based upon your notes and interaction, you have failed to achieve the level of understanding necessary to continue to serve in the temple. Bathenosh—you are dismissed from all further duties."

"Could you have stopped it?" Lameck was shaken, still wanting to trust in his grandfather's abilities.

"No—only God," said Enoch.

"Why did He allow it?" asked Lameck.

"What were your thoughts?"

"That I might die."

"What else?"

"I was powerless against it."

"Good."

"How is that good?"

"You learned an important lesson."

Lameck was trying to understand.

"You cannot fight a spiritual enemy in your own strength," said Enoch, continuing to explain.

They were both tired and, with daylight ending, decided to stop and rest for the night. They gathered some wood and started a fire, continuing to talk about the event. Though not needed for warmth, the firelight served to keep animals from intruding, and the smoke helped to repel insects.

Lameck lay awake thinking of all that had happened, and how he had been deceived. Spiritual realities beyond his comprehension had broken into his world and his perception of life had changed. He was thankful to no longer be the way he was.

The gurgling of moving water could be heard through the trees as they continued their walk in the morning light. The trail had straightened and was taking a gradual slope back up the Ridge. Soon they came to an opening that allowed them to approach the stream.

Enoch waded in and picked up a stone. "What do you see?" he asked, handing it to Lameck.

Lameck rolled it in his fingers feeling its smoothness, "a good slingstone."

On the bank was another stone, rough with jagged edges. Enoch took it up and tossed it into the middle of the rapid current. "This is what is happening to you," said Enoch. "As the water acts on the stone to remove its resistance, God has been using challenges in your life to bring about change."

"Even Lucifer?"

"The Creator has power over His creation. Angels—both good and evil—are part of it."

As they continued up the trail, Enoch pointed to the trees, some greener and more fruitful than the others. "What do you think makes the difference?" he asked.

Lameck noticed their location. "The greener trees are closer to the stream."

"It is where you must learn to abide."

"What are you saying?" asked Lameck.

"The flowing water is like the Spirit-will of God. Continually seek it, and you will prosper in all that you do."

Enoch kept teaching as they went. It seemed that everything around them was full of wisdom waiting to be discovered, and the grandfather who had studied it for centuries was able to reveal it. Rocks, plants, insects and animals—all seemed to contain revelation from the One who fashioned every detail.

In the distance, the roar of the falls grew louder as they approached. The waters sprang from fissures near the summit—collecting and cascading down the Ridge rocks, emptying into streams which wound their way into the river and finally the sea. It was not the first time Lameck had seen it. He had been to the pools at the top and watched the arrival of the great silvery fish. It was a sight that had made an impression. "What about the fish?" Lameck asked, wondering if there was more to learn.

"It is the lesson I was saving until now."

A natural overlook offered the perfect opportunity. Before them was the panoramic splendor of the blue-green waterfall sparkling and spilling over ledges of rock, crashing and rushing with such swirling force that, as the waters came by, Lameck looked beneath to make sure that where they were standing was not eroding.

In the rapids below them, several long silvery streaks could be seen racing against the powerful current and breaking the surface with great leaps, upward to fifteen feet. Lameck watched one fish fling herself up into a downward barrage of water, setting her back momentarily…then with a violent thrash of her tail—up again, fighting her way through to a higher level.

"Do you know why they swim in such a difficult direction?" Enoch asked.

"They are going home," answered Lameck.

"True, they return to their birthplace where they will reproduce, and it takes all their energy to fulfill their purpose." Enoch paused. "Likewise, when we align ourselves with the will of God for our lives, we face a struggle against great opposition.

"See how the fish wait in whirling currents for the water to fall, using that very force to help boost them to higher levels." Lameck took notice. "In the same way," continued Enoch, "success requires the recognition and wise use of existing opportunities, taking what the adversary intends for destruction and using it to your advantage."

Lameck considered his grandfather's words, hiding the truths in his heart. "I have also wondered," he asked, "how these fish find their way back, so far from the sea."

"How does the small iron bar, when struck with a lodestone, swing to the north?" asked Enoch. "In the same way, would the Creator not put a sense of guidance within His living creation? In the natural there is sight, sound, smell, as well as taste and touch. But in the spiritual dimension there is guidance. You will know the right direction when you are submitted to God's will."

They stood awhile longer just watching. The sight and sounds of the thundering waters gave evidence to the far greater invisible power and glory.

After leaving the falls, they followed the trail to the top of the Ridge, the site of the sacrificial altar. On the way, Enoch stopped at a nearby home and obtained a lamb from a family's flock. The shedding of blood using an innocent animal had been initiated in Eden by Holy God. The descendents of Seth had continued to offer sacrifices in obedience to the directive communicated by Adam. While other offerings were sometimes brought, the use of blood was needed as a covering for sin, and to signify the setting apart of individuals for service to the Lord. As Enoch had explained, this was the time for Lameck's sanctification to the mission for which he was destined. This was the culmination of their preparation—the point at which Lameck would be consecrated into the hands of Holy God.

Taking blood from the slain lamb, Enoch smeared it on Lameck's forehead, and also on both of his hands and feet. "Father God," spoke Enoch, looking to heaven. "By your covenant blood, I dedicate Lameck, son of Methuselah, to your service and invoke your protection upon him. Guide him and grant him wisdom and strength in carrying out your purpose for his life. Into your hands, by faith, I commit him."

Lameck knelt as Enoch placed his right hand upon his head.

"In the name of the Lord God, I bless you with success in all to which you are called. As your name means conqueror, so shall it be that through your life victory will follow you and many lives will be saved." The words conveyed authority and power.

Until now, the desire to gain information and to stop the advancing of the Nephilim had seemed an impossible burden, but for the first time Lameck had confidence—faith in the God of his fathers that it could be done—and that he would be God's instrument.

Enoch sensed that they should return before dark to the hidden place of prayer, and remain there for the night.

Father Jathron did not enjoy the ride through the tunnel on their way to Phlegra. It was more than the danger of water breaking through, though he had considered the weight of the river on the ancient archway. He was unable to attend the temple council meeting that had been scheduled on the same day as the priests' tour. With Lucifer presiding, he suspected that it was planned that way in order for the gods to discuss matters secretly among themselves. Druana had been upset over recent events involving Trog and one of their flying reptilians—she had cursed the family of Methuselah and someone named Enoch. Whatever happened had also changed Azazel—Jathron had never seen him looking so riled.

"Do you ever wonder about them?" asked a shaggy-haired priest who was seated across from Jathron, referring to the giants whose homeland they had entered. The Nephilim gazed curiously at the six priests seated in their open-sided cart as they moved through the street.

"Wonder what?" asked Jathron.

"Whether they belong."

"They are part of the plan," said another priest next to Jathron.

"What if they rebel?" asked the first.

"They won't," said Jathron. "The gods control them."

"I hope so. There is no way we could."

The cart jerked and turned, continuing on as the driver prodded the harnessed beast. In the distance on a lush green hilltop, Jathron observed a tiered palace with flowery vines draping over the levels. Surrounding it at the base of the hill was a high wall bordered by trees.

"Welcome to the palace of the gods," said the Nephilim guide. With a buttoned uniform and mid-level voice, it was difficult to tell if it was male or female. "Follow me."

They entered through an ornate iron gate topped with spikes like the walls. Inside, Nephilim workers were busy on the grounds, swinging sickles and tending shrubbery. It was an immaculate landscape. At the door, an armored guard stepped to the side, permitting them entrance to the palace.

Jathron was covetous. Luxurious marble floors with exquisite furnishings stretched before him with intricately carved staircases connecting the levels. The open area in which they stood provided a view all the way to the pyramidal ceiling which was laced with gold artwork. Beautiful young women in light flowing garments were moving about leisurely. The high priest gave the other priests a visual check of self-restraint.

"This is where the chosen daughters of men are prepared for their nuptial unions with the gods," said the guide with a grin. "What you smell are some of the fragrant oils."

"Where are the ceremonies held?" asked the shaggy-haired priest.

"The nuptial feast and fire dance, on the lower level. The daughters are then carried by the gods to the consummation chambers at the top."

"Can we move on?" asked Jathron.

Departing the palace, the priests returned to their transport, accompanied by the Nephilim guide, for the next part of their tour. After traveling a short distance, they came to a place most unlike the one they had just seen, flat with no foliage. Three long wooden structures sat parallel with a low brick wall around them.

"This is the birthing and development area," said the guide.

"Why is it so barren?" asked a priest.

"There is no need for attractiveness," said the guide. "The Nephilim are being born."

Stepping into the first hall, Jathron saw rows of open wooden boxes, four feet in length, lining the walls. Within them there was movement. He looked closer at the stocky red-headed infants with six fingers and six toes, unique to Nephilim. The odor of urine along with a piercing whine prompted him to catch up with the group being escorted to the next building for birthing. "We cannot linger," said the guide.

Not wanting to be pushed, Jathron let the other priests go first. Women were lying closely spaced on one side of the long room, all but their faces covered. It seemed strange that they were so still. Eyes were either glazed or closed, and expressions were lifeless. Then he recognized the look and smell—a corked bottle of liquid pharmako sat alongside each bed. At the other end of the room their guide was motioning, hastening the group out of the building—but not before the shrill cry of a woman could be heard. It came from behind a cloth partition in the corner. There was no way to hide the agonizing labor pain.

Jathron took one last look before leaving. A cover had been lifted on one of the women's beds, exposing the wrist and ankle restraints. Perhaps it was necessary, he thought. Giving birth to a giant, even as a baby, was obviously no easy task.

The third building was not visited.

The guide accompanied them to their final stop in Phlegra—the weaponry range in the northwest area, just south of the river Pison. Stair-stepped benches were in place for viewing the demonstration of the Nephilim's latest weapon. Jathron was standing to the side, waiting for the others to move upward, before sitting in the front.

"We are certain you will be impressed." The words were unexpected. Jathron turned. "I am Semjazza, the god of Phlegra." His stature was greater, with a demeanor darker and more intense than Azazel.

"My priests have enjoyed the tour," said Jathron, trying to show no surprise.

"It was a personal favor for Azazel. He has something we want."

Jathron knew of the plans for transferring the Sethite daughter. "It is being arranged."

"Good. Enjoy the demonstration," said Semjazza, and he vanished.

After they all were seated, a uniformed Nephilim captain, fully decorated with insignia, strutted before them. Behind the captain, in a field, was positioned a catapult-like device on wheels, about forty feet in length. A bird shaped object with wings and tail projections was attached to the throwing arm. It reminded Jathron of the small glider toys carried by the merchants. "As captain of military operations, I extend greetings to the Eridu priesthood. The demonstration you are about to see will reveal that we are more than ready to purge the northern land of human-kind…that is, the ones who are in resistance to the plan."

Jathron understood his reference to human-kind as meaning the Sethites, although he would have preferred the more specific term.

Shifting his weight, the captain glanced behind at the catapult. Two Nephilim soldiers were helping another one, much smaller, to climb up and into the winged object.

"Is that a child?" asked a priest.

"They are all soldiers, well trained and fully capable of carrying out their mission," said the captain

His small head could be seen protruding from the top of the craft, and then an arm extended with a clenched fist.

"We are ready," said the captain. "Look to your left. In the distance, do you see the white brick building?" He waited for nods, then continued— "That is the target. The D-craft is lightweight, designed to travel well beyond the range of a projectile and to deliver far greater damage. With controls, it can be maneuvered in flight to strike any target, even if surrounded by trees. The mobile launcher has been built to—"

"Isn't it just a catapult?" interrupted the shaggy-haired priest.

"An ordinary catapult lacks the thrust," said the captain, with strain in his voice. "Notice the angled metal against the lift. By combining molten elements, we forged a spring. With the stone counterweight, it gives us all the power needed."

"What elements did you use?" asked Jathron, wanting the formula.

"All weaponry secrets are kept by our general and god, Semjazza." The small fist was raised again. "Attention to launch," bellowed the captain. At his signal, the two soldiers standing at the launcher began to slowly turn a notched wheel.

It was only a moment and there was a click. With its release, the great beam shot upward, the counterweight descending with a thud against the ground. The launcher jumped as the D-craft soared away through the sky.

Jathron let out his breath as he followed the path of the wooden bird and its tiny occupant. Some of the priests stood and applauded. Semjazza had been right. It certainly had been impressive.

"Prepare for impact," shouted the captain.

As the craft glided above the white building, it dipped a wing and swooped in a tight circle, then went into a steep dive.

Jathron had trouble imagining what a glider of light wood could do to a solid brick building. Everyone watched as it continued to gain speed downward.

"BARROOOOM!!!"

There was a flash of blinding light and a deafening roar. The ground and benches shook. Hands tried too late to cover eyes and ears. The captain was the only one who stood without moving.

In the distance was a huge plume of black smoke, nothing remaining of the white building or D-craft. Even the trees were gone. Only flickering flames across the concave ground could be seen.

"The purpose of the D-craft," said the captain, to the ashen-faced priests, "is to destroy. There are many of us willing to sacrifice."

13

After time alongside Enoch in the hidden place, it became clear to Lameck that he did not know much at all about praying. In a good way he was jealous. He wanted the same relationship that his grandfather had with God—to be able to speak as with a friend, and with assurance.

As Enoch had been directed by God, they had not returned to the house. The need for sleep had been satisfied early. Most of the night had been occupied with prayer, praise, and some singing to their Father and Creator. It was not yet daylight.

"How did you learn?" asked Lameck.

"God is only hidden to those who will not seek."

"Can I?"

"Do you hunger?"

"I want what you have."

"There is no greater joy."

"Why does He make us wait?"

"Few cry out. Many seek their own desires."

"Is that wrong?"

"As you walk with Him, you will learn His ways of wisdom."

"How can I?" In the light of his past, Lameck felt incapable.

"In your weakness. It is the place of His strength."

"Your words are not weak."

"God's power is released through faith."

"To stop the Nephilim?" Lameck was still determined.

"Agreement with His purpose is the prayer that moves God to act." Enoch stood, his right hand resting on Lameck's shoulder. "Holy Father, you have called this one to a great mission. We thank you and praise you for all that you plan to accomplish through his life. Now I ask that you come upon Lameck, son of Methuselah. Send forth your Spirit in power—Hallelujah. Let your righteous Name and Word be exalted. Protect him as he follows you. Let the plans of your enemies be overthrown, and show us your mighty salvation."

Lameck felt an inner warmth, and after Enoch finished his prayer, an indescribable peace.

"Stay in prayer," said Enoch, "until I return from the house."

Lameck lay face down, listening to the trailing footsteps and the dawn call of a songbird. He felt different—lighter—and without the strain that had been part of his life. But most significantly, he knew that he was no longer alone. He sensed a comforting presence, like a father's arms. "Holy God?"

"Be still," the Voice spoke to Lameck's spirit, *"and know that I AM your GOD.*

"Lameck, son of Methuselah, I knew you before you were formed in your mother's womb, even before you were born. I, THE LORD, search the hearts of man, and have full knowledge of your thoughts and ways.

"I felt your grief when the one you loved was taken away. I have watched your struggle with the fallen ones, and the prayers of the righteous have prevailed.

"You have done well to hide my words in your heart. By my Spirit, they will strengthen, encourage and guide you. Do not be afraid of those who are against you. It is I, THE LORD, Who will complete the work I have begun within you, to bring glory to My Name."

"My Lord, am I to act alone against the Nephilim?"

"You are not alone. I am with you, and have others, even within the enemy's gates. The battle is not yours. It belongs to Me. Trust in THE LORD and you will see My victory."

There was no image, no angel of light as in the forest, nothing but a profound peace and inner witness that the words Lameck had heard were spoken by the One True God. The message brought understanding and hope. It satisfied deeply and promised direction. And the writings that Lameck had studied testified to the truth of what he had experienced.

Lameck's face was wet. He did not try to control the tears of joy and adoration. To know that the Creator of the heavens and earth knew and cared about him was the greatest revelation that he had ever received. Furthermore, Lameck realized that God was not finished…that He had a righteous purpose and plan for mankind, and that Lameck had a part. But something still bothered him. "I am not righteous," said Lameck, "I have committed evil."

"You are wise to acknowledge your sins," said the Lord, *"There is always a payment needed for remission. It is through the life-blood of the sinless."*

"The sacrificed lamb?"

"That will cover you until the Perfect is sent. Then sins will be removed.

"Lift up your head, son of man. I do not see your sins. Be strong in My righteous Word."

Lameck sat up with wonder. He felt so free, yet so indebted for the forgiveness and acceptance he had received. "What can I do, Lord, for you?"

"Love Me, with all your heart, mind and strength."

Yes, he thought. He wanted to do that and more. "I love you, my Lord."

"Obey the promptings of My Spirit."

"I will—" The rustling of bushes caused him to turn.

Enoch had come back with a horse. "You must go without delay."

"I have heard from Holy God," said Lameck. "His Spirit is with me. What is the matter?"

"There are men who arrived yesterday from the Grove who seek your life. Your brother, Aril, and sister, Riana, have been missing and they believe that you killed them."

"You know they are wrong."

"But you must go and find them."

"How?"

"By the Spirit of God." After embracing his grandson, Enoch handed him the reins and he quickly mounted.

"Take the south trail from the Ridge," said Enoch. "Your mission has begun."

"Thank you, grandfather, for everything."

"Remember all you have learned."

"Keep praying for me."

The strips of leather stung as they slapped repeatedly across Enoch's bare back. His wrists burned from the cords that stretched him between two trees.

"Where are you hiding him?"

More painful than the physical flogging was the hatred Enoch was seeing from Sethites against their own family. They were spiritually blind men, angry and unrestrained. The four had come from the Grove with intent to kill Lameck and had been directed to Enoch's house by the bitter parents of Talisha.

"Just tell us, old man, and we'll cut you loose."

Enoch had tried earlier to reason with them and suspected that their reasoning had been affected by pharmako. Before their arrival, a friend had run to tell him that they were coming, enabling him to get the horse to Lameck just in time. His grandson's mission was all that now mattered to him.

Again it came. His body involuntarily arched. He felt no hatred, only sorrowful compassion toward the ones striping his flesh. They were not aware of what they were doing. If somehow they could have known what Enoch knew, they would never have allowed themselves to be used. It was Lucifer.

"How many lashes will it take?"

"It is enough," spoke a Ridge-dweller to the attackers. "He will die before he speaks."

"Then let him."

"He is a Sethite elder. It will bring retaliation."

The one with the leather straps paused.

"He is no good to you," continued the Ridge-dweller. "Release Enoch to us and we will try to get the information for you."

The four looked at one another. "Let's go," said one, that had been silent, "We are wasting time here." Murmuring, they mounted their horses.

As soon as they were out of sight, two men from the Ridge untied the cords and helped Enoch inside his house and to his bed where they tended to his wounds. The others who had gathered returned to their homes, the reason for their presence now past.

"We are sorry for this," said one, dabbing Enoch's back with a wet cloth.

"It was not your doing," said Enoch. "They were stirred up by another."

"Is Lameck guilty?"

"No more than you or I."

"Do you know where he is?"

"On a journey."

"For what reason?"

"To bring peace to our families."

"Is he safe?"

"Our time will be best spent praying instead of talking."

———————

The South Ridge River did not require dismounting to cross. It crept up to Lameck's knees and rippled around the horse, pushing westward and emptying into the Gihon. Just below the water's surface ahead, he noticed a streak of silver racing eastward on its way upstream.

Concerns for Aril and Riana and questions about the men seeking to kill him had been on Lameck's mind since his rushed departure, but this time was different. There was a comforting Presence, and he knew that the One whose presence he sensed was able to deliver. He had experienced enough in his own life already to have hope for the safety and future of his family. Lameck thought of the fish as he purposed in his heart to keep going.

He felt the empty saddlebag. Except for a water skin which he had filled in the river, there was nothing—no T-bow, nor any weapon. He had been thrust out with nothing but his faith. There was no way of knowing what difficulties and dangers lay ahead, but he knew that it was best. Now he had no choice but to trust God.

Eridu—the word came as clearly as if it had been spoken, confirming the direction in which Lameck had been proceeding.

It was a two-day journey and the merchant roadway that he was taking was the most direct way from the Ridge, also the most open. Some called it the salt-way because of the spillage from merchant carts and camels. The pilgrimage was past and Lameck could see no one to the north or south. He knew that Sethites were not welcome on the roadway. There was prejudice among the Cainites and hatred from the Nephilim. Given the use of pharmako, the people were easily stirred to evil against one another. He had seen attacks from the Ridge. There was a hood on the clothing Enoch had given him, but Lameck had not yet used it. He quickened his horse's pace, wanting to cover as much distance as possible before sunset.

Some time later, to the south, the sight of travelers caused Lameck to consider his options. There was a byway through the fields to the southeast. It would also take him to Eridu and offer better concealment. Rather than risk confrontation, he decided to take it, but tested his move by questioning the will of God. He felt peace as he left the roadway and continued.

His new direction passed close to one of three temple-towns. They were farming settlements outside of the city, important sources of food to the Cainites, and under the control of the Eridu temple. The Sethites were aware of them but never bartered with them, having plentiful food supplies of their own.

Eventually the byway narrowed and Lameck entered a thicket of trees. He was thinking of a place to rest when he heard a noise from the branches above. Tightening the reins, he stopped the horse. He did not see anything and wondered if he was being overly cautious. Starting ahead, he heard it again, like something brushing the leaves. Then, suddenly, he saw the long shadow moving through the air toward him—a log swinging from a rope. Pulling back, Lameck made the horse rear, just as it passed in front. It was a huge weight that narrowly missed knocking him and his horse down, possibly killing him. Frantic voices and scurrying motion through the trees quickly revealed the situation. They were juveniles and were now hastening to escape. Lameck watched them drop and flee out of sight, not impressed to pursue them. He was thankful that he was not hit.

The log was still swinging and one last boy, his foot caught in a vine, was struggling to get down. With a crack, a branch broke and he fell—twenty feet—dropping head first, still clinging to the loose branch. Then just before hitting the ground, the boy's body jerked upward, the taut vine entangled around his ankle. Lameck rode over to him. If the prank had not threatened his life, he might have laughed at the sight of the boy bobbing upside down, eyes wide with fright.

"Wha—" the boy gasped. "What'r you gonna do?"

"What do you think I should do?" asked Lameck.

There was no reply.

Reaching out, Lameck took his hand and helped him onto the back of his horse, slackening the vine. Quickly, the boy worked his foot free and slipped to the ground.

"Why'd you do that? You're a Sethite," said the boy.

"Go tell the others that the God of the Sethites spared your life."

Without delay, the boy turned and ran, and Lameck continued on. He pulled the hood over his head.

Harvested grain fields were visible through the trees to the south, and in the distance, a settlement that he would bypass.

To the north, a pride of lions played on a hill in the tall grass. The setting sun filled the sky with fiery pink and streaks of crimson.

Lameck was ready to find a place of rest for the night. A Grove of palms offered the opportunity. Taking the strands from two long fronds on opposite trees, he spliced them together to form a hammock and tested it. It was perfect. God had known and provided just what he needed along the way, including fruit trees.

It was not much longer before the stars began to appear in their myriad splendor. Lameck was reminded of Enoch and the star lessons. He recalled the wonderful story and considered it as it unveiled above. He had heard the prophetic events as a child, but had not given it much thought. Now, through the circumstances of his life and the intervention of his grandfather, God was revealing new things. Lameck knew that the One who held absolute power to determine future events had to be trustworthy…and that the place of communication long ago established with man was still there.

An unexplainable peace overshadowed any concerns Lameck might have had for the mission ahead. The unknown was swallowed up in the glorious known.

14

A bag of candles for a sack of grain. Bathenosh had traveled to the trading center before and knew what to say. This time, due to an accident on his job, her father had been unable to go. Despite his objections, she had insisted on taking the cart herself to get the extra grain needed for their family.

Her hair was tucked into a red scarf, the kind that field workers wore. She had thought of field work since the loss of her position in the temple. There were other ways to earn goods to help her family, but most she would not consider. Her parents had taught her to have a higher view of her worth than to allow her body to be used to satisfy the lusts of men, even if they were priests.

The empty cart clattered along the dimpled trail. Having departed early, Bathenosh planned to reach the temple-town, make the barter, and be back before dark. Two carts had already passed her on their way back to Eridu with their loads. They had been covered to conceal their cargo.

Idle and curious onlookers gave her an uncomfortable feeling. The trader scowled down from the platform as Bathenosh pulled her cart alongside. She had arrived and it was her turn.

"Candles of delightful fragrances made to temple standards," said Bathenosh, holding one up in clear view.

"How much for the bag?" asked the trader

"Two measures," said Bathenosh.

"One," the trader replied.

She nodded her consent, trying not to appear anxious.

The trade was made and Bathenosh quickly started home, satisfied with the outcome. After a short distance, she stopped long enough to pull the cover over the grain. She did not feel any danger in the middle of the day, but it was the wise thing to do.

Time seemed to go faster on the way back. Already, she was nearing the bend at the big tree, halfway home, and had seen no other travelers. She thought of her father and anticipated his proud smile and complimentary words at her return. The trip had been relaxing, the flowing greens and golds of the country providing a peace not found in the city. Bathenosh loosened her scarf letting her hair fall naturally. The rhythmic sounds of her horse-drawn cart had a lulling effect as she gazed ahead, unaware of any problem…until the sudden sound of pounding hooves behind her. As she turned to look, she felt a dull blow against her head. Her last thought was *grain thieves*.

Disoriented, Bathenosh opened her eyes and felt a piercing pain in her head and shoulder. Blood was on her hands and clothing. Every attempt to move hurt. From where she lay alongside the trail, she remembered the sudden attack. Bathenosh slowly lifted herself and looked around. There was no sign of her cart. They had taken everything but her life. For awhile, she just sat and wondered at her circumstances. Then she noticed a distant figure—a rider coming from the west. *She had to move out of sight.*

———————

"Son of man, I am sending you into the midst of an idolatrous and corrupt land. They do not seek the truth and their minds dwell on evil continually. Do not be afraid of them or dismayed by their looks, though they are a rebellious people under the sway of the wicked one. But hear what I say to you and follow the leading of my Spirit."

Lameck meditated on the message from God. He was on a trail he had never traveled, heading in a direction he never would have chosen. But there was no turning back, nor could he go home, for his own people were seeking to kill him. He knew that if he had been wiser, he could have avoided the evil that had affected his behavior and driven his brother and sister away. But it was done. And God's presence was now with him.

His thoughts were interrupted by the sight of a red cloth in the middle of the trail. Remembering his surprise encounter the day before, Lameck slowed and cautiously looked around. There were trees as before, though not as thick. No movement could be seen. He felt impressed to dismount.

Upon closer examination, the cloth looked like a head covering. Lameck looked at the trail. A set of fresh cart tracks veered from the center to the edge, then back again. Walking to that area, his attention was drawn to a path of grass that had been pressed down, leading up a slope, and some reddish-brown spots that looked like blood.

Exploring further, Lameck walked up the slope. He began to circle the tree… Suddenly, he drew back. Facing him was a woman, crouched and holding a stick, defensively. "Are you hurt?" asked Lameck.

She just stared and looked frightened.

"Are you going to strike one who would help?" asked Lameck, while removing his hood.

"How do I know that?" She swayed against the tree.

Lameck reached to offer support and felt the stick sting his arm. She looked surprised that she had done it. He met her eyes quizzically.

"You are a Sethite. What do you want?" Her voice was weak.

"To meet a Cainite." Lameck extended his hand again slowly, but before he could reach further, she collapsed.

After she opened her eyes, Lameck got some water and gently poured it on the wound near the back of her head. Her hair was matted from the blood. Tearing a strip from his garment, he applied and knotted a bandage. Then he helped her sit up against the tree and to lift the container to her mouth. She drank, and then asked, "Did you say that you wanted to meet a Cainite?"

"My name is Lameck."

"Mine is Bathenosh."

"Bathenosh," Lameck repeated, thinking of the name. "Can you eat a piece of fruit?"

She nodded, so he got one from the saddlebag and sat down across from her. He rested and watched as she ate and drank some more water. She appeared less threatened.

"Do you live in a temple-town?" asked Lameck.

"I was on my way back to Eridu."

"What happened?"

"Thieves stole the grain that I had come to get, along with the horse and cart belonging to my family."

"Were you traveling alone?"

"My father was not able to come."

"You could have been killed."

"He wanted me to stay home, but our family needed the grain."

Lameck wondered at the young lady's industrious and sacrificial qualities, giving less thought to her own safety than to the care of her family. It was rare to see, even among Sethite women. "Are we far from Eridu?"

"About a half-day's ride."

"Let me help you get safely home."

"Why would you do that?"

"We are both children of Adam."

Bathenosh was hesitant, but with Lameck's assistance, climbed up on the horse. He sat behind her where he could give support if she started to fall. Leaving the bend they proceeded south, the pace of the horse unaffected by the added rider. If the movement was painful, Bathenosh did not show it. She rode well.

"It is not often that a Sethite rides into the city," said Bathenosh. "What is your reason for coming?"

"To find and ask forgiveness of my family."

"You have family in Eridu?"

"Possibly."

"Eridu is large and hostile to Sethites, because of our different beliefs."

"Do you know what we believe?"

Bathenosh was silent.

A small temple-town was visible to the east, its fields stripped bare and few workers in sight. A little way further, Lameck stopped the horse, dismounted and walked to the edge of the roadway. A set of wheel prints crossed through the loose dirt into the grass.

"Is it our cart?" asked Bathenosh.

"It seems to match." Both the spacing and width of the impressions were the same as Lameck had seen earlier where he had found Bathenosh. Since there had been no other travelers, the lines had been noticeable in the roadway. Now it looked hopeful that his investigation might be of help.

Following the trail through a field, they came to the edge of a wooded area. Voices could be heard, so they slipped from the horse and tied it out of sight, and then continued walking in the direction of the sounds. There was no sight of people, but at the end of a pathway in a clearing Lameck saw horses and next to them, a cart.

Bathenosh squeezed his arm. "It's our grain cart," she whispered.

Lameck made a gesture of silence as they moved forward, cautiously scanning for lookouts. At the back of the clearing was a high wall of reeds. Through some gaps, a pond could be distinguished and, within the pond, movements.

Clothing had been strewn on the ground between the cart and the pond. Shrill laughter, shouts and splashing revealed the carnal activity and told Lameck that the thieves were unguarded. There had been no reason for the revelers to suspect that the woman left for dead would be able to come after them, and locate them in such a secluded place. They were apparently unsuspecting and unaware of any intrusion.

Wasting no time, the two moved in unspoken unison, gathering the clothes into the cart, retying the horses, and leading them back through the woods. Lameck thought of the flint-rock and igniting the foliage around the pond, but was satisfied. They had gotten the cart, along with their clothes, and would trail their horses far enough away that they would be left on foot.

"I'm not a horse thief," said Lameck, as they rode away.

"What about the clothes?" asked Bathenosh, smiling.

"Do you want them?"

Lameck had the cart reins as Bathenosh turned around and stepped into the back. Gathering the clothes she flung them from the sides. Stepping back over the grain, she sat down again alongside Lameck.

"What do you think they will do?" asked Bathenosh.

"Leaves worked for Adam, temporarily."

"Was that true?"

"It's in the fathers' writings."

"We are not allowed to have those, but I have read it."

"Where?"

"I should not talk about it."

Lameck decided not to press the matter, though interested. When far enough away from the wooded area, they released the revelers' horses leaving only Lameck's tied behind.

Eventually, the roadway merged with the broader merchant roadway from the west and the gates of Eridu could be seen in the distance. With people in sight, Lameck pulled up his hood. It was an unnecessary risk to leave it down.

"Am I putting you in danger?" asked Lameck. He was willing to part company at this point, if it was best.

"What are you thinking?" asked Bathenosh.

"I can ride separately if—"

"We are both safer together. Do you know where to find your family?"

Lameck could not say. The city was unknown to him.

"Please allow me to return some kindness," said Bathenosh. "You can come to our house."

"How will your family respond?"

"Were it not for you, I would not be here, nor the grain cart. They will be grateful."

Her family lived in a working-class structure on the north perimeter of the city. The arrival went as predicted. Lameck helped Bathenosh and her brother off-load the grain. Her bandage and the presence of a male Sethite required some explaining, but after awhile her parents' consternation changed to congeniality and Lameck felt welcome. A place was given upstairs on the roof for him to bed. It was flat and open, with a view of the temple. The home was modest and simply arranged. A few plants and a colorful tapestry gave the main room warmth. It was the first time Lameck had entered a Cainite dwelling or sat alongside a family other than Sethites. Somewhat surprisingly, they were courteous and hospitable, and appeared quite interested in learning more about the Sethite way of life, especially the activities of Lameck's family.

Lameck listened as the father, a kind-hearted man, described his humble work, his recent injury, and the difficulties they were having in procuring a sufficient supply of grain. In turn, the father leaned forward with interest when Lameck described the Grove and the tree homes in which they lived. The father did not show surprise when he heard of the terror the Nephilim were causing to the Sethites. He told of their own fears, even though the Cainites were supposedly aligned with the Nephilim's purposes. Their religious beliefs were not discussed, but Lameck was impressed that this Cainite family might be receptive to the truth.

A platter of strawberry pastries was brought out by Bathenosh and her mother. As they ate and continued to talk, Lameck felt relaxed. He liked these people, despite what he had heard. They were not so unlike his own family.

"Tell us," said the father, "why you think that some of your family may be here."

Lameck was not sure how to respond. "It was a crisis that forced my brother and sister to leave—"

"Did you say brother and sister?" interrupted Bathenosh. "Please describe them."

As Lameck described their features, Bathenosh took a sudden breath. "There were two Sethites matching your description. I saw them while serving in the temple. They were taken by guards to a holding chamber."

"When was this?"

"One week ago."

"Where were they to be taken?"

"Your brother, to the arena—"

"And my sister?"

"She was to be taken to Phlegra…for bridal preparation."

Jathron had never felt the atmosphere so charged. He was back in the inner council meeting, in the company again of the gods. It felt euphoric.

The assembly listened intently as Azazel told of their victory over one of the Sethite fathers—a spiritual leader named Enoch. Azazel revealed how they had incited an uprising among the Sethites to execute a scourging and to bring a humiliating defeat of this one who was suspected of actively opposing the plan. Elated creature shrieks filled the room as the details were touted—the agonizing pain, the spectacle of human weakness, and the issue of blood as the lashes severed the flesh.

As the sound of elation subsided, the Queen Mother, Druana, raised a question— "Where is the Sethite named Lameck?"

"You can rest assured," said Azazel. "It will only be a short time before his own people locate and kill him."

"I want to know the moment it happens," said Druana, pursing her lips.

"You will, my Queen. But tomorrow it will be the Sethite brother you can gloat over as he is ripped apart by Gorgon in the arena, along with the other dissidents." Azazel looked at Jathron. "Have they been transferred?"

"It is being done this evening, my lord."

"Be sure that Nephilim guards are assigned."

"Of course," said Jathron.

Azazel took a deep breath and unfurled his dark wings. Jathron had noticed that it was his way of showing authority and drawing attention to himself. "My fellow rulers…and high priest, this is the eve of a great celebration as we approach the fulfillment of the Luciferian plan."

"Why is our lord not here?" interrupted one of the dark angels with a stern look.

"You are aware," said Azazel, "that Lucifer goes to and fro, gathering information, and at such a critical time must oversee his earth ever more closely to assure success. Let me continue."

"We heard of a disturbance at a temple-town," said one of the others.

"It was nothing," said Azazel. "merely a brawl of workers with too much pharmako."

"Naked, it was reported…and mysteriously separated from their horses."

"We are looking into it," said Azazel. "As I stated, we are on the eve of history, about to see the greatest transition ever to happen on this planet. With the advance of the Nephilim and the northern siege of the Sethites, the purging will begin. The weapons are ready, being lined up near the tunnel in Phlegra. At Lucifer's signal they will be deployed. Such destructive power will be witnessed never imagined by mortal man. Our priests got to see a demonstration of the D-craft recently. What was your impression, Jathron?"

"There can be no possible resistance to such a weapon," said Jathron. "Nothing was left."

"Once the results are seen," continued Azazel, "all mankind will melt with fear. There will be no opposition. No further lies from the writings of the Sethites. The Luciferian doctrine will be embraced by all. Then our own kind—the Nephilim—will fill the earth."

Again, came the prideful banterings and whistlings of the creatures, anticipating the Luciferian conquest.

But something in Azazel's last phrase caused a churning in Jathron's stomach, a question that had to be asked by the human representative. "Azazel, my lord," said Jathron. "As the earth is filled with Nephilim, what will become of the human kind?" At the completion of his question, there was a period of silence. Jathron felt the tension in the chamber as Azazel took his time to speak.

"Father Jathron," said Azazel, "as high priest you are privileged to the knowledge of the council. Deep secrets have been entrusted to you as well as powers. You are no longer the man you once were. Whatever may happen to the humans will not affect your future place in Lucifer's kingdom…and your position one day as a god."

Azazel paused, his demeanor darkening, and then continued. "It has been a long time since we have mentioned it and it will continue to be held in confidence, assuming you maintain your loyalty to the council, but your Sethite origin is a matter that is well documented. If such a truth were released, the consequences would be too terrible to imagine. Now let us put all this behind us, and prepare for tomorrow. The Nephilim are preparing a small weaponry demonstration for the Cainites. It will be the first event in the arena."

Jathron's insides felt like they were in his throat. All he wanted to do was to fill himself with pharmako and drink.

15

"How long do we have?" asked Lameck.

"Until daybreak," said Bathenosh.

"Where can I find him?"

"In the arena, underground."

"Under?"

"There are corridors and chambers below the arena floor."

"Can you show me how they are arranged?"

"I have seen them once. I will try." Bathenosh brought a writing slate to the table and lit two more candles. Her family was occupied in another room. She scratched an elliptical shape, and then added details, enough that Lameck could see the most likely location of his brother and how to get to him. "They will be guarded," she said. "You will need help greater than I can give."

"I have confidence in the One who brought me this far," said Lameck.

"Is He the God of the Sethites?"

"He is," said Lameck. "Are you on His side?"

"If your God is able to deliver your brother and sister... then, yes."

Lameck wished there was time to talk but knew that he could not delay any longer. "Thank you for the help you have given. Do not put yourself in danger by doing more."

"If I do no more and you perish, your blood will always be with me. Let me take you to the arena." Her pleading brown eyes were clear and innocent like a child's.

Lameck consented.

Bathenosh spoke briefly with her parents and tightened a scarf around her head in place of the bandage while Lameck took a final look at the slate. They were ready. As they departed the house, he felt her slip the hood up onto his head.

The moon was waning but reflected enough light, with the few city lamps still burning, to see the way. Lameck heard singing. It was coming from a small group of Cainites sitting in a circle on the grass, two with stringed instruments. The message was sad and the words were slurred as they passed by.

"How long did you work in the temple?" asked Lameck.

"Almost four years."

"Why did you leave?"

"I got too curious and was caught."

"Was it worth it?"

"If what I found is true."

Their conversation stopped. A giant walked by.

"Are there many of those in Eridu?" asked Lameck.

"Not at night. They usually return through the tunnel to their own land."

"Phlegra?"

"Birthplace of the giants."

"Have you been there?"

"I have no desire to mother a giant."

"Neither does my sister."

"The arena is just ahead."

As they continued walking, Lameck could see the structure silhouetted against the night horizon. The prominent attraction had been built on a high area, with steps angling up from both sides meeting above the main archway. He knew where he had to go.

"Bathenosh," He touched her arm gently. "Thank you."

"Be careful, I will wait."

The way around the outside was easy to follow, because of the earlier sketch. He tried to stay in the shadows of the trees to avoid being seen, but sensed no fear. Things had so changed since his time with Enoch that there was no longer any place within his thoughts for such a spirit. There was still the unknown; but in place of anxiety, Lameck possessed a peaceful confidence that the one true God was with him. He thanked Him for Bathenosh and her family.

At the far end was the carrier entrance which was now visible. Two carriers with four large stallions were tied to one side, like the ones that he remembered. The horses were calm as Lameck approached; but then, suddenly, one whinnied and reared back pulling against its reins. Opening the iron gate, Lameck stepped past the horses to the inside.

In the shadowy moonlight before him was the vast arena with its surrounding stadium, something he had never before seen, although he had been given a description. In an eerie sort of way, he could picture the crowds and the Nephilim. To his left was the closed door that led to the underground chamber where the prisoners were kept. To his right was another door, but wider. According to Bathenosh, it was the way they moved the beasts to and from their subterranean cages. It was the door Lameck would enter.

He pushed the heavy door inward then felt along the wall as he slowly descended the steps. Everything was dark. Reaching the underground corridor, he continued forward cautiously. There was a foul odor like a decaying carcass. Then he heard breathing, heavy and regular. Lameck reached into his pocket and felt the flint-box. Whatever it was, he decided to see. Removing the flint, he struck it.

The flash of sparks revealed a barred cage door and, behind it, the glistening green scales and spines of a large creature. The breathing paused, then, when it became dark, started again as before. He struck the flint again.

This time there was a hissing snort and movement.

With the third shower of sparks, Lameck saw the wide head and open jaws baring teeth the length of his forearm. The creature raised and moved in his direction—it was Gorgon—the beast that Bathenosh had described.

With the flint-light, an unlit torch had been noticed on the wall, which Lameck lit and repositioned. By its light, he made his way around the corridor. As the light behind grew dim, the glow of another light was seen ahead, coming from the side where the prisoners were held.

Reaching the corridor's second bend to the left, Lameck peered around the corner. Two Nephilim were seated on a bench playing a game with their hands. Facing them was the outer prison chamber. *God had given him a plan.*

Lameck stepped into full view. It was enough. Both giants suddenly stood and started toward him. "Who is this?" bellowed one.

Quickly, Lameck turned and rushed back through the corridor. There was just one way for them to come, one passageway with two turns. The growling beast was waiting. Reaching the cage, Lameck pulled the restraining bar, grabbed the cage door and swung it wide open as he sprinted up the steps, closing the outside door behind him.

He dashed to the prisoners' entrance and descended to their corridor. The Nephilim were out of sight. Going to the prison-chamber door, he released the latch. Faces of astonishment flowed from the room as Lameck motioned them out and up the steps. "Hurry, move quickly!"

Among the last to step out was his brother. "Lameck?" Surprise was on Aril's face.

"There is no time to talk. We must get out."

As they hastened to leave, the pounding of footsteps could be heard from behind. Lameck turned to see one of the Nephilim with his sword raised. *There was nothing they could do. No time to climb the steps.*

Suddenly there was a deep growl. The giant stopped. Gorgon was crouching behind him and with one leap landed on his back, sinking its teeth into the giant's shoulder. The sword dropped and clanged against the stone floor as they both fell backwards, the giant unable to shake the beast's lock.

Aril and Lameck scrambled up the steps and outside, closing the door behind. The carriers bumped and squeaked as the horses jerked back and forth. Past them the brothers ran, retracing the path Lameck had taken earlier, through the trees, around and away from the arena.

Soon Lameck saw the one coming toward him who had waited for his return.

"You are safe." Her voice breathed relief.

"It was close," said Lameck. "Aril, this is Bathenosh, the one who helped me to find you."

"I am grateful," said Aril. "but our sister is now the one in danger."

"If she is still in the temple there may be hope," said Bathenosh.

"She was there when they came for me," said Aril.

Lameck looked at Bathenosh. "Can we get in before sunrise?"

"You will need help to get past the guards."

"If we can get inside, I think I can remember how to find it," said Aril.

"Let's go," said Lameck.

"Why would a Cainite do this for us?" asked Aril.

"We can talk about that later," said Lameck, thankful for the help that Bathenosh was giving.

The peak of the temple was visible from any point in the city. Its height testified to the builder's belief—that man can reach into the heavens and become like God. Lameck was aware, through Enoch, of the false teachings and distortions of truth. Luminaries outlined the temple entrance. Within the shadows, the three watched. Only one Cainite guard was stationed by the double doors, adjusting his armor.

"We can overpower him," said Aril, starting to move.

"Wait," said Lameck. The temple door had opened and a second guard was coming out, taking his place on the opposite side.

"Let me distract them," said Bathenosh. "You can slip in by the bushes along the side."

"This time, you be careful," said Lameck.

As Bathenosh began her walk toward the temple entrance, the two brothers moved through the tree cover to the side. There was enough space behind the shrubbery to remain concealed as they crawled closer to the doors. Lameck heard Bathenosh call to the guards. He watched as she removed the scarf from her head and let her hair fall. More words were spoken. Soon both guards had abandoned their post, swaggering down to where she stood. It was time to move. Quickly they darted up the side, past the vacant guard station, and through the doors.

Inside, faint oil lamps flickered from the stone walls. Lameck followed Aril through tunnel-like corridors and up several sections of polished stairs. They walked rapidly, his brother recalling the way.

The final corridor sent a shiver up Lameck's spine. It looked like the others, but the farther into it they walked, the more conflict he sensed within his spirit. He thought of returning but had no reason. They were so close.

Aril stopped at the next to last door. The slide latch was open.

Hinges creaked as the two pushed through, expecting to find their sister—But, it was not Riana who met their gaze from across the room—

"How delightful for the Queen to finally meet both sons of Methuselah," said the woman in red, "Were you expecting your sister? Pity, she is on her way to Phlegra."

Lameck and Aril stood silent.

Suddenly, behind them was a rustling noise and the doorway was blocked by a dark figure with wings.

Enoch's arms stretched upward. Through faith, he reached to the One who dwelt beyond the visible heavens and starry hosts—the omnipotent One—the self-existent One—the Great I AM. Bothered no longer by the stripes from the lashings, he was in communion in the place where he knelt, the secret place of prayer. Instead of hindering, the pain had surprisingly helped to open his eyes. It had caused him to see the condition of the world with fresh intensity. The present world was clearly no longer the world once created.

The rebellion had begun within the spiritual creation and spread to the physical. Adam had fallen and, with him, his descendants. Like a thorny intrusion, it had worked its deadly tendrils throughout the family of man. *Were the angels to blame for leaving their given domain, or man for believing and following a lie?* Enoch considered the question but concluded that all had fallen. *All were equally guilty and no one had escaped the effects.* Even the descendants of Seth, who were taught of God, had allowed the evil to spread. Forgetting the One who gave life, many had become self-sufficient and proud—fertile ground for the enemy.

Enoch's own Ridge family had failed to see the root of the problem. They only wanted vengeance—to repay evil for evil. He had pleaded with them not to go strike their brothers in the Grove, knowing that it would only have fed the forces of destruction. He knew that the power needed to move God's hand upon the earth was accessed by forgiveness. It was not man's place to retaliate. Vengeance belonged to the Lord. He had forgiven his attackers, including the ones who had helped or stood idly by, and the Presence that surrounded him bore witness that he could ask and he would be heard.

"Almighty and Holy God, I am as unworthy as my countrymen to come before you. Father of mercy, thank you for seeing our desperate condition and hearing my cry. We have violated our consciences and transgressed your holy will. We have given ground to the enemy. Now our very existence is threatened by those who deny your Name. They are like brute beasts that give no thought to your ways, strange flesh that rejects your authority."

"*I have allowed the Nephilim,*" said God, "*for all mankind have corrupted their way. They defile their bodies, pursue violence and fix their minds on evil continually. There is none righteous. Why should I not let them all be destroyed?*"

"All that you speak is true, Lord," said Enoch. "and you would be perfectly just in doing so; but, for your Namesake, I beg you to have mercy. If the promised Seed of the woman perishes, how will your word be fulfilled? How will your creation perceive your faithfulness? I implore you to cover our sins by the blood of the sacrifice, even as you covered our first parents."

"*Very well,*" said God. "*I have heard your humble cry of faith and, because of my word, I will raise up and spare a righteous remnant.*"

"Take vengeance, my Lord, upon those creatures who have left their proper abode, who deceive and plot to destroy mankind. Separate them and give us your protection. I especially ask for your hand to be upon Lameck and the members of his household."

Enoch sat on the ground and looked up at the sky sparkling with stars. One star cluster was brighter than usual. It was the constellation and sign of the Virgin holding the sheaf of wheat in her hands—the Seed of the woman.

———————

Any hope of rescuing their sister had been foiled, and now even their own escape was impossible. Lameck had been unable to resist the force of the winged creature, the so-called god named Azazel. Both brothers' backs were against the wall of the chamber, held fast by wooden stocks across their necks, arms and legs, which were secured to the stone by long metal spikes. In front of them stood their captors—Azazel, and the woman he called Druana, the Queen. It was obvious to Lameck that they had been expected.

"How did you know we were coming?" asked Lameck. Words were difficult with the wood against his throat.

"Have you forgotten the stallions," asked Druana, "the ones you took after killing my son?"

Lameck listened. Aril had a fixed stare.

"You were seen then. And you were seen again by the same embodied ones, tonight at the arena. Nephilim spirits don't forget a face."

"A spirit came and told you?" asked Lameck.

Druana almost smiled, then her face tightened viciously. "We finally have you both."

"What have you done with our sister?" asked Aril.

"As the Queen already told you, she is on her way to Phlegra," said the dark angel, "where there is great demand for Sethite daughters."

"What do you want from us?" asked Lameck.

"I will tell you exactly what I want," spewed the woman. "Vengeance! To see you all destroyed!"

Azazel stepped closer. "Let me begin by telling you of the imminent fate of your Sethite families." He paused as though waiting for a reaction before continuing. "Already, the Nephilim are prepared to advance northward with weapons so destructive that none will survive. The onslaught will purge your kind from the earth."

"And you," interrupted Druana, her voice crackling with hate. "Your destruction will be first."

Azazel continued, "It seems that Gorgon is not able to be used, so we have made other, more impressive, arrangements for your removal. Following the arena celebration, the two of you will be taken to the sacrifice platform. There, in full view above the river, you will dangle together by your feet, so that you can watch with terror as your doom approaches. You may have eluded the mob on the Ridge, but you will never escape the jaws of Leviathan."

Lameck and Aril both looked blankly as the two walked out, slamming and locking the chamber door.

"If you had only left us alone," said Aril.

Lameck was searching for something to say, but could only sense a churning sickness within.

"The blame is all yours." The voice was not Aril's.

Lameck strained to see where it was coming from.

From the light of the wall lamp, the features of one he remembered came into view—it was Lucifer.

"Lameck, you are a fool for renouncing me and trusting in the lies of your deceived fathers. If only you had remained loyal, all this could have been avoided. Instead of being bound and doomed to die, you and your brother could have been free to enjoy all the pleasures of my world. As the destruction of you and your family draws near, think of the feasting and fleshly delights, the riches that would have brought fame, and how you have foolishly thrown it all away. Did you really believe that your Sethite God could save you? You and all the world will soon see how little power He has."

16

The glass lamp cover rattled in its base. A rumble could be felt through the wall awakening Lameck from a daze.

"What was that?" asked Aril.

"I am not sure," answered Lameck, trying to shift his weight within the stocks.

"We could die here."

"We are not going to die."

"I am not ready to die."

"Aril—"

"What can we do?"

"Aril, I am sorry for getting you and Riana into this. Forgive me."

"Sure, but how does that help us now?"

"It helps inside."

"What we need is outside help."

It occurred to Lameck that he had not looked to God since their capture. Even the earlier warning that he had felt in the corridor, he had ignored. He wondered if it was too late, but then his thoughts returned to his circumstances that seemed inescapable.

He had heard tales of the great fiery sea serpent as a child. When first heard, the description had made the children curious, and it had caused Lameck to ask the question—why

God had created such a monster as Leviathan. Grandfather Seth had tried to explain that its purpose was to reveal the limitations of man and the terrible nature of pride. Everyone knew that it was not a beast to arouse or to catch. The last thing he wanted to think of was being dangled as its meal.

Lameck's hands tingled and his arms were numb, pressed motionless against the wall. He tried to push up with his feet to relieve the pain in his neck, but could barely move. He closed his eyes, and then reopened them. He wondered if it was day, but there was no way to tell with no light from outside, only the flickering lamp. How much time had passed since their capture was indiscernable, even the amount of time he had been conscious.

A click came from the door. The latch slid open, and in walked a man in a long gray robe. A guard stepped inside with him. Standing a few feet away, the man studied them curiously. "So, these are the two who have caused all the problems?"

"Yes, father," answered the guard.

"You can step out. I will call you."

The guard obeyed, closing the door behind.

"Sethites." It was not a question. "You have somehow succeeded in slaying three Nephilim—the first by yourselves, the other two by Gorgon. You also managed to set our captives loose.

"I have just come from the arena where we have had a demonstration of the Nephilim's weaponry. Perhaps you heard it. One fully-charged weapon is enough to devastate your homeland. With forty launchers ready to move, there is nothing that can stand in the way.

"Your foolish acts have only served to incite their determination to eliminate every one of you from the face of the earth. Their only delay is their demand to see the ones responsible pay for the Nephilim blood that has been shed. Do you have any idea where you are about to be taken?"

"We were told," said Lameck.

"As the high priest, I will be officiating. Are there any last words?"

"May I ask your name?"

"For what reason?"

"There was a baby, many years ago, that was born into our family, the result of a Cainite merchant violating one of our daughters. As a young man, he left the home in anger and…we heard, entered the Cainite priesthood."

"An interesting story, but what difference would it make to you, even if the priest could be found?"

Lameck coughed from the pressure of the stock against his throat.

"Guard," the priest called. "Bring some water." Shortly, the guard stepped in with a container. "And take a turn off the upper stock on this one." The priest waited for the guard to leave. "Was there anything else?"

With his neck loosened, Lameck continued. "The reason the young man ran away was because he had been falsely accused of stealing a family scroll. It was found a week later. Father was deeply grieved and tried to send word, but there was no way to reach him."

"I have never heard of such a one, and such a lie will not help you."

"Your words—some have a Sethite pronunciation."

"Nonsense."

"And your features—"

"Enough of this—Guard!" The door swung open. "I will see you both on the platform."

"Why did you say that?" asked Aril, after they had gone.

"I believe it is him," answered Lameck.

"Do you think he will help us?"

"Not likely. He has changed."

It was not long before they heard the latch slide again. This time four guards entered. Two went to Lameck and two went to Aril. They began to remove the stocks. As soon as the brothers stepped away from the wall, they were bound again with leather strapping, but able to walk. With a guard on each side, they were pushed out of the room, prodded through the corridors, down the steps, and out of the temple.

Waiting at the road was a black transcart bridled to a three-horned beast. The door on their side was open. As they approached the enclosed carrier, Lameck was jerked to a stop by the guards. A sack was pulled over his head.

"Step up," came the words of the guard.

Lameck slid across the bench seat and felt the cart give as another took a place alongside him. "Aril?"

"Who did you expect?" his brother replied.

He heard the cart door close and latch.

———————

Bathenosh had heard the talk of those returning from the arena. An announcement had been made of the capture and the fatal punishment of the two Sethites that would take place before dusk. The news was grievous but had come as no shock to her since they had failed to return the night before. She knew the danger, but still hoped that the God of the Sethites would prove Himself.

A special transcart was used for security when moving prisoners and those who were to be sacrificed, due to the chance of attack by vengeance seekers or of rescue by dissidents. The driver sat up on the front with two riders, one on each side, armed with projectile bows that were deadly enough to stop a rogue Nephilim, if necessary. Bathenosh had seen where the transcart was kept when not in use, and knew that if there was any chance of helping Lameck, it had to be part of the plan. She had taken advantage of an unguarded moment and the hollow bench inside.

There would not be much time as it traveled around the perimeter of the temple and down the southern slope to the river. She waited from her cramped position until the right moment. Covered by the noise of the moving wheels, Bathenosh bumped the base of the seat, trying to lift with her back. The weight of them was too great. "Lameck, it's me," she spoke, hoping to be heard. Slowly the board lifted and inside the transcart she could see two hooded figures bent toward her.

"Bathenosh?" came Lameck's muffled voice.

"Do you think the Sethite God might like some help?" asked Bathenosh, as she struggled to climb out of the open bench. Hastily she pulled the hoods from the wide-eyed captives and, with her knife, severed the leather cords.

Aril pushed against the door, but there was no give.

"There is little time," said Bathenosh. "We must open the bottom." Together, the three of them pried and grappled the boards from below the bench seat, making an opening large enough to fit through. "I will go first," said Bathenosh. "Roll into the bushes and stay hidden."

She waited until the transcart made its final turn and, with Lameck's help, lowered herself through the hole. As soon as she was clear, she rolled under the temple shrubbery and watched as Aril and Lameck followed, dropping and rolling to cover.

With the transcart out of sight, the group rejoined at the northeast corner of the temple. She had not expected the hugs but enjoyed them. They were feeling like family.

"The guards could be back soon," said Lameck. "We cannot stay here."

"What about Riana?" said Aril.

"You heard them," said Lameck. "She has been taken to Phlegra."

"If you want to go, I can take you," said Bathenosh.

"How?" asked Lameck.

"In a load of grain." Bathenosh pointed to the approaching cart. "Aril, meet my younger brother."

As instructed, Rushton had been following the transcart at a distance, and was just in time, pulling the cart to a stop.

"We're going to Phlegra," said Bathenosh.

As Lameck and Aril climbed on, Rushton stepped down from the cart. "Be careful, Bathy."

"Take care of mother and father," said Bathenosh, as she climbed up and took the reins.

The road to the tunnel passed near the sacrifice tower. The crowd of Nephilim was greater than she had ever seen in one place, stretching from the base of the tower across the road and nearly to the temple, blocking the way.

She continued ahead. Bathenosh was wearing her old worker's uniform to look like a delivery worker and had tightened a scarf around her head. The Sethites were well concealed beneath the grain. She hoped that nothing would arouse suspicion. The Nephilim were there to see the sacrifice and, from their looks, were not likely to notice anything else, until it was discovered that the prisoners had escaped. How soon that would be, she had no guess. "Grain to Phlegra," she shouted. "Let us pass."

Gradually, the wall of giants parted and allowed them to roll through to the tunnel entrance. "That load won't feed a dog," scoffed one, as they passed.

A few Nephilim were still arriving through the tunnel entrance. As they pulled up to the check point where one of their guards was stationed, Bathenosh tried to look relaxed, while sounding official. "A spare load," she spoke, without meeting the giant's eyes.

"This time of day?" asked the guard.

"It was missed earlier."

The giant was scrutinizing the cart closely. As he walked to the back, a cheering roar erupted from the crowd behind, causing him to turn his head.

"Pass on. I must see this."

Jathron braced himself against the trembling platform rail as Leviathan dropped back into the river, throwing water upward into the structure. Two frayed ropes dangled from the sacrifice arm above. A cheer resounded from the Nephilim below.

It was done and no one knew but the three apprentice priests. Jathron would talk with them later to make sure that they were sworn to secrecy. Neither Lucifer nor Azazel had shown up, which was most unusual, but it would all work to his advantage, Jathron felt. He was proud of his ingeniously desperate plan to save himself from a shameful embarrassment.

He scanned the massive crowd which had begun to break up. The Nephilim were returning through the tunnel to prepare for their advance, the next day with full weaponry. Stacks of explosives had been laid from the tunnel to the temple, where the bulk was stored for later use. The chemicals used in the D-craft were volatile and had to be carried separately until the time of launch.

With nothing more to do until the meeting, Jathron climbed down the tower ladder and headed back to his chamber office. His thoughts were on the two Sethites that he had spoken to that same day. Escape did not seem possible, knowing the procedure for moving captives. They would have to be found and silenced, their bodies secretly disposed.

A few other loose ends needed tending also—the repair to the transcart, and the notification of the two riders' families. It could have been an accident with their projectile bows, a heated argument between them. To Jathron it all seemed believable.

Fortunately, the hoods had been left behind and no others knew of the sacrificial switch.

Back in his private chamber, Jathron continued to ponder the circumstances and to consider his plan of action. He was confident that he could put the matter behind him. The growing concern that he had was with the advance of the Nephilim. He did not trust them or the gods' ability to control them. If it had only been the elimination of the Sethites, he would not have been concerned. But he had heard the slip of the captain's tongue and had a fear that the Nephilim surge would not be satisfied until all mankind was removed. *Was it Lucifer's plan to replace mankind...* he wondered. Something inside Jathron was signalling that it was a sacred breach.

It was time for the inner council meeting. Not wanting to play the part of the puppet, he purposefully delayed his entrance, just long enough to be noticed. Sounding the brass knock, father Jathron waited. No one opened the door. Pushing the heavy door forward, he stepped inside. The long dark table was empty. There was no sign of Azazel, or any of the others. At first, he wondered if the time of the meeting was correct. Then, why he was not contacted. While puzzling over it, the door opened on the back side to Azazel's private chamber—it was Druana.

"Jathron, what has happened?"

"I just arrived."

"Tell me where they are."

"If my Queen does not know, how should I?"

"Don't be belligerent with me, Jathron."

"It is not belligerence, but ignorance."

"Are you insulting me?"

"I am only trying to communicate that I do not know their whereabouts."

"Are you not the high priest?"

"Yes, my Queen."

"Then find my Azazel!"

Druana, who had been in his face, then turned abruptly and stomped from the room, leaving Jathron in bewilderment and with a multitude of questions. *How was he to know where the gods had gone? Could they have had a higher level meeting somewhere else? Where could he possibly go to get such information to satisfy the Queen?* The other priests came to mind.

"Assemble the priesthood," said Jathron to his messenger.

"The apprentices as well, father?"

"Everyone, immediately." Jathron returned to his chamber and shortly there was a tap on the door. "Enter."

"They were already assembled," said the messenger.

"Very well." Why they had taken the liberty for a general assembly without his authorization concerned Jathron as he hurried through the corridor and down the steps.

A guard at the door ushered him in. One of the priests, Sanchon, stood at the front. The others were seated throughout the room.

"Jathron—" said Sanchon.

"Father Jathron," he corrected him.

"Jathron," Sanchon continued, "be seated here." He pointed to a chair facing the assembly.

"That is not the position for the high priest," Jathron replied.

"Your position is the reason we are meeting."

"By whose authority do you speak?"

"By our own."

"You are transgressing Azazel's chain of command."

"Then let Azazel speak. He and those like him are nowhere to be found."

"He will return," said Jathron.

"Perhaps—but, until he does, we will decide the laws."

"What of the Queen's authority?"

"She has none apart from Azazel. Now be seated," reiterated Sanchon, giving a nod to the guard.

Under duress, Jathron took the seat.

"There are three charges against you which have come to our attention through our own priesthood." As Sanchon spoke, Jathron was forced to meet the stern gaze of all the assembled apprentices and priests.

"The first charge concerns your Sethite origin which has long been suspected. How can one who is part Sethite, having been raised among Sethites, govern fairly over Cainites?"

There was a heavy moment of silence.

"The second charge stems from the first—that you privately met with and assisted two Sethite captives to escape."

Jathron felt the sting of the unjust accusation, like the opening of an old wound.

"However, the most condemning charge is the last—that you attempted to cover your crime with one far worse, the murder of two loyal Cainite guards."

"I say we make Sanchon our high priest," shouted one, standing.

"Sanchon, Sanchon, Sanchon…," the whole assembly stood and echoed the name.

"Very well," spoke Sanchon, "I humbly accept your unanimous decision to be the new high priest of Eridu. As my first official act, I hereby order you, Jathron, to be removed from this temple and the priesthood. You have shamefully desecrated the holy position that was once entrusted to you and are now declared *ANATHEMA*. You have until morning to gather your personal belongings and be gone."

The realization penetrated Jathron like a lance. *There was nothing left.*

17

Lameck could have slept, cushioned within the grain, had they been traveling anywhere other than to Phlegra. A raw grain cluster was the only food he had tasted in two days, munching while staring through the cart slats counting the flames on the tunnel wall. *Thirty*. It was taking longer than he had estimated. He thought of Bathenosh and how his perception of her had developed. Through her courage and resourcefulness, the brothers had been delivered from a horrible fate. Her commitment to their cause along with other qualities had endeared her to him.

"How much longer?" asked Aril from under the grain.

"Stay hidden," said Bathenosh. "We are almost through."

Lameck prayed silently. They were about to enter the land of the Nephilim, a place that none of them, and reportedly few humans, had ever seen. If they were going to save their sister…and if the Nephilim threat were to be stopped…Holy God would have to intervene.

The steps of the horses quickened as the cart angled upward, leaving the river bed and the bricked archway behind. The sky appeared and, along the riverbank, something else— catapults. Lameck recognized their construction, something he had played with on a smaller scale. But he had never imagined so many so large. They were lined up and ready to move. *Was it the weaponry of which he had heard? And what were the bird-like objects on the tips of the launching arms?*

As Lameck strained to see through the narrow opening on the right, the cart took a turn to the left, passing uniformed Nephilim. The main road was blocked, forcing them onto a side trail bordered by high structures, making the way darker. Another turn, then the cart slowed and stopped.

"We need to find the palace," came Bathenosh's voice. "Can one of you direct us?"

Lameck heard no answer.

"We have grain," she added.

There was still no answer.

"Lameck. Aril." Her voice was tense.

They raised their heads through the stalks. Surrounding the cart were six young giants. Their clothing was black and their faces and arms were covered with serpentine markings.

Lameck slowly climbed over the side clutching a handful of grain and faced one, about nine feet tall. "Tell us the way to the palace, and we will give you grain," said Lameck, extending his hand.

The one he faced shifted his eyes to a taller one that looked coldly back. He then reached out and seized Lameck's wrist, dumping the grain into his own hand and stuffing it into his mouth.

Lameck decided to approach the taller giant that appeared to be the leader. Taking another handful he walked over to him, displaying the grain. "Can you help us?"

"Watch out Lameck." He heard Aril's warning but had no time to respond. A blow to the back of his neck made him lose consciousness as he felt himself collapse in the darkness.

"Where are we?" asked Lameck. "...and where is Bathenosh?"

"Behold, the Lord comes with ten thousand of His saints, to execute judgment on all...that are...against Him." Enoch pushed the scroll back, placing the feather quill beside it. The prophetic words had been recorded and described a future event, though he knew not when.

He put his head down on the table. The burden that he felt was too great to allow for sleep. *How much longer*, he wondered, *could such a state of mankind continue, with no apparent conviction of sin or awareness of accountability? At what point would God's patience give place to judgment?*

Earlier intercession had been laced with grieving—a sensing of the Father's heart for man and His desire to pour out far greater love and blessings. But man had ignored his God-given faculties and had turned to godless ways, searing his conscience and becoming at enmity with his Maker.

Enoch sobbed deeply within, alone in his house, engulfed by the darkness outside. He lay still, unable to think.

Something crawled up the back of his neck. He brushed at it, but felt nothing.

There it was again, but all over—a wind.

The flame on the table lamp flickered and went out.

Enoch sat up, wondering at this strange occurrence. It had never happened before.

Then he saw light, beginning from above and filling the room—light with such purity and brightness that Enoch shielded his eyes.

Suddenly, in the midst of the glorious light, appeared a figure like a man, with his hands outstretched toward him. Perfect peace and understanding radiated from his countenance. *"I AM,"* He spoke, *"Do not be afraid, Enoch, my faithful servant."*

Enoch had turned in his chair, but quickly dropped to his face, trembling on the floor. "Lord, depart from me. You are most holy. I am unclean and unworthy to be in your presence."

"You are well-pleasing to me, Enoch. Stand up and know that I have covered your sins with my covenant blood." The Lord reached out and took his hand.

Enoch felt his spirit strengthen and he got up from his knees.

"Come with Me," said the Lord.

There was no hesitation. Leaving the house behind, Enoch went with Him, the light encircling them, separating the darkness.

As they walked, Enoch listened. There was great comfort and joy just being in his Lord's presence. Everything for which his soul had yearned was satisfied. His Master's words conveyed such tenderness and compassion toward humanity that tears flowed from his eyes.

"The prayers of the righteous bring needed change, but not always immediately," said the Lord. "Your intercessions served to send warring angels upon ones that rebelled—those Watchers that left their given domain by taking human wives. They have now been seized, bound and delivered to the pits of darkness, until their final judgment."

"And the Nephilim?"

"The fruit of their ungodly unions will continue for a time."

"Will man find peace, as in the beginning?"

"Man searches for peace in the wrong way. There is restoration, but apart from My Word he will not find it."

The two had walked to the summit of the Ridge where they now stood. Enoch looked out into the darkness. "What will become of mankind?"

"It is appointed unto man once to die and after this the judgment. His faith will determine his destiny."

Enoch was grieved, for he knew the ways of man. "Are there none who seek to know you, Lord?"

"There is a remnant."

"And the promised Seed?"

"It is a mystery yet to be revealed."

The Lord again took Enoch's hand as the encircling light became a shaft, piercing the sky above. Together they arose from the darkened face of the earth. Into the atmospheric earthly heaven, then on and into the celestial starry heaven they traveled, soaring upward at incredible speed through the shaft of light until finally they entered the indescribable glory of the highest heaven and the company of myriads of angels. Enoch was immediately drawn to the praise and worship of the One True God for Whose glory all creation existed. He was home.

"We are in a cage," said Aril.

Lameck put his fingers through the slits of the hardwood enclosure. There was barely enough space for the two of them to sit. "…but how?"

"The Nephilim brought us here."

"Where is Bathenosh?"

"Their palace… they sold her as a servant."

Lameck felt the back of his neck, still throbbing. He was surprised that he had been unconscious so long.

"Did you really think that we could bargain with them?" asked Aril.

"We were desperate."

"Not as much as now."

"What is this place used for?" Lameck tried to focus beyond their cage. Next to him was a glass tank, about twelve feet square, filled with water, and something inside.

"I couldn't tell. It is one of three long buildings."

Lameck was watching the movement in the water—a dolphin-like creature with four stubby, dangling appendages jointed like legs, each tapering to six pointed digits. "Did they say anything?" An eerie moan resonated through the glass. Its partly opened mouth was wide and filled with fangs. It had sleek green hair and rough gray skin.

"The one who paid for us was called a breeder."

"Did you see what they have in here?" In front of the creature's gills were ears and a nose like a human. Greenish-gray eyes with large pupils were coldly detached like a reptilian.

"Animals." Aril replied.

"…like no kind I have seen." In front of their cage was a long wooden counter with stools, and shelves lined with glass containers and trays. Unidentifiable instruments could be seen on the counter.

"There is a door on this side," said Aril.

Leaning over, Lameck peered through Aril's bars. There were more cages by the door, and open bins along the wall next to them. The light was not enough to see what they contained but the smell was musty.

"They're returning," said Aril.

Footsteps could be heard coming from the other end of the building. Around the end of the tank stepped a tall male and a shorter female Nephilim. He was thin with big eyes and scraggly red hair. She was stockier, though similar in appearance. They both wore black full-length tunics.

"See?" The female pointed at Lameck. "He was not damaged."

"They need to be more careful," said the male, "if they expect to be paid."

"These are Sethite specimens."

"Very useful." He studied them. Removing a pole from the wall, he rapped the side of the cage. They jumped.

"Responsive," she said.

"Not bad."

"Should I feed them?"

"After we take blood."

"And elemental parts?"

"When the fertilized eggs are ready."

Lameck pushed his foot against the cage door, but felt no give. "What do you do here?" he asked, hoping for some answers.

"The humans have curiosity," said the female.

"It matters not if they know," said the male, returning the pole to the wall. "They will not be leaving." Clearing and deepening his voice, he continued, "For your information, as humans, you are being used as part of a breeding plan that will change the face of the earth. I and my assistants, we are proud to say, are uniquely qualified and endowed with the abilities to recombine and manipulate the reproductive chemicals of humans and animals, producing entirely different kinds."

"How?" asked Lameck, believing that the kinds had been distinctly created and unable to reproduce outside of their own boundaries.

"The knowledge is a complex secret imparted by the angelic gods and beyond your ability to understand. As the appointed breeders, we receive what Semjazza has taught—the ability to alter the shape and function of nature."

Lameck had never heard of this but knew that the angels were a higher order of creation. Perhaps they did have access to certain knowledge that could be misused for destructive purposes. He remembered being told of their rebellion.

"Look around you," the breeder continued. He reached up and took an oil lantern from the wall and walked over to the bin closest to them. The uncertain shadow Lameck had seen earlier suddenly took form, causing him to hold his breath. Curled up in the bin, was the upper part of a child covered with hair, but only to the waist, where it connected to the body of a goat. Aril gripped his arm as they both stared. The breeder grinned, seeing their reaction, and walked back to the counter.

"What will you do with these?" asked Lameck.

"When they mature, release them," said the female assistant.

"It is the completion of *Lucifer's plan*," said the breeder. *"...the evolution of the kinds with the dissolution and victorious termination of the human seed."*

Lameck was silent. The threat was far greater than he had thought.

More footsteps were heard approaching. It was another Nephilim assistant. "Quickly," she motioned toward the back. "A complication has developed."

The other two turned and followed her, leaving the brothers alone.

At first they just stared at one another. Lameck was distraught. He loved the creation—had always loved it—and loved the Creator even more. These strange beings were threatening to distort and destroy not only his life and surroundings but future generations as well. He looked again at the fanged creature in the water and around the room at the others, gripping the bar of his cage in frustration.

"Is it possible?" asked Aril. "Can they do that?"

"Look around us Aril. They have already begun."

"But why would they want to destroy all humans?"

"It seems that we have a powerful adversary with a grudge against the Creator and His laws of operation."

"How can they change what God has done?"

"Their powers are being misused."

"If our God has all power, why would He allow it?"

"One day I hope that we can ask Him."

Lameck was cramped and dazed...his head still aching. It all seemed impossible to understand—so opposed to everything he had been taught to believe—how created beings of any kind could thwart the Creator's plan. Tired and leaning his head against the cage, Lameck went to sleep while pondering.

"Son..." His father appeared in a dream. The two of them were seated in a river craft that was tied to the bank of the great forest. "Let us go for a walk." Methuselah stepped out and started through the towering trees.

Lameck followed. He was young, about twenty. As they proceeded into the shadows of the forest, he felt fear. Where are we going, father?"

Seeing his son's hesitation, Methuselah slowed and walked alongside. Lameck felt the comforting hand upon his shoulders. "There are creatures upon this earth that you have never seen, but there is no reason to fear."

They had not gone far before the stillness was broken by the sound of rustling foliage. Movement was seen. They continued, pushing aside branches and large leaves.

"Walk normally. Creatures can sense if you are afraid."

Through the trees, thirty feet up, a huge head moved slowly. Its jaws pulled on the leaves with a ripping sound. The body of the beast was immense. Low bellowing noises came from beyond.

"Have we gone far enough?" Even with the presence of his father, Lameck was ready to return.

"Just ahead. Stay close."

Shrill cries of birds warned of their intrusion. More massive dark shapes came into view. Soon they were standing almost close enough to touch the skin that seemed like tree bark. All were busy stripping and consuming vegetation, showing no concern for the humans in their midst.

"We are no threat to them and they are no danger to us." Methuselah gazed upward. "Amazing creatures—all created after their kind—made the sixth day, the same day as man."

Lameck was in awe at their size, the way some of them stood on two feet, and the use of their teeth. He was thankful that they were designed to be vegetarians. He was also glad that they could dwell in peace according to God's plan on the same earth.

"What can we do?" Aril's voice awakened Lameck. He was no longer on a nature walk. The reality was that they were

trapped—in a cage for humans—surrounded by creatures never intended by the Creator.

Lameck's arm rested against a lump in his pocked, barely an irritation but noticeable—it was his flint box. He slid it out and opened it, then tapped the tender into a pile at the base of the cage gate. "Move back." Aril gave him space as he struck the flint repeatedly—first, a wisp of smoke, and then a tiny flame. Lameck blew on it, then watched it climb and spread, finding fuel in the hardwood, slowly enveloping the end of the cage. As they waited for the flames to climb, Lameck spotted a glass jug across the room that contained oil for the lamps. The plan was obvious.

Aril coughed. The smoke was filling the cage and clouding the air in the building. There was stirring within the other cages and bins, as the flames leaped higher. Lameck knew that they did not have much time before the fire was detected.

"I hope that we can find the palace," said Lameck.

"I know the way," said Aril.

"Ready?" He looked at his brother. "Let's kick it."

18

"Let this one clean up the bones." The brutish Nephilim female shoved Bathenosh toward one of the servants, a Cainite girl.

"Come." Bathenosh followed the servant girl through the palace atrium, below the terraced gardens. She reminded her of a temple worker with her rigid demeanor.

"How many of us are here?" asked Bathenosh.

"Servants?"

"Cainites."

The girl kept walking without reply. Bathenosh was only interested in finding Lameck's sister and getting out.

After entering a hall they paused at a doorway where there was a strong smell of food. "You will bring it all here," said the girl, motioning inside. "Dump the leftovers in the holes and stack the platters."

Continuing through the hall, they came to a set of double doors. They were bronze with gold inlaid dragons. The girl opened one slowly. "They are sleeping. Do not disturb them." Looking around, Bathenosh saw that the room was immense with a stone arch ceiling. Scattered lamps reflected like faint stars from metal goblets and platters spread across the tables. Reclined shapes behind the tables filled the incensed air with rasping snores, signaling that the feasting of the palace Nephilim was finished.

The servant pointed to the table that she wanted her to clean. Picking up a platter and knife, Bathenosh scraped off the uneaten parts and worked her way around until she had a stack to carry out. It was no quick job. Back and forth they went until the tables were cleared of all but the big bones.

A large bag was handed to her—"The bones are your job." Bathenosh looked at the girl. Her expression was not arrogance, but seemed more like pity.

Carrying the bag, she returned to the feast room alone. The sight of gnawed bones and carcasses was not familiar or pleasant. Animal meat was rarely served in her home, and the thought of slaying one was disturbing. Holding the bag open in one hand, she reached out with the other and dragged a bone off the edge, letting it drop. There was no way to avoid touching them. She pulled another into the bag. They could have been pigs, or field animals. She tried not to think about it.

Another bone, longer than the others. She began to pull. Suddenly, she drew back her hand. Her whole body tightened. At

the other end, was a foot like her own, with five toes—
HUMANS! The Nephilim were eating HUMANS!

Bathenosh felt her heart throbbing. Dropping the bag,
she turned and left the room. The servant girl was in the hall.

"Why didn't you tell me?" Bathenosh tried to look her in
the eyes.

The servant girl was looking away. "We do our job."

"Who were they?"

"Ones brought in."

"Like us?"

"Sometimes."

"The brides?"

"If they fail to conceive."

"Will you help me?" asked Bathenosh.

"Where is the bag?"

"I will get it, but do you know of a Sethite bride?"

"One."

"Is she still alive?"

"Finish the bones."

Bathenosh returned to the room. Cooperation with the
girl was her only way. Nauseously, she slid the rest of the bones
into the bag and carried it back.

"Empty it in the hole," said the girl.

Bathenosh did as she was told. "Can you show me her
room?"

After pausing a moment, she nodded and began to walk
with Bathenosh back through the hall into the atrium. There she
stopped, facing the back interior. "The bridal chambers are there.
Her's is the corner room. Now, we must return to the servants'
quarters"

Bathenosh followed the servant girl back again, all the
way to the end of the hall to the darkened sleeping quarters.
Positioned just inside the doorway was the occupied bed of the

female Nephilim overseer who blinked at them with half-opened eyes as they walked by.

Bathenosh lay awake, waiting, until the steady breathing of the others could be heard—then, slowly, carefully, slipped from her bed and quietly moved past the sleeping overseer and back through the hallway.

There was an impulse to leave, to quickly get out and save her life. But something stronger within her heart told her not to leave without Riana. Her connection with this family had changed her. She now believed that she had a purpose that transcended her own self interests. While thankful to be alive, Bathenosh was more concerned for Lameck and his family. Surely the God who had miraculously delivered them earlier from certain death, was able to do it again.

The way looked clear. Bathenosh crossed the sea of marble, stepping softly so as not to make sounds. A brass loop with a key hung on the wall near the bridal rooms. Taking it down, she went to the corner door, inserted it and twisted. It clicked and released. She pushed it open.

Through terrace vines, moonlight splayed its patterns, revealing a canopied bed in the center of the room and a young woman, asleep. Bathenosh touched her shoulder, and then gently shook her. "Riana, I am a friend of Lameck, your brother."

She turned and lifted her head, "Did you say Lameck?"

"My name is Bathenosh. I came with your brothers from Eridu to help you escape."

"Semjazza will not allow it."

"Do you trust your God?"

"I am a Sethite. What is our God to you?"

"I am learning to trust Him. We must hurry." Bathenosh took her hand to help her up from the bed. "Let's go."

Riana sat very still on the edge of the bed, not moving a muscle. She was staring at something behind Bathenosh. The door had been left open.

"What a surprise." The words sent a shiver up her back. Bathenosh turned around.

"I see that losing one job did not keep you from finding another," said the Queen Mother. "My first night in charge of the palace, and already there are servant problems." She paused. "And what business would one of our workers have with a Sethite? Speak, Bathenosh."

Bathenosh had no words for such a malicious woman.

"It will not matter. Both of you will be food for my children tomorrow."

Druana stepped out and one of the Nephilim guards stepped in, closing the door behind.

———————

From the top of a tree, Lameck scanned the moonlit palace grounds looking for any movement. A Nephilim guard had just returned to his post by the front entrance.

"Do you see any others?" asked Aril, from a lower limb.

"Only the one."

The spiked wall in front of them was impassable and the gate was barred. But Lameck was waiting. The hand of God had been powerfully demonstrated already in his life, and he had no reason to doubt that his God would complete the mission. Just how, he was not sure.

Lameck was wondering how they might get inside when he noticed something moving in the distance, approaching the gate from the main road. It was a carrier. "Let's get down, and break off some branches." The two dropped to the ground, working quickly, and before the carrier arrived, were crouched alongside the gate with the loose branches pulled tightly around themselves. As the horses and Nephilim rider moved through, so did the bushes. Once inside, the brothers stayed in the shadows and crossed the grounds to the palace wall, out of sight from the guard.

Grabbing one of the longer terrace vines, Lameck began to climb with Aril close behind, pulling, and pushing with their feet against the tendrils. About thirty feet up they reached a ledge that opened to the palace inside. There was room enough to walk around the perimeter. It was evenly spaced with supporting columns and planters of lush greenery. Peering over the ledge to the palace interior, the brothers began their search, checking spaces that might contain the two they sought. Aril moved ahead, but not too far. The atrium below was vacant, its pools and lounging areas unoccupied. It was the sleeping area that Lameck wanted to find. Getting down inside had already been considered and he had a plan in mind.

Aril signaled, pointing down. The walls of a chamber room could be seen, a canopied bed in the center. If anyone was in it, they could not see. Lameck motioned him on. There were two more rooms like the first and each time they kept going. Soon Aril stopped again. It was a fourth room like the others, near the corner of the palace.

Suddenly, Aril stooped and moved around the ledge behind one of the plant containers, his hand waving and motioning for Lameck to hide. Lameck dropped to his knees and crawled toward the edge, just far enough to see down into the chamber.

Standing in the center of the room below, next to the bed, was a Nephilim guard. Lameck watched him jerk the bedding from under the canopy and slide it across the floor to the wall beneath Aril, then walk over to it and sit down. Lameck's hands tightened on the ledge as he looked. Across the room from the guard, sitting against the opposite wall, were both Riana and Bathenosh. They were both alive and together, but the presence of the giant changed the rescue plan. Obviously, the guard was not moving, and the brothers had to act before daylight. Lameck looked over at Aril's face, just above the planter—he was straining, and in front of him there was movement.

Little by little, the large stone planter budged forward. Lameck checked where the giant was positioned. He was directly below, and Aril seemed aware as he pushed. Closer and closer, it slipped to the edge. Then finally, it tilted, and toppled.

The women looked up in time to see it falling, but the guard had no chance to move. With a crunch the planter impacted, rolled from the slumped body, and broke in two on the floor with a crack. Lameck saw no further movement.

Quickly, Lameck took hold of a vine from the outside ledge, and pulled it inside, letting it down. Aril stood at the top while he descended.

Riana and Bathenosh were speechless. Lameck quickly hugged them both.

"How did you find us?" asked Bathenosh.

"I will have to tell you later," said Lameck.

"Aril?" Riana looked up to see him for the first time.

"Hurry and come up, sister," he replied.

Bathenosh looked at Lameck with fright. "They are eating humans."

"We can talk later," said Lameck, guiding Riana's hand to the vine. "Now, we need to climb." Lameck and Bathenosh both lifted Riana as she pulled and worked her way up slowly within reach of Aril. Though it took some effort, the way they got in seemed the safest way out.

Next, it was Bathenosh's turn. Lameck helped her to get started and watched as she pulled herself up. Once she reached the ledge, Lameck took hold of the vine to begin his climb when a sound from behind startled him—a creak from their chamber door as it swung open. It was too late for him to escape.

In the doorway stood a big woman—the same one that had surprised them in the temple—the one who called herself Queen Mother. With piercing eyes she looked at Lameck, then to the top of the vine at the others. Then she turned and saw the Nephilim guard lying in a pool of blood. The scream that came through her mouth, Lameck knew, must have alarmed the entire palace. Her face was contorted with hatred as she twisted and stomped back through the doorway. "GUARDS! GUARDS!" she yelled, then screamed again as before.

Lameck knew there would be no second chance. Grabbing the vine and clutching tendrils, he yanked himself up, moving desperately. Reaching the ledge, he was helped to his feet by Aril. "We need a quick way down," said Lameck. "Follow me." Moving around the corner, they crossed the rear of the main palace, concealed from the outside by the vines. Parting them, Lameck looked down. Below them was a short sloping roof and on the ground were horses and carriers. Several were rigged and ready for use. It was a short drop from the vines, then another drop to the ground. No one was in sight. Lameck knelt at the edge and helped the others down—Aril first, then Riana, then Bathenosh.

Suddenly, there was a grunt and scuffling noise. Lameck watched as a guard they had not seen ran toward the three on the ground, trapped beside a carrier. His huge arms seized them and despite their struggles held fast, dragging them back to the palace entrance, below Lameck. They were all about to be recaptured and killed.

There was just one chance. Breathing a prayer and stepping back, Lameck sprang forward with all his might, leaping outward feet first. The Nephilim guard was backing in his direction with his attention on his captives and just the right distance from the roof. Lameck's body came down at an angle, his legs tucked. Precisely before impact, he thrust both feet straight into the neck with all his strength. He felt the crack of bone as together they all collapsed to the ground. The giant lay limp as Lameck helped the others up.

"This is our way out," said Lameck, his hands already on the reins of a carrier's horses. Quickly, they all got on. Responding to his signal, the horses pulled them away, past the stalls, and around the side of the palace. Lameck increased their pace as they reached the front, and headed across the grounds in the direction of the gate.

Shouts were heard. Looking back, they saw two Nephilim guards running hard after them from the palace entrance. From the far side, more could be seen emerging with weapons in hand. Popping the reins, Lameck worked the horses. Just ahead were the gates, still open, as they had left them.

"Are we going home?" asked Riana.

"As fast as we can travel," said Lameck.

Leaving the palace grounds behind, the carrier with its four fleeing riders raced along the main road, the pre-dawn darkness surrounding them in all but one place in the distance where there was a glow from a fire.

"What is burning?" asked Bathenosh.

"Be glad that you don't know," said Lameck. It was a place he never wanted to return.

"Can it be any worse than what I have already seen?"

Jathron buried his face in his hands. *There was nothing left. No further authority. No further honor or recognition. It had all been snatched away. "What had happened? Where were the gods who had forsaken him?"*

His blurry gaze fell upon the crystalline apple at the table where he sat. A gift of the god, Azazel, it had been presented at his ordination as high priest. Just above the jade base, etched into the crystal, were his name, and the word, *immortality*. He had believed Azazel that his future was secure, that he too would be a god. But now, all the gods were gone, even Azazel. All of his hopes, everything for which Jathron had invested his life, had been ripped from him, suddenly, by a usurping priest. Gripping the apple in anger, Jathron threw it hard and watched it smash against his chamber wall. Spread across the floor, the glittering pieces broadcast his foolishness. *It had all been a lie.*

A fear that Jathron had not experienced for awhile was returning—the fear of an unknown God being in control of his destiny. *What if the foolish teachings of the Sethites were not foolishness, but the wisdom of God? What punishment would await one, like himself, who had ignored and later opposed the teachings of truth?* His knees shook involuntarily at the thought of facing such a judgment.

A stark choice suddenly came into focus—something he could do for the good of humanity, and at the same time—a way to avenge himself upon those who had robbed him of his position. He sat still, examining the decision. The intensity of the moment and his emotions were at work. Finally, with resolve, Jathron got up. Taking nothing with him, he shut his office chamber door behind and proceeded briskly through the corridor, down the steps, and out the main temple entrance.

"Good morning, father Jathron." The temple guard had not heard the news, neither was it full morning.

Jathron turned and continued walking by the temple toward the river. No others were in sight. At the corner, inside the temple storeroom, he located a hand cart. Removing two barrels from the stockpile, he positioned them on it and used his knife to open a hole in the bottom end of one.

From the storeroom down the trail to the river, he pushed, leaving a path of powder close to the other barrels that had been stacked along the way. At the entrance to the tunnel, the Nephilim guard was gone, as expected. The Nephilim were lazy and lawless in nature. Without their god to enforce the rules, structure had quickly broken down. They would probably reorganize, but it would take time. Hunched over, Jathron strained against the handle, slowed by the bumps in the tunnel bed. As high priest, his life-style had not profited him physically, and it was taking all his effort to keep going. His chest tightened with pain and his breath labored for air, but he was determined to reach the middle.

While struggling, he tried to recall his life before coming to Eridu, but everything was enshrouded in anger over the offense. He had been unjustly accused by the family. They were the ones to blame for driving him away. What if Methuselah had discovered the truth and forgiven him, as Lameck said? How could it matter at this point? His half-Sethite ancestry had followed him like a chained weight. Unable to cover the truth, he was finally forced to face it. But the most painful part, that Jathron now realized, was that the ones he had rejected were the only ones who had ever demonstrated love toward him. Perhaps that had been the hidden motive that brought him to this place.

He stopped the cart and returned a short distance through the tunnel. He went to the wall. There, he reached up and removed a lantern. With the flaming lamp in hand, he walked over to the trail of powder and bowed his head. "Creator God, Whoever You Are, have mercy on my sinful soul."

The instant it fell to the ground, a blinding flash of light raced through the tunnel in both directions, followed by a deafening roar and erupting force.

19

The sudden stop threw them all forward. Lameck tried to steady the frightened horses—the ground had shaken. Gripping the edge of their carrier, the four occupants stared across the Pison. On the distant shore was a flash of intense light—and a moment later, a rumbling blast. A rising plume of smoke followed, like a mushroom.

"Oh, God," said Bathenosh. "That is Eridu."

"What happened?" asked Aril.

"Look," said Riana. "—the river."

As they watched, the water erupted from one shore to the other, sending high waves rushing east and west. Like a dark wall in the dawn light, one swept past them crashing against the bank and ripping into structures. Lameck looked for the tunnel entrance, but it was gone. The place where it had been was now engulfed by the river. The Nephilim had been aroused and were beginning to gather.

"Where can we go?" asked Aril.

"How will we get home?" asked Riana.

"They have boats," said Bathenosh.

Lameck wheeled the carrier around—the horses again under control—and moved closer to the riverbank to investigate. Connected to the shore was a floating dock, bobbing on its angled pilings, with an oar boat still moored, but underwater. Two other boats had broken loose and lay smashed on the bank. Nothing that Lameck could see was useable.

"They had boats," said Aril. "What now?"

"We may have run out of escapes," said Lameck.

"There is a God who delivers," said Bathenosh, "and I am putting my trust in Him."

Lameck felt a wave of shame for failing to look to Him. "Help us, Lord, to find a way home," he said. "…and thank you for bringing us this far."

"I promise to never play with those powers again," said Riana.

"And I promise the same," said Aril.

Lameck felt the presence of the One he had come to know. His eyes focused on the huge catapults that were lined up side-by-side near the river, and the glider-like craft mounted on the projecting arms. He had seen them on the way in and knew that they were designed to soar, but was uncertain if one could carry four people across the Pison.

"Any ideas?" asked Aril.

"Possibly," said Lameck, driving the carrier over to one of the catapults. "Do you feel like flying?"

No one spoke.

Stepping down from the carrier, Lameck walked over to the wheeled structure while the others watched. The beam was positioned for release with enough weight for lift. Under tension was a metal spring device for added force. Lameck climbed up, being careful not to turn the gear. Standing alongside the craft, he looked into the opening. On both sides were control bars connected to metal rods. When he pulled one, he noticed that it lifted the rear edge of one of the wings. He understood the principle but wished that he had some actual practice. Lameck climbed back down to look again at the gear. Though it was designed for release from the ground, there was a line that could be stretched upward and used to turn it. It all looked workable.

"Aril," said Lameck. "Help Riana up into the rear of the glider."

"Are you sure about this?" asked Aril.

"Do you want to stay?" asked Lameck.

"Come on," said Aril, urging Riana to move.

"Can I shut my eyes?" she asked.

"After you are in," said Lameck, helping them as they stepped up and into the glider. "Your turn," he said, turning to Bathenosh.

"Can I trust you?"

"Not me, remember."

She gripped his hand tightly. Lameck provided support as she climbed up and lowered herself into the front section. Aril and Riana were seated with their feet to the rear and looking behind. Lameck was reaching to get the gear line when he heard his sister's frightened voice—

"The Queen Mother is coming!"

"They see us!" shouted Aril.

He heard the sounds of the horses and realized the danger. Grasping the line, Lameck hastily climbed up the structure to the craft's opening and slipped in.

"Hurry," said Aril.

Lameck pulled on the line and felt the gear begin to move. Then it stopped. He pulled harder, but nothing happened.

"What's wrong?" asked Aril.

"The gear must be locked," said Lameck, scrambling over the side and down. He could see the carriers approaching. The wheel was in front of him, but he could spot nothing that prevented it from moving.

"Look underneath," said Bathenosh.

Wondering how she could know, Lameck looked and was surprised. Inserted in a hole at the base of the wheel was a lock pin. He seized it and yanked it loose, then scrambled back up the side to the glider and into the seat alongside Bathenosh. Line in hand, Lameck again pulled... and this time felt the wheel keep turning. He heard Druana below, shrieking orders to her guards, then a click—

Meadows of greens with sprays of gold surrounded Enoch as he rested on a blanket of grass. It was all more perfect and beautiful than anything on earth. Soothing fragrances of cassia, cedar, juniper and roses calmed and pleased the senses. Trees cast no shadows. Neither death nor anything that threatened was present. Animals moved about freely. The only sound was the gurgling of the crystal clear stream that branched through the rolling hills after cascading from the central mountain. The overflowing love and kindness of the Creator was abundantly evident in Paradise. It was the fulfillment of Enoch's deepest yearnings.

He asked a question, looking into the face of Adam, sitting with him. The first father's countenance reflected wisdom and maturity far beyond the appearance of his youthful spiritual body. "Is it usual to feel shame for failing to reckon such love to our God?" The contrast of Paradise with the earth was far beyond anything Enoch had imagined. He regretted his earlier inclination to regard the place he had once lived as his home. Now it was obvious how much the original glory of earth's creation had faded. How much decay had taken place.

The first human father was silent, a sadness in his eyes —then he spoke, "Please forgive me."

Sitting up, Enoch felt the depth of Adam's emotions. As the representative of the human race, he needed release by his own family for subjecting them all to the dire penalties of the first sin.

"Of course I forgive you, father Adam, but you are not alone. We all have sinned. What you have done, we too have done, and in no small measure."

"It is true…but the nature and propensity to sin as well as the tragedy of death and the curse might not have been—had Eve and I obeyed. So, I thank you for your forgiveness."

"That old serpent has tempted us all," said Enoch.

"And taken many souls captive," said Adam.

"Praise the Lord for providing a way of escape."

"And great blessings."

"Great indeed." Enoch's eyes had focused upon the source of the crystal river—the seat that was crowned with a glorious white aura and magnificent bow of colors. It was the throne of all power in the center of Paradise. Music and voices of praise could be heard surrounding it.

"Were it not for the blood, none of us would be here," said Adam.

Enoch knew that he referred to the sacrificed animals which covered them when leaving Eden. It had been the beginning of the sacrificial system which was still in place upon earth. "Praise the Lord for making a way of entrance into His eternal presence and fullness of joy." In the light of Paradise,

Enoch finally realized, the most beautiful places in the world were but temporal shadows—imperfect forms prefiguring the perfect. Even if Eden had remained in its pristine beauty, apart from God's presence it would have been a flowered grave. Truly the best part of Paradise was the fullness of the glory of the Lord, the one true Creator God Almighty, and Love. Every living spirit, every creature, and every blade of grass had its existence for the one supreme purpose of magnifying His glory.

"What is the condition of Methuselah's family?" asked Adam, concerned and knowing that most of mankind had hardened their hearts. He also knew of the angelic rebellion and the efforts of the adversary to rule the creation.

"Lameck has become a vessel of honor. It was a struggle. Lucifer almost succeeded in dividing and destroying the family."

"Time is drawing near for the judgment."

Enoch had sensed it and knew that Adam's words were true. "Let us return to the court of worship with Eve and Abel."

"Yes," said Adam, as they arose and headed joyfully in the way of the sparkling river into the glorious light. "The angels need our strengthening."

Praise was known to empower God's ministering spirits.

With its release, the beam sprang to its limit and the weights hit the ground with a thud. Lameck had never felt such force, even from the slidecart. He was transfixed, slammed against the seat, as the air rushed against his face.

Up, and higher up they soared, far above the trees, into the sky of the eagles. Below them was the Pison, and in the distance ahead, illumined by the partly risen sun, the shoreline of Eridu. The smoke was gone.

"Is everyone all right?" asked Lameck, his hands on the controls. Bathenosh met his eyes and smiled. He glanced around at Aril and Riana, who had no comment, still sitting and facing the rear. Behind them stretched the now isolated continent of Phlegra. He could see the tiny garden palace and the smoke still rising from the fire that they had started. Further away, protruding through a blanket of greenery, could be seen the pyramids—the constructions of the Nephilim.

"Are we changing direction?" asked Bathenosh.

Lameck looked back to the front. The glider was slowly banking, turning eastward into the sun. Pulling on a lever, he tried to adjust but nothing happened. The left wing angled upward.

"What is happening?" asked Aril.

"The controls are not responding," said Lameck. "Are your feet against anything?"

"Try it now," said Riana. "I just moved."

Lameck tried it again. This time it worked, but they were in a spiraling dive. With little time to correct, he pulled back on all the controls. Gradually, the horizon returned and the wings stabilized. "We have lost most of our altitude," said Lameck. "It will not glide much further."

"We are only halfway," said Bathenosh.

"At least we should float," said Lameck.

"Are we going down here?" asked Aril.

"I am sorry," said Riana. "If we die, it is my entire fault."

"Brace yourselves," said Lameck. Holding the controls steady, he kept the nose of the glider up as they descended to the level of the river. The water hit the tail and contacted the underside, dragging them to a stop with a final splash from the front wings.

"Any new ideas?" asked Aril.

"Get a fish to pull us to shore," said Riana. "At least we are alive."

"And we escaped," said Bathenosh.

Aril looked around at Lameck. "Why are you tearing it apart?"

"Making some paddles," said Lameck, leaning out on the left wing while disconnecting the rear flap. It was long enough to break in two and both flaps provided four. "Here," said Lameck, handing them out. "With some effort, we should arrive before sunset."

"That won't be fast enough," said Riana. "A boat is coming."

Lameck looked back. An oar-boat was pulling from Phlegra in their direction. It must have been lifted from the water.

"Start paddling," said Lameck, although he did not see how they could outrun their pursuers. The glider was not built to travel in water. The wings dug in, creating too much friction. Even with all four paddling, it seemed futile.

"We cannot lose hope," said Bathenosh.

Lameck was thankful for the reminder. They continued to paddle, glancing back occasionally.

Plunk.

It was not the dip of a paddle, but an arrow hitting the water close to them. They were within range of the boat. He could see the giant archer standing in the bow and the other Nephilim pulling on the oars, with the Queen Mother in the center giving orders.

"We need to take cover," said Lameck. It was their only recourse, so the four pulled in their paddles and lowered themselves inside.

Thunk.

Lameck saw the arrow sticking out of the right wing.

"What will they do to us?" asked Riana.

"They want to kill us here in the river," said Aril.

"Is Bathenosh the only one who has not given up hope?" asked Lameck, "We should not believe that the God who brought us this far will now abandon us."

There was no reply, just a swell in the river that lifted and resettled.

Lameck looked again at the approaching boat, less than a hundred feet away. The archer was readying for another shot when a roll of water caused it to pitch, interrupting the rowing. The giant lowered his weapon to steady himself as the Queen continued to shriek orders.

All four heads rose from the glider to see what was happening.

The rolling had passed but something else was taking place. The river was moving in a circular direction around the boat, swinging the bow with it, the oars unable to stop it. Druana looked frantic, trying to keep her eyes on those they were pursuing while the boat turned.

"Can you see what that is?" asked Aril, pointing down into the water.

Lameck leaned over and saw an immense shadow, circling in the same direction as the water. "Whatever it is, we need to be still and not draw its attention."

"It is Leviathan," said Bathenosh, after peering down.

"What is it doing?" asked Riana.

"It seems to be playing with them," said Lameck.

The turning slowed as the water around the boat stilled. They seemed unaware of what was taking place below. With a shrill bark from the Queen, the oars began to stroke together. Then, suddenly, the whole boat bumped three feet in the air and splashed back down. The Nephilim let go of their oars and crouched toward the inside, huddling around the Queen.

Leviathan's coiled tail could now be seen on the surface, with its glistening green scales, tightly wrapped around the waterline of the boat. As the occupants gazed in horror, the creature's head and neck suddenly burst upward from the depths alongside. Swaying above them with smoke streaming from its nostrils, the watery serpent studied its prey through fiery eyes. Its jaws were closed.

"I demand that you release us, in the name of Lucifer," said Druana, standing in the midst of her Nephilim guards.

The head stopped swaying and reared back, shadowing the rising sun.

"Do you know who I am?" asked the Queen Mother.

The jagged jaws parted as its coils tightened with a terrifying crunch. With nowhere to go and their boat disintegrating around them, the Nephilim climbed onto the monstrous tail like flooded ants onto a branch. Druana stood stiffly in the center of the constricting coils glaring upward defiantly.

Baring its fangs, Leviathan sprang forward again and again, seizing and swallowing the Nephilim one-by-one from its coils. Then, with its tail entwined around the lower half of the Queen, it jerked her into the air upside down, above its head. Slowly it turned its open mouth upward and dropped the dangling prey. The piercing scream was quickly muffled in the closing jaws, and the crunch of bones was heard as Leviathan's head retracted in the river.

Incredulous, Lameck watched the tail uncoil and whip across the water toward the glider. "Hang on," he said, bracing himself and Bathenosh.

He felt the craft lift and was expecting it to fall. The nose of the glider angled up and it continued to climb, higher and higher. They looked with surprise at one another, then back at the craft. Below the wings of wood was another set of wings, radiant white, bearing them up and in the direction of Eridu.

"Praise the God of all creation," said Lameck.

"Praise the One True God," said Bathenosh.

"Praise the God who saves," said Aril.

"Praise the God of mercy," said Riana.

After setting the glider down gently on the grassy slope, the large angel helped them out. Standing before Lameck and Bathenosh, he opened his hands to them and spoke, "The Lord God Almighty declares these words unto you both—"

"Do not say or listen to those who say, 'I am Sethite' or 'I am Cainite', but know that it is God, the I AM, who has found you faithful and decreed that you will bring forth a righteous remnant from this earth. Out of your seed will come the Promised Seed, the One whose goings forth are from and to eternity."

As Lameck wondered upon the words of the Lord, the angel vanished before them.

In view of what they had been through, Bathenosh was grateful to be back; but the thought of seeing the devastation within Eridu was unsettling. The explosion they had witnessed from across the river had seemed ominous, and Bathenosh was concerned for the survival of her family. She walked quietly. There was comfort in Lameck's presence and she was glad they were with her.

As they approached the temple area, the sight confirmed what Bathenosh had imagined. Rubble was everywhere. The entire area was leveled. Not a single wall remained, and the place where the tower once stood was now overlapped by the widened river. People wailed with grief as they wandered aimlessly through the wreckage, while others, possibly merchants, slowly worked to clear sections.

"Bathy—" It was the voice of Rushton. Over the razed site he came running and threw his arms around his sister. "—you are still alive."

Bathenosh returned his squeeze. "And you—what about mother and father?"

"They are safe, but grieving. We feared you were dead. How did you—"

"I will tell you everything. Let us go home now."

Away from the temple area, the damage from the blast had been minimal. As they approached the house where her family lived, everything looked the same. Bathenosh was thankful. Her mother and father had been anxiously waiting and wept when they saw her.

"We thought we might have lost you," said her mother.

"The explosion looked devastating from Phlegra," said Bathenosh.

"It was an evil alliance by the priests," said her father. "Somehow, the Nephilim's weaponry was detonated."

"For the good of humanity," said Lameck. "Their plan would not have ended with the Sethites."

"None of us trusted them," said Rushton.

"Lameck, we are thankful that your brother and sister are safe," said the mother. "Please sit and talk and let me bring you all something to eat and drink."

Bathenosh excused herself to help her mother, while the others described what had happened in Phlegra. The two of them listened as they prepared, and then brought everything to the table. Bathenosh set a vegetable cake and cup of juice down for Lameck. She thought about him as they ate and continued to talk. In some ways he was like her father, in other ways uniquely himself. His personality complemented her own, and the adventures they had been through had allowed her to discover many things about him. She watched how well he related to her family, and her family to him, her father and Lameck even walking outside together for awhile. After returning inside, Lameck came over to her. She did not want him to go, but the time had to come.

"Can we talk alone?" asked Lameck. They walked up the steps to the rooftop, where he had stayed on his way into Eridu. "Your family has been gracious to us. Horses and provisions for our return trip have been readied." Lameck paused, looking into her eyes, "I have never met anyone like you, Bathenosh. Not only have you saved our lives, but you have unlocked my heart with your very presence. It is as though I have known all these years that there was someone like you, but such a person had never been revealed until now."

Bathenosh was silent.

"With God as my Witness, I confess my love for you and the longing of my heart for our lives to be as one. Will you covenant with me to be my wife?"

"Oh, Lameck—" She forced her eyes away. "I cannot."

"Is there someone else?"

"It is my family. I cannot abandon them."

After a brief silence, Lameck drew her to him, embracing her tenderly. For a few moments they held each other, and then returned down the steps to the others. Before leaving, Lameck gave a parting hug to all of her family, as everyone exchanged farewells. Bathenosh watched the three mount their horses and ride out of sight.

After they had gone, she had to turn away from her family for the fullness of her tears. Her heart felt like it would burst as she rushed to her room and fell face down on her bed.

A short while later, she felt her mother's gentle hand on her back. "Do you love him?"

"No."

"I saw differently."

"It cannot be."

"Lameck will make a fine husband."

"He will find a Sethite woman," said Bathenosh, trying to separate herself from her feelings.

"Lameck has requested my permission for you to be his helpmeet," said her father, just entering her room. "I gave it. He is a good man and will look after you."

Bathenosh lifted her head and sat up. They were both standing next to her.

"If your concern is for us, it need not be," said her mother. "Rushton is old enough and able to help."

"The grain will be more plentiful now that the Nephilim can no longer take it," said her father. "Do you want to be with him?"

"I do."

"Do you understand that, with the Sethite God, the marriage covenant is for life?"

"Yes, father. Haven't you always believed that?"

"In my heart I have always believed that the true God of our fathers was the Sethite God. And now, after the destruction of the temple, I am even more convinced."

"Are you sure you will be all right without me?"

"The God who safely returned you to us will also watch over us."

"Do you love him?" asked her mother again.

"I am sure of it."

"Then gather the things you will need and go to him."

It did not take her long. With her mother's help, she hastily prepared for her departure. Bathenosh hugged each one dearly; then, before she left, her father called her to him. Placing his right hand upon her head, he gave her his blessings.

"Your horse is ready," said Rushton, standing in the doorway.

"Where did you find the extra horses for everyone," asked Bathenosh, as her brother helped her up. "...and the two big stallions for the grain-cart we took to Phlegra?"

"Just wandering loose," said Rushton with a smile.

20

The three riders stopped at the bend. Following the road would take them northwest toward the Ridge, but there was also a trail to the northeast that connected with the coastline.

"The beach will be a faster way home," said Lameck. "…and safe, now that the Nephilim are gone."

"What should we tell father?" asked Aril.

"I will be home a day later, after seeing Enoch." He watched his brother and sister take the trail heading northeast. His plan was to go on to the Ridge, but he did not have a sense of peace yet about leaving the bend. Getting down from his horse, Lameck walked to the big tree where he first found Bathenosh, and sat down.

Resting his head against the trunk, he reviewed his experiences in the light of the truths he had been taught by Enoch. It was all happening just as he had said. As the streaming water acted on the stone to remove its resistance, God had used challenges to bring about needed change. Lameck had grown in his faith, seeing God take him through insurmountable difficulties.

He had tried to abide in the awareness of his Creator and, like the trees that grew greener closer to the water, he had succeeded in his mission. The Nephilim were cut off and his family was rescued.

Then he recalled the silvery fish that used the pools within the falls to propel themselves to greater heights. God had guided him in the same way, to make wise use of existing opportunities, to take the catapult that the adversary had intended for destruction and use it to save lives.

Like the lodestone compass, the Creator's guidance system had worked well up to this point. But now Lameck wondered—"had the purpose for Bathenosh in his life been fulfilled with the escape…and nothing more? Had his feelings and words been mere self-expressions?" The prophetic words of the angel gave Lameck peace and he determined in his heart to wait upon the Lord.

"Would you like to meet a Cainite?" The familiar voice caused his heart to jump. She was there, more beautiful than he remembered, looking at him from her horse. Her pack of belongings was on the back, affirming her intentions.

"My name is Lameck," he said, remembering their first dialogue.

"And mine is Bathenosh." Her eyes were teared.

Lameck got up from beside the tree. "Are we beginning again?"

"I do not want it to ever end." She slipped down and walked up the slope to him. He reached out, took her in his arms, and pulled her close. Bathenosh responded warmly to his embrace. "I wanted to leave with you," she said.

"No words are needed. It is enough that you are here."

As they held tightly to one another, Lameck closely looked into her eyes. Filled with love, they sparkled like the morning dew and radiated joy. Never before had he felt such oneness with another person. It was as though a part of his life had been missing until this very moment, and now he was…and the two of them were both…complete.

Lameck lifted a strand of hair from her face. It was moist from the tears that continued to trickle down to the smile on her lips. How grateful he was for such a precious gift that transcended anything he had ever known, mentally and emotionally. How awesome God was to use such events in their lives to bring them together.

The return to the Ridge with Bathenosh seemed to take far less time than when he had traveled alone. Lameck anticipated seeing Enoch again, and introducing his betrothed.

As they approached the rock house, Lameck was surprised to see vines on the doorposts and the animals missing from the stalls. There were no signs of life.

"Is this where he lives?" asked Bathenosh.

"It no longer looks like it."

They dismounted and walked to the door. Pushing it open, Lameck stepped into a room that had been stripped bare. There was no furniture, nor lamps, nothing but a few dirty rags that lay in the corner. The rest of the house was the same.

"What has happened to him?" asked Bathenosh.

Recalling his last visit and those who had caused him to flee, Lameck was struck by the thought that Enoch's life had been taken, along with his possessions. There was another place he had to see that could tell him more—Enoch's secret place.

"Come with me, outside," said Lameck.

"Among the trees?"

"It is his hidden place of prayer."

There was no path but Lameck remembered the direction as they went. Sweeping branches to the side, they stepped through the undergrowth into the open area—then halted. On the ground in front of them, lay two men on their faces in prayer. "Nathel?"

His cousin raised his head, "Lameck?"

"Bathenosh, meet my Ridge cousins, Nathel and Abinar."

"When did you get back?" asked Nathel.

"We just arrived. Where is Enoch?"

"Please sit down," said Nathel.

"Is he alive?"

"Very much so," said Abinar.

"Then where?"

"With God," said Nathel. "…in both body and spirit."

Lameck and Bathenosh sat down on the log bench across from them. He had not heard of anyone escaping the penalty of death, and listened with intrigue as his cousins took turns describing what they had seen happen. They had been on their way to pray, as Enoch had taught them to do…very early, before daylight. When almost to the summit, they had seen an angel standing with Enoch and a shaft of light surrounding them, when suddenly through it they ascended into the heavens.

"He walked with the Lord, and God took him," said Lameck, his spirit affirming the truth. "Have you told any others?"

"We told a few," said Nathel. "but they did not seem able to believe."

"They found it easier to think that he was dead," said Abinar.

"And some from the Grove probably wished it," said Nathel. "after what they did to him."

"But they were after me," said Lameck.

"When they could not find you they took out their anger on Enoch. He took a lashing in your place.

"Then, like vultures, many came when they heard he was gone and picked his house of anything they wanted."

"As Enoch said, the people have filled their hearts with the stuff that perishes and left no room for the things of God," said Abinar.

"Did you come here with him for prayer?" asked Lameck.

"A few times," said Nathel.

"It is a peaceful place," said Bathenosh. "Enoch must have had a great awareness of God."

"Enoch knew Him in a way that no one else seemed to," said Abinar.

"Did he leave his writings with you?" asked Lameck.

"He gave us some that he had re-copied," said Nathel. "The others, he wanted you and your family to have."

"They are still in the hidden enclosure," said Abinar.

"Is it safe to stay in the house for the night?" asked Lameck. It was getting late.

"There is no reason for anyone to come back with everything gone," said Nathel. "Take one of our lanterns. We can pick it up later."

"Thank you," said Lameck. "We will remember you in our prayers." With darkness encroaching, Lameck lit the lantern and walked back with Bathenosh to the house. They brought in food, then knelt and expressed their thankfulness to God for His continued goodness. After they finished eating, Lameck opened the wood panel to the hidden enclosure and took down the scrolls.

"Do they contain the creation account?" asked Bathenosh.

"Yes. Were you taught of it?"

"Not by temple instructors."

"How did you hear?"

"I discovered the inscriptions on some tablets."

"Where were they?" Lameck was deeply interested.

"Within a lower chamber of the temple, behind a curtain. They were kept hidden by the priests. After finding them, I lost my position as a temple worker."

"Would you remember what was written, if you saw it again?"

"I am sure."

Lameck opened one of the scrolls and set the lamp alongside it. For awhile, Bathenosh studied it, and then looked up. "It matches word-for-word. Where could the tablets have come from?"

"Adam," said Lameck. "The fathers told of such tablets on which our first father recorded the revelation, as given to him by the Creator God. They were entrusted to Seth, and then later mysteriously disappeared. Fortunately, the inscriptions had been carefully copied in time to preserve the words for later generations."

"Now, the tablets have been destroyed with the temple," said Bathenosh.

"But not the truth."

"Why would the priests not have wanted to reveal such wonders to us?"

"For the same reason the Nephilim attempted to erase the kinds and make their own—Like their false gods, they envied the glory of the creation, and wanted to claim the power of the Creator for themselves."

"Our family never believed their lie. Can we give them a copy of these writings?"

"We will have it for them when they come for our covenant ceremony." Lameck rolled up the scroll and placed it with the others. "But now we should get some sleep for the journey home tomorrow."

"Lameck?" Bathenosh spoke softly. "Please forgive my ignorance of Sethite customs, and allow me to ask a personal question."

"Anything."

"How many wives do you plan on having?"

The question surprised him. Polygamy had never been a practice among the Sethites, only among those Cainites that disregarded the instructions given to Adam. "If I could ever find another woman so designed for me as you, I could only introduce her to my good friend, Albo. Did Adam provide more than one rib?"

Bathenosh relaxed and smiled. "It is as I thought. But, one other question...When two people are ready for covenant, is it permissible for them to lie down together?"

Then, it occurred to Lameck that he had given no thought to their sleeping arrangements for the night. He had no intent of violating the timing and sacredness of their union. Their proximity for the night, in the same house, could allow for temptation. "Forgive me, Bathenosh, for allowing the question to arise. Nathel's home is near and you will be comfortable with his family overnight."

"If it is too late, perhaps I can stay here in another room."

"Nathel's family will still be awake." Lameck offered his hand. "Shall we go?"

Taking his hand, Bathenosh stood before him and looked into his eyes. "Lameck, have you ever loved another woman?"

"Once," he said. "But I never knew her."

"Neither have I known another man."

"What are you feeling in your heart?" he asked.

"The joy of knowing that the one I love is one who knows God."

The morning sunlight streamed down through the window, warming Lameck's face, and opening his eyes. He had not heard the door, but Bathenosh was already there, looking at him.

"Did you get enough rest?" she asked.

"Like a rock. And you?"

"I am ready to meet your family."

Lameck gathered and packed the writings, while Bathenosh took care of the provisions. Soon they were back on the trail, but this time headed home to the Grove. Hopefully, his family would not be too upset over his past behavior. It would take time, but he planned to make the necessary restitution for the damages he had caused.

On the way down the Ridge, they saw the stream that led up to the falls and stopped for a moment while crossing the bridge. Bathenosh was fascinated by the sight of the fish as they jumped and struggled against the current.

"Does it remind you of us?" she asked.

"How true. I like your thoughts."

"Those fish must have an important mission."

"To fill the waters with more of their kind."

They watched a little longer before finally leaving the Ridge and entering the grassy plains. Ahead of them the landscape rolled like a river of gold. Lameck enjoyed being back in familiar territory, but most of all with Bathenosh. She shared his appreciation for the beauty of creation and his love for the Creator.

Multitudes of animals along the way added intrigue to the homeward journey. The taller reptilians fed on leafy trees near the edge of the plains, while other kinds wandered through the grains. Some rested while others played. Herds of horned cattle dotted the grasses, peacefully grazing.

Coming to a natural spring, they let their horses drink while they tasted some of the fruit that grew near the water. "Was it God's command for us to be fruitful?" asked Bathenosh, picking one that was plump and orange.

"You recall the tablets well."

"Is it in order to fill the earth with our kind?"

"Not just to fill, but to fill with good fruit—children who will follow their consciences, filling the earth with the goodness and glory of the Creator."

"Do you think that your parents are ready for a Cainite family member?"

"They will love you. Besides, you are not the first."

"Oh, really?"

"Jathron, the high priest of Eridu, lived with us when he was younger. His father was Cainite."

Bathenosh had partly bitten into the orange fruit, but removed it from her mouth and tossed it to the side. "Bad fruit."

"Here," Lameck offered her another. "Have a good one."

Bathenosh savored the sweet fruit and the close companionship of one who shared her heart…Pondering what she had heard, it seemed incredible that father Jathron had been raised in Lameck's family, yet turned out the way he had—denying any mention of his part Sethite origin But now, it seemed that *Bathenosh was the odd one. Would Lameck one day feel strangely toward her?* The thought had not even entered in, much less bothered her, until this time and she would rather have ignored it—but it was there—and now they were enroute to a permanent home within a totally Sethite community. She wondered how the family members would feel toward her.

"Is something bothering you?" asked Lameck. There was nothing in his eyes to confirm the feelings that had come upon her.

"It is nothing." Bathenosh wished for a moment that Lameck had been a Cainite, and then felt foolish.

"Is there any unhappiness. Please tell me." He was searching her eyes.

"It only concerns my Cainite heritage. I do not want to bring division to your family."

Lameck turned fully toward her and took her hand. They walked to a soft rise and sat facing each other. "Bathenosh, it makes no difference to me if you are a Cainite or a Sethite—nor will it affect my family, once they know you as I do. I love you." Lameck looked upward at the bluish-pink sky, then back at Bathenosh while clasping her hand. "Before I departed from your family's home in Eridu, your father confided in me—not that it made any difference in how I felt toward you—perhaps he needed to tell someone and did not know what our future might be."

Bathenosh studied Lameck's face, curiously waiting to hear the words that followed.

"…When you were a baby, you were taken to be used as a sacrifice and placed in a basket by the priest. While working on the temple, Milcah, who is now your father, saw you. At the risk of being killed, he took you to their home where they raised you secretly, as their own daughter, not knowing the identity of your natural parents. Eventually, they had a son of their own who became your brother. I promised only to tell you if it was necessary. I feel that it is."

It was almost too strange to comprehend. She had been adopted—actually saved from the jaws of Leviathan as a baby. And the family that had raised her—as a Cainite—had loved her as a natural daughter...but, *Was she a Cainite? Would she ever know?* Apparently, Lameck did not have the answer—but neither did it matter—as he reached out and drew her to him. They held each other tightly as tears flowed. *Everything would be all right.* She knew deep within.

The time had passed quickly and the day, though spent traveling, had been relaxing, contrasted with the days past and all they had recently been through. Their journey was coming to an end as the sun settled behind them. Pointing at the distant trees, Lameck let Bathenosh know that they were close to arriving. She looked happy.

Lameck, however, was bothered by the uncertainty of what to expect. Remembering the hostility, and with concern for the safety of Bathenosh, he wondered if they should wait until dark, or circle the Grove and come in on the side nearer home.

As they got closer, the sound of a ram's horn trumpeted from the trees. Lameck had last heard it as a signal for approaching Nephilim.

"What is it?" asked Bathenosh.

"A warning sound," said Lameck, though uncertain.

"There is a rider coming this way."

Lameck watched, while moving his horse in front of Bathenosh. He decided to meet the rider. As the horseman came into closer view, Lameck breathed with relief. It was his friend, Albo. "Is it safe to come home?"

"It has not been this safe for a long time," said Albo. "Is this the woman we have heard about?"

"This is Bathenosh, my helpmeet and future bride. Why was the horn sounded?"

"To announce your return."

"Am I being taken before the elders?"

"You are being welcomed home as a hero. The entire Grove has heard of the rescue and the separation of the Nephilim. Follow me to the feast that has been prepared in your honor."

Lameck and Bathenosh looked at each other. Not only did he no longer have to worry about redeeming himself, but favor had been restored to his family. His heart expressed deep gratitude toward the One responsible for it all. Side-by-side they accompanied Albo back into the Grove, while the ram's horns continued to trumpet above. People cheered and waved from their tree dwellings and children ran alongside, growing in numbers as they went.

At last they arrived at his family home. Tables had been spread throughout the area, filled with more food than at a Sethite gathering. Torches were being lit for the feast that was ahead and families were coming from all directions. After they dismounted, Albo took the reins and led their horses to the stable while Lameck guided Bathenosh to the steps leading up to their home.

They were halfway up the steps when he heard his father's voice from above—"Lameck, my son, welcome home." He looked up and into his father's face. It was the same warmth and unconditional acceptance that he remembered through all the years.

Bathenosh was received graciously by everyone, especially his own family, which made her feel very much at home. The news of what she had done, along with Lameck, was well known, thanks to Aril and Riana.

The evening had grown late when Lameck went to his father's study, carrying the saddlebag with the scrolls. There had been little time to talk following their arrival or during the festive meal. On the way to the room, he could hear his mother talking with Bathenosh from the guest quarters. It would be her place to stay until the ceremony, at which time Lameck's own dwelling would be ready to occupy.

Methuselah was waiting for him as he stepped inside. "Lameck, my son, let me welcome you again." Both father and son reached out to one another and embraced. The separation that Lameck had felt earlier served only to magnify the closeness he now realized that had always existed between them. They sat down.

"You have fulfilled your name, as conqueror," said Methuselah.

"I have learned to trust in the ways of God."

"And you have gained wisdom."

"From the fathers," said Lameck.

"I have felt the turmoil of the enemies you have faced."

"The one within was the most difficult."

"The victory is evident," said Methuselah.

"Finally, yes, but Lucifer used me for awhile. I beg you to forgive me for the damages I caused."

"How can I hold anything against you?"

"I want to rebuild the altar."

"It is not necessary. Gimlet and his brother have done it."

"Gimlet? I would not have thought—"

"I was also surprised, but they seemed to understand the need for a sacrifice better than most. Can we talk about Enoch?"

"Did you hear of his ascension?"

"From the man who returned. The others who pursued you to the Ridge did not."

"What happened?" asked Lameck.

"It is reported that they were mauled to death by a bear."

"They were the ones who lashed Enoch for my offense."

"Justice sometimes occurs without mercy," said Methuselah. "What more can you tell me of our father, Enoch?"

"That will take days," said Lameck, as he reached down into the saddlebag and presented the scrolls. "These are his writings which he wanted us to have."

Methuselah cradled them for a moment in his arms, and then placed them on the shelf along with the others. "It is late and you need your rest," said his father. "But, before you go, I want to show you something"

Lameck watched his father carefully unfold a white cloth from a rectangular object on the center of his table.

"Come closer and look."

Lameck rose and walked to the table. There, on the cloth, lay a flat piece of clay with words inscribed upon it.

"Aril said that he found it in the rubble of the Eridu temple," said Methuselah.

Lameck's eyes widened as he wondered, *Could it be… one of the tablets of Adam?*

"I saw them once as a child, before they vanished. It is as I remember, and a most significant part of the original record of creation—God's promise of the coming Seed that would crush the head of the serpent, mankind's spiritual adversary."

For Lameck, this was greater than all of his temporary victories. It was verification of the ultimate conquest, and the exaltation of Holiness, The Creator LORD GOD Almighty.

21

Praises flowed from Enoch—with hands lifted—and were magnified by those around him. The weight pressed him low—the Glory always present in Paradise, but heaviest when close to the throne. Voices rang in harmony, angelic and human together. Time was of no concern. Everything moved in accordance with the Holy Spirit in appreciating splendor for the One who was seated in Absolute Holiness. Enoch's head was bowed and eyes closed to the light—too intense to gaze into. The love and peace that he felt was beyond understanding, like that of an infant being held within the arms of the perfect father and mother at once. Every part of Enoch's being was sensing complete fulfillment in expressing his thankfulness to his God— the One who had spoken all creation into being—the One who reached out with mercy to restore fallen man.

He was impressed to look up. The magnificence radiated with force. Enoch was first overwhelmed by the absolute whiteness—then an image appeared—a Lamb, positioned and standing on the throne. As suddenly as it appeared, it vanished, and One like a man began walking toward him from the light. Enoch wanted to bow again and, as he did, felt a comforting hand rest on his shoulders.

"Enoch, rise and come with me." It was the face of the One he knew—the same One he had walked with while on earth.

"Yes, my Lord."

"My friend, it is time for you to see the place of the separated. You need not be afraid." At His signal, a large angel came alongside. "This is Teroch. He will take you and bring you back safely. Then we will talk again."

Enoch was aware of the place known as Hades and saddened to think about it. For whatever reason, he knew that the visit must be necessary, though he would have preferred to remain in the peaceful presence of the Lord.

With a rush of wind they went out. Teroch's arm held him firmly. Away they flew from the glorious light, departing the beauty of Paradise through clouded streaks of gold. Soon they began to descend.

Lower and lower they dropped like an arrow—the surroundings no longer bright and glorious but grayish and growing darker. Through whirling celestial matter they descended—passing planetary bodies with their own peculiar reflections. At one point Enoch recognized earth. Teroch drew his sword and extended it.

Below and in their way was a disturbing black cloud with erupting flashes. As they got closer, a churning movement of dark winged creatures could be discerned—some like angels, others like brute animals—with claws and long tails. Enoch had no fear as he recalled the Lord's words. Straight down they kept going leaving a shaft of light through the scattering cloud of creatures—the gleaming sword tip barely missing some.

After passing through, Enoch gagged from the odor of burning sulfer. The scene below was one of horror. Spread across a flat barren wilderness was a great fire—like a forest burning without trees. As he gazed down within the flames he saw bodies of people twisting and groping, faces contorted with pain. Enoch clutched his heart as he felt such grief rise within that he had never known. There were human persons, descendants of Adam—some he recognized—being tormented without relief. Included were the same ones who had persecuted him during his final week on earth. Their cries were the most desperate he had ever heard, causing him to tremble and his insides to wrench.

Slowly they passed over the flames and through the yellowish smoke. Enoch was recognized by those below but was helpless to answer their cries for even a drop of water. There was nothing that he could do. They had been warned. Their own choices had sealed their eternity.

Another descent opened before them. Torach's wings lifted above a wide pit, then down they went with great speed into a place of utter darkness.

"Where is this?" asked Enoch.

"The tunnel to Tartarus"

The only illumination was from Torach's sword as they slipped vertically through the blackness. The pressure from the depth felt thick like mud pushing in against him. More and more it increased, until finally they stopped.

Below the subterranean darkness was another realm of flames—greenish blue—even hotter than where they had been. Winged creatures of evil countenances were held down with chains. Spiteful groanings gripped Enoch's soul as these beings pulled in torment, beating against jagged rocks.

"These are the angels…" Torach was not able to speak easily. "…the ones who rebelled as God's Watchers and took human wives, teaching the abominable. Your prayers were answered."

Enoch remained silent. These powerful once-glorious creatures would no longer be allowed to exercise the higher purposes for which they had been created. Obviously they bore great responsibility for the well-being of mankind, but had turned their powers to evil.

"They will be held in chains under darkness for the judgment of the great day." Torach turned and extended his sword upward. "Now we must return."

Enoch felt the thick darkness slide by as they sped back…flying up through the pit…out of the realm of Hades… and into celestial space. The horror was behind but the images remained vivid. The oppression was gone and the great light was ahead. His appreciation for Paradise had been magnified, though questions loomed within.

His eyes looked away from the place of worship. Enoch was troubled at what he had seen as he wandered down the grassy slope to the water's edge, his mind on issues of justice and mercy, wondering if he would ever understand the unending torment. The lashings he had received certainly did not seem to warrant such a fate. He had been able to forgive…and knew that God was far greater…that there had to be much that he did not yet comprehend.

Shimmering reflections within the water interrupted his attention. Three fish swam by. A full spectrum of colors radiated from their silvery sides, more glorious than any earthly fish he had seen. Their movement was effortless as they glided along—no striving, no ledges to leap, and no falls to climb—already where they belonged.

"Teacher?" The word of the Lord was gentle. He stood near, smiling with warmth.

"Not I, Lord. You are the Teacher." Enoch turned and began to walk with Him along the bank. "There is much I do not understand."

"Humility is the mark of a good teacher."

"But Lord, I…" The words that expressed his concern fell silent as they started to cross a small but beautiful bridge. It sparkled with diamonds, rubies, emeralds and every precious stone—its value no doubt exceeding all the riches on earth. Together they walked to the center and paused.

"Do you trust your Creator?" His eyes looked deeply, searchingly into Enoch's.

"Who am I to question, Lord?"

"You are my friend."

He had heard the word before, but it sounded out of place coming from God. "Lord, how did I become your friend?"

"We chose each other."

The Lord allowed Enoch to consider what He said, and then continued, "I have set before every man choices which lead to life or death, blessings or curses, joy or sorrow. Like the angels, man was created an eternal being. When the body dies, the soul continues and another body takes its place. The present earth is a test of man's heart to determine his destiny. As you know, there are vessels of honor and vessels of dishonor. While on earth they dwell together, in eternity this can never be. The place you have seen was never the Father's perfect will. Man was created to enjoy eternal fellowship with God. Hades was not prepared for mankind, but for man's adversary—Lucifer and his angels.

"Forgive my ignorance, Lord…but why did you not prevent your creation from making such choices?"

"If man had been a mere animal, it would have been prevented. But our desire was to create a special being, in God's Holy likeness, which would exercise love and find oneness of the highest order with us. Man was made with the power of choice. Though he fell—if he wills—he can be restored. Whosoever will, may freely come. Those who seek righteousness, will find Me. Great mercy is offered to those who seek it, though it comes at great cost—the substituted life-blood of the innocent.

"The animals?"

"The sacrificial blood of the animals points ahead to what I alone must do." The image of the Lamb stood alongside Enoch.

"Welcome home, Enoch."

His heart leaped. It was the one familiar voice he had not yet heard. Standing at the edge of the bridge looking more beautiful and happier than ever before was Edna, his earthly helpmeet.

———————

Children squealed with delight as the wet sand trickled through their fingers dripping in towering shapes on the beach where they played. The sun shone brightly. A month had passed since Lameck's return, but it had been years since Methuselah's family had been able to safely enjoy a family outing away from the Grove, and to catch fish in the daytime. The donkey cart, with a few boards replaced, was half-full. Lameck had made another beach bow to replace the one that had been broken.

Dropping the net, Lameck smiled and took the fruit that Bathenosh brought him.

"Your father is ready to speak," she said. The family had begun to gather around Methuselah. "I will help you fill the cart afterward."

"You are a blessing and our house is blessed because of you." Lameck's hand cradled her waist as they walked. He was indeed thankful for the gift of her presence and anticipated their future union as husband and wife. Bathenosh had surprised him by offering to go with him on one of their honey hunts. She had caught on quickly to the technique, being the first to spot the comb. At fishing she had also proven helpful, and not afraid to get in the water with a full net, a task that Aril had been reluctant to do at first.

The family sat on the sand in a semi-circle facing the father. Behind him spread the graceful green palms, with colorful birds perched on the stalks filled with berries. It was good to see Methuselah looking so peaceful.

"My family…" His face turned to the south, then back. "It has been too long since we have had a day like this, together without fear at our cove. Hopefully, there will be many more.

"Let us never cease to give praise and thanks to our God and Creator for His Holy Watchers over us. Recently we have learned some valuable lessons in a painful way. God has helped us to discover things—certain activities—that can weaken His protection and permit entrance to the enemy of our souls.

"The adversary of man is a liar and deceiver. Although he once acted loyally, his pride caused him to fall from his heavenly position of great power. Now he uses his abilities in an attempt to steal, kill and destroy the very creation that God has made—especially mankind. His invisibility as a spirit makes him more dangerous along with those other spirits that have aligned themselves with him. We do not have to fear as long as we seek to please and obey Holy God.

"With the destruction of their tunnel, there is no longer a passage from Phlegra for the Nephilim. We have been spared. The destruction they had intended for us has fallen back upon them. How long they will remain isolated, I cannot say. But let us be thankful for the time we are granted. Let us make the most of it—enjoying the abundant provision of our loving God—and being careful to behave righteously.

"As I look upon my beloved family, and future family, represented by Lameck and Bathenosh, my heart is blessed. I have done my best—though less than perfect—in trying to communicate the faith of our fathers, the sacredness of creation and the seriousness of covenant. We have seen the damage that can be done by listening to the lies—by playing with the occult, indulging in pharmako and in sexual transgressions.

"So, let us have fun and enjoy our freedom—but let us beware. Freedom is not passage to sin. If we are to survive, we cannot live as many of the others do. We must follow the writings and wisdom of the fathers and stay alert, for our time in this world may be brief, and every person will be held accountable on the day of judgment.

"Because mankind has fallen from glory, we must not forget the need for the blood sacrifice—something the angels do not have. It is the payment we have for our sins that will satisfy divine justice. Let us as a holy remnant retain this hope. Let us be strengthened and encouraged by the promise of the Seed who is yet to come."

Methuselah extended his hands over the family group. "Now, let the Lord bless you and keep you. Let the Lord cause His face to shine upon you and give you His everlasting peace."

It was time for the family to go home. Lameck took Bathenosh's hand and helped her up. Aril and Riana stood next to them. "Are we ready for one more cast?" Lameck looked at the three.

"I heard that once before," said Aril.

"This time there will be no intruder," said Lameck.

"I am ready," said Bathenosh.

"Me too," said Riana.

As the rest of the family returned to the Grove, the four of them remained and readied the net. Aril seeded the water with bait, and soon the surface of the bay was teeming with fish— swelling and erupting with fins and flashings.

"Now—" Lameck gave the release and the beach bows sprang loose, hurling the net over the water. With a splash it landed in perfect position. "This one should fill the cart. Keep tension on the lines."

Lameck and Bathenosh worked one end while Aril and Riana teamed up on the other. The floats made a wide arch in between, containing the bulk of the fish. A few escaped by leaping the net but most were being swept in. The weight of the pull was heavy.

Bathenosh held firmly to the lower line. Lameck noticed the sparkle in her eyes. "Is there anything you do not enjoy doing?" asked Lameck. He was refreshed by her enthusiasm in all the family activities.

"Visiting Phlegra," she replied. It was the one thing they should never have to do again. "Have you thought of a name for our first son?"

"What do you think of Noah?" asked Lameck. "It means rest?"

"I am ready for that."

Lameck then noticed Aril. He was in chest-deep water behind the net. A couple of floats were submerged and he was trying to raise them to prevent fish from escaping. The pull was too much for Riana and the line was slipping through her hands. "Can you hold this end?"

"I have it," said Bathenosh.

Lameck hurried to the other end and took the lines, pulling shoreward. From the seaward side, Aril gripped the net and pushed upward. Bathenosh held her lines steady, and then with Riana's help, began to move their end. With all of them struggling, slowly the net crept with its load to shore.

Once in the shallows, the immensity of the catch was apparent, more than enough to fill the cart. One-by-one, they carried the big fish, stacking the cart until it could hold no more. Then, from both ends of the net, they proceeded to free the smaller fish, releasing them back into the bay. It was almost done.

Suddenly, a scream came from Riana. She was pointing at a dark bulging object entangled by the net in the shallows— the same place along the net where the floats had submerged. Aril was standing like a statue, staring. As Lameck approached, a strange feeling came over him, like something he had felt within the cage in Phlegra.

"What kind is it?" asked Bathenosh.

Lameck was silent. His eyes followed the fish-like tail up the scaley body, past the stubby appendages with shell-encrusted fingernails, to the sleek green hair and the head.

"It is like the one in the tank," said Aril. "

Gills were closed behind its ears. The nose was human in appearance as were the greenish-gray eyes, now glazed and clouded. The mouth was a slit spread wide, slightly parted and lined with fangs.

"They have infected God's creation with their corruptions." Lameck stared into the bay waters.

"Is it alive?" Riana had been unable to speak until then.

"It is dead," said Aril.

"Can we show it to father?" asked Riana

"It is not necessary for him to see," said Lameck. "He is aware of the evil."

"Do you think there are more?" asked Bathenosh.

"How can they be stopped?" Riana's face reflected the concern they all felt.

"The Lord has His way and His time," said Lameck. "Let us hold fast to the promise of the inscriptions."

Their eyes met with consent. The future was in God's hands.

THE TIME OF THE FLOOD...AND LATER

"Noah—Come, and your entire house, into the Ark..."

Darkness had overtaken the afternoon sky. Inside the cypress tree-dwelling the old man lay motionless, a small clay tablet in his hand. Lines of grief were still embedded in his face, traces of the tension the family had borne for the past century. Methuselah had lived 969 years

The white haired father sat erect as he listened to the words of his Lord. By faith he had built the Ark according to the instructions issued by God—300 cubits long, 50 cubits wide and 30 cubits high (the cubit being a forearm's length). It was huge, encompassing three levels with numerous cubicles and stalls—enough space to take in over 35,000 animals, leaving plenty of room for Noah and his three sons and all their families. It was time for the father to take a final step of faith.

Seven days had been given and it was exactly seven days later—on the second month and seventeenth day of the year—that it happened. As the last two of the animals were secured in their stalls, the ground trembled. The water had started to fall—a mist at first, then increasingly harder. The people gazed upward with puzzled expressions, but soon their faces reflected annoyance. And eventually they disappeared from sight.

The families of Noah were aware of the approaching judgment and already clustered inside the vessel. Noah proceeded up the ramp. There was nothing more that he could do. He had known all along that such a moment would come and suddenly it had. His throat tightened uncontrollably and tears mixed with rain dripped from his beard as he took his last step into the Ark. He could not bear to look back.

As he entered, a sweeping darkness caused him to turn. The wide open doorway was no longer there. A solid door had taken its place—tightly shut. Even the pitch had been applied as a seal, like that used throughout the vessel, inside and out. They were separated from the world, and in a way that no man could have done.

Oil lamps mounted on bulkheads illuminated the interior so that the family of eight could make their way past the cages and up the ladder to the third level where they would live. It took no persuasion for them all to gather in the center for prayer. In a close circle they joined arms and knelt. The Spirit of God was strongly sensed and His grace was needed for what was ahead.

Soon the skylight from the narrow upper window grew dim. The trembling earth was felt, intense flashes were seen, and overhead rumblings were heard. Noah's wife drew closer and he held her more tightly. Looking around he was thankful for the courage evident in the faces of his sons. Noah knew that they would be kept safe as Holy God had promised. The place of scorn had become their shelter.

It was not long until a different kind of movement was detected—with the creaking of beams. At first the weight of the Ark shifted, and then it began to swing in position. Then, with a battering crash of water against the side, it lifted, and floated free. Noah realized that from this time they had totally placed themselves in the care of their Creator.

Tremblings continued within the earth below as fissures cracked open and mountain tops erupted, spewing their fiery red rivers into the climbing seas. Torrential outpourings continued to build as churning waters whipped and driven by powerful winds raged across changing land masses. With the bursting of deep fountains below and the deluge from the waters above, soon all mobile life forms scrambled to survive, climbing ever higher, until their last stronghold was swallowed—then they too perished. Everything with the breath of life that had lived on dry land was washed from the face of the earth. Nothing could challenge the merciless waters that stood fifteen cubits above the highest peaks.

The very good earth that God had created was carved and sifted by the waters of judgment. The perfect design and marvel of nature was ripped apart by catastrophe. With each successive wave, layers of death accumulated and were left as a witness to subsequent generations. The primal giants of vegetation and animal kind were crushed and compressed beneath tons of roiling debris. The palaces and places of ingrown pleasure with their temptations to unrestrained evil were taken away as easily as dust with a broom. Fleshly transgressions that had manifested as Nephilim and other creature abominations had been left as legends.

It was a full year before the ark settled and the family and animals were able to re-occupy the earth. Noah's first act was a blood sacrifice using those animals that God had specified. God stated to Noah that never again would He destroy the earth with water, and as long as it remained, seed-times and harvests would continue for the benefit of mankind. The rainbow was the sign.

The generations that followed the flood were marked by sharply declining longevity. Noah lived another 448 years to a final age of 950. Shem lived to 600. But within four more generations, the human life span had decreased to 239 years with Peleg. Abraham, who was born 352 years after the flood, lived 175 years (150 of those years, Shem was still alive). Joseph, the third generation from Abraham, lived 110 years. Records of ages were carefully preserved by the Hebrew descendants within the sacred Scriptures.

Gone were the days of the towering reptiles. Yes, they hatched and dispersed from the Ark, but the post-flood climate had changed—no longer able to supply the oxygen and food requirements for the growth of such beasts. Gradually, they too declined in size and number, hunted and destroyed, until they became so few that they were labeled extinct. Neither could the great winged warriors develop the span once obtained, in an atmosphere unable to provide the lift needed. The bones of their ancestors layed down in the flood provided testimony to their once spectacular presence. And stories continued to be told around fires, captivating the imagination of those with child-like faith.

Within the nature of man, even after such a judgment, there still existed a tendency toward evil—even from childhood, in thoughts and actions. While the flood had buried the physical corruption, it had not changed the human heart, nor had it removed the roaming spirits of the Nephilim which were driven to seek, inhabit, and manipulate other bodies. Also, still present, were many of the unchained fallen angels that had sided with Lucifer in his rebellion. Their evil hierarchy would continue and their judgment would be future.

The identity of the Seed had been mysteriously concealed, and continued to be, for over two thousand more years—until the fullness of time. A prophet of God, Micah, hundreds of years before it happened, had declared that out of Bethlehem He would come—the Ruler whose origin was from eternity. Another prophet, Isaiah, provided a further clue, foretelling that as a sign from God, a virgin would give birth to a Son. Over three-hundred prophecies had predicted the arrival and workings of mankind's Savior, the long-hidden Seed of the woman that would crush the head of the age-old serpent, Lucifer.

Because His arrival and ways were without a show of outward force, most failed to recognize the One who came down from Paradise. He did not choose the existing world's kingdoms, but declared His Own—offering entrance to those who would turn to Him.

After four thousand years of waiting, Lucifer and his angels realized that the Seed had arrived. Enraged with pride, after repeatedly being eluded, they made their move, throwing all their powers to the task of human manipulation with the goal of destroying the Seed before He could gain any further human following or threaten their own worldly dominion. Driven by an ancient hatred of the Holy, they seized the Son and subjected Him to the cruelest, most torturous form of death devised. To the cross-members of a tree they nailed Him, then lifted Him, and finally drove a spear into His side, watching His Life Blood as it spilled to the ground.

For a moment in time, Lucifer believed himself the victor, but had he realized the plan of God, he would never have crucified the Prince of Glory. For in carrying out their vengeance, the rebelling angels committed the one act that, by the legal decree of God, both sealed their destruction and provided release for their prisoners.

Beginning in the garden with the clothing of Adam and Eve, and continuing through ancient times, a blood sacrifice had been required. Without the shedding of blood there was no remission of sins—no right-standing with God. The outpouring of innocent blood from an unblemished animal had been established by Holy God to provide a covering of forgiveness for those who looked to it by faith. But concealed in the use of such animals was a far greater promise, one that would loose human captives and restore the glory that had been lost—the walk and oneness with God that by faith Enoch and others had obtained.

The fulfillment of all the law and sacrifices had arrived. Because the promised Seed had no biological human father, He did not inherit sin—His blood was Holy. And because He committed no sin, He was able to become the unblemished Sacrifice for man—to whom all the slain animals pointed. With the offering of the Perfect Sacrifice, there would need to be no more. Because He was a man, He could take man's place—providing a like substitute for all who would believe. Because the Son of God bore man's sins in His own Body, mankind could be released from the penalty and separation of sin, and be rejoined to God.

On the third day following His crucifixion, Jesus was raised from the dead, validating His identity as the Son of God and prophesied Savior of mankind. He appeared to over five-hundred eye witnesses before ascending back to heaven. He demonstrated God's love for man and promised that those who repented and placed their trust in Him, would also live eternally. Lucifer's greatest weapon of fear—death—suddenly lost its power.

The doorway to the kingdom of righteousness, joy and peace was opened on the cross. The victory that the serpent had been able to achieve through Adam in gaining dominion was turned to defeat by the second Adam, the only begotten Son of God. Mankind could enter that spiritual kingdom—which would one day be observable—now by faith. By repentance from sin and faith in the Blood Sacrifice—the finished work of Jesus on the cross—man would be kept safe from the final judgment and outpouring of God's wrath, and restored to the relationship and blessings intended for man from the beginning.

"Therefore if any man be in Christ, he is a new creation: old things are passed away; behold, all things are become new." (2 Corinthians 5:17)

THE NINTH GENERATION

About the Author

John L. Owens and his family were full-time missionaries to the former USSR in the early 90's where he served as Academic Dean of a leadership training school, equipping nationals to start new churches. He has received degrees from F.S.U. and Luther Rice Seminary and has ministered as a pastor, seminar speaker, and through Christian films with Worldwide Pictures. His home is in Coastal Georgia, USA, where he remains active as a teacher and writer, with one published novel, *The Ninth Generation*, and a non-fiction book, *Positioned for Victory*.

More information about the author and the novel can be found at **www.theninthgeneration.com**

Recommended Resources

There is no resource more highly recommended than the Bible; but for further exploration into the subject matter of this novel, the following should be of considerable interest. These were helpful research tools to the author—

Randy Alcorn, ***Heaven***, Tyndale House Publishers, Wheaton, IL, 2004

Walt Brown, ***In The Beginning*** – *Compelling Evidence for Creation and the Flood*, Center for Scientific Creation, Phoenix, AZ, 1995

Bill Ligon, ***Imparting the Blessing*** – *Your Biblical Heritage*, The Father's Blessing, Brunswick, GA, 2000

Henry M. Morris, ***The Genesis Record***, Baker Book House, Grand Rapids, MI, 1976

George Otis Jr., ***The Twilight Labyrinth*** – *Why Does Spiritual Darkness Linger Where it Does?*, Chosen Books / Baker Book House, Grand Rapids, MI, 2000

Made in the USA
Charleston, SC
11 April 2012